For you, Mom.

"Oh, guy!"

Seattle Singer-Songwriter Amy Nguyen Dead at 29

By Marcia Blain
July 23, 2018 at 11:47 pm

Seattle indie rock star Amy Nguyen died from what the King County medical examiner has confirmed to be a self-inflicted gunshot wound. Her body was found in her home yesterday morning by her housekeeper, who immediately called 9-1-1 and alerted Nguyen's family.

ORB, the band of which Nguyen was co-founder and lead singer, had been on its first European tour. According to ORB co-founder Mohamed Ahmad, Nguyen had taken advantage of a scheduled break to return home to Seattle.

Speaking for the family, Nguyen's brother, Bill, said that they are devastated by her loss. Before departing for Europe, "Amy was tired and stressed out about maintaining under the pressure of live performances in front of their first international audiences. I told her I was worried about her, but she said she'd be all right, she'd take care of things. I had no idea what that would ultimately mean." He further revealed that the family first learned of his sister's return to Seattle when contacted by authorities about her death.

The American-born daughter of Vietnamese refugees, Amy Nguyen showed early gifts as a multi-faceted artist. In high school she won prizes for her original spoken word poems, several of which she later put to music. One such composition, the anthemic 'Enigma,' became ORB's first hit, drawing serious attention from fans and critics alike, and earning the band the first of its three Grammy awards.

In an interview with *Rolling Stone* magazine, Nguyen spoke openly of her history with depression and anxiety, and of having been in therapy for many years. "My family experienced incredible trauma during and after the Vietnam War," she said. "My parents and older sister were boat people who barely made it to a refugee camp in Thailand. I'm the first member of the family born in the States. Some of that residual pain and suffering got handed down."

Upon hearing of Nguyen's death, rock critic Cyril Jenson said, "Amy was a luminous force. We can only guess at what she would have accomplished."

In a 2017 op-ed piece published in the *Seattle Times*, she urged young people, especially members of traditionally marginalized communities, to "trust your guts and use your voices. The world needs you."

DAY ONE

• •

I only go downtown when it's unavoidable. Being sued is one of those occasions.

Since the day I got served I can't eat, can't sleep, can't think straight. But I'm proud to say my clients haven't seen me squirm. That's the advantage of being a marriage and family therapist; it's all about the other people in the room. And they're not aware of the energy it takes to sit still, focus, and respond in a semi-rational way. I'm happy to leave it like that.

At least my malpractice insurance company came through. Sort of. The lawyer they found for me is definitely not the minority issues specialist I'd lobbied for, and the weird vibe during our initial call had my therapist radar spinning three hundred sixty degrees. As soon as we hung up, I called my insurance rep to press my original request. She hinted I was lucky the guy took the case, claimed it would be near impossible to replace him on such short notice.

Oh well. His twenty-seventh floor office with the vertigo-inducing, wall-to-wall view of Elliott Bay must prove he's good. Unbelievable that this stranger now holds so much power over me and my future. My breath catches this same way every time I see a police officer. My brother used to call it the "minorities and authorities reflex." MAR for short.

I scoot forward in the heavy leather armchair so that the soles of my shoes lie flat on the carpet.

"I read through the clinical record," he says, his tone brusque, official. He's not even trying to put me at ease. Form your opinion already, sir?

I mirror his business-like manner. It's hard to do with my hands clenched in my lap. "Thank you for seeing me so quickly, Mr. Lagergren."

"Please," he says, "call me Wayne. May I call you Jackie?" No energy's wasted on eye contact. I want to say no but am too slow and miss the moment. We both know who's in charge. "Today's the seventeenth of May. You have nineteen more days to answer the complaint and summons."

"That's my understanding."

"How did you hear about Ms. Nguyen's death?"

"I saw it online."

"Were you surprised?"

There's a dumb question. Is this where he expects a no?

"I thought it must be a sick joke, one of those phony April fool's headlines. Only it was July."

He leans forward in his even heavier chair, taps a fancy-looking fountain pen on the broad oak desktop that separates us. "The girl from ORB," he says, skepticism in his face.

Yeah, buddy. Me and Amy Nguyen. Doesn't quite compute, eh?

"My son likes them," he says. "I don't know why." He looks comfortably smug. Yo, Lagergren, there's a person of color sitting across from you. Is this some kind of test, or do you really not realize how you come across?

Amy once brought in a harsh early review. The byline photo depicted a Euro-American man, maybe mid-thirties, with a don't-even-bother expression. The critic had fixated on the fact that the family of each ORBer had arrived in the US as refugees, and had doubted the band's ability to sustain interest in what he'd termed "refugee rock." ORB's rapidly increasing, ever more diverse fan base went ignored.

"Narrow-minded and condescending," Amy had said. "Our music is not refugee-only. He either forgot or never knew what it is not to belong."

Wayne and that critic could start a club. I'd love to interview him: Tell me, Wayne, how long has your family been in this country? Do you know what it took your immigrant ancestors to succeed? When was the last time you felt uncomfortable in your own skin? Do you even try to understand how uprooted your clients feel, how I feel?

For someone trained to keep her head down and draw no attention to herself, this is as bad as it gets. A quarter century I've been at this job, fighting off my worst professional nightmare. Every day already begins with a battle for confidence and courage, the enemy swirling through my head: It's only a matter of time before you're found out. You, a mental health professional? Pretender! Fraud! Your poor clients.

Unbeknownst to them, my clients have witnessed some Oscar-worthy performances. I should've been a theatre major. I've been method acting my entire life. Now the whole world is privy to my failures. Schadenfreude is alive and well; the emails sent by shocked, if-you-need-a-shoulder colleagues, a couple of whom I've never even heard of, drive that home.

"You mention trauma in the family history," says Wayne.

"Yes, surviving the Vietnam War, then years in a Thai refugee camp."

"This was before Amy was born." His nostrils flare like there's a bad smell in the room. I guess that would be me.

"Trauma like that isn't healed by an entrance visa."

"The lawsuit alleges that because you met so soon before her death, you should have known she was suicidal and therefore taken legally-mandated steps to prevent her subsequent actions." He sits back. My skin prickles as if I'd just walked into a swarm of gnats.

"I *knew* Amy," I say. "She would not have shot herself."

"The sheriff and medical examiner beg to differ." He refers to the thick open file before him. "The poems, lyrics, drawings you received from her over the course of treatment, they're quite dark."

"That perspective is based on a lack of understanding of Amy's worldview. You have to look at the arc of her work to know what it meant. Then you can properly assess the progression of treatment."

"The most concrete information we have is from the police report. A single gunshot wound to the head. The evidence ruled out an accident and clearly indicated suicide."

I massage my hands and slow my breathing, conjuring the current scents in my garden. Lilac, honeysuckle, rose. "Amy was not at risk for suicide, hadn't been for several years. She still struggled with anxiety, but she had it under control."

Oregano, peppermint, pineapple sage.

Wayne taps the file with his pen. I wonder if he actually writes with it or if it's just a prop. "There's nothing in here that either condemns or exonerates you. Are your notes typically so … sparse?"

"I document the minimum to maximize client privacy."

"In this case it may work against you. Her death was ten months ago." He raises his eyebrows. "Have you had any difficulties with the media?"

You mean besides that nasty news story with the less than flattering photo? "There were some calls the first few days. I hung up on them."

"Nothing more?" He seems disappointed.

"No, thank goodness."

"Attention spans are short." He tries a vague smile. "And she's not Elvis."

That's his idea of reassurance? What would happen if I got up and left? I swallow. Focus, girl. Breathe from the diaphragm. Lilac, honeysuckle, and … and what? Oh yes, and rose.

He tilts forward, the smile a distant memory. "There will be more scrutiny if this goes to trial. How prepared are you for the spotlight?"

If, not *when*, plus a dash of intimidation. Dude, you're transparent. Thanks for letting me know where we're headed. One last try.

"The media made it sound like I've already been tried and convicted. When we first spoke, you mentioned an expert witness. Have you found someone willing to testify on my behalf?"

"Based on her review of the materials, the psychologist I consulted questioned whether her testimony would be of help. She, too, wished your notes were more detailed." He settles back again. His back and forth adds to my nausea.

"The Nguyens want more than a pound of flesh. Amy's brother filed the lawsuit."

"Bill Nguyen is no longer involved. He stepped away to avoid any conflict of interest. A senior partner is taking the lead. Jackie, the insurance company wants this to go away as quickly as you do. Now it's a matter of the right number."

"I don't want to settle. My work with Amy Nguyen was solid. How can this be cleared up before the deadline?"

Wayne squints, points his fountain pen at me. "Then I'll need something more from you, Jackie, something persuasive that corroborates your opinion of Amy's mental state."

"I'm not going to falsify the record. What kind of person do you think I am?" I dig the fingernails of my right hand into my left forearm. Time to shift the balance; I fight my inner nature and go on the offensive. "Who's your client, me or the insurance company? My policy's maximum payout is five million. The Nguyens won't settle for that. This will destroy my practice. My family depends on my income."

"Your husband is an architect."

"Who's recovering from a major stroke. At this point we don't know if or when he'll be able to return to work."

Wayne stiffens slightly, pulls a newspaper article from the file and reads. "According to leading local mental health expert Dr. Earl Richmond, 'Jacqueline Kessler ignored clear and repeated warning signs of Amy Nguyen's suicidal tendencies, showing a complete and callous disregard for the well-being of her client.'"

I continue the imaginary stroll through my garden. Lily of the valley, columbine, rosemary, my hot pink azaleas.

"'She may not have pulled the trigger, but her substandard, harmful treatment methods ultimately led to the untimely, tragic, and completely avoidable death of a great talent.'"

He read the passage with such gusto. Maybe the high profile was why he took the case. Great – if I can't trust my attorney, I'll need other allies.

My throat clogs, making my voice hoarse and thick. "I have to fight this. I have to set the record straight. For myself *and* Amy." I raise my voice. "Amy didn't kill herself!"

"Are you suggesting it was indeed an accident?"

"It was no accident. I'm saying she was murdered."

He sits back and looks at me like I'm insane. "If you want to fight this, your assertion will have to be proved. You have nineteen days to do it."

I hate being late. Being late for an appointment is unprofessional and just plain rude. Hell, today we'll all have to live with it. I wait for a woman in a swamp green SUV to vacate a parking space. I hope she got a good deal on that fucking ugly vehicle.

The windshield wipers scrape and squeak across the not-quite-wet-enough glass. This is my least favorite weather, the obnoxious, smeary excuse for precipitation that has earned the Pacific Northwest its reputation as the depression capitol of the nation. The only positive of this relentless misery is nature-made job security.

I spot them through the restaurant's picture window. They're in our usual end booth, waiting to hear the verdict. Rachel fiddles with her omnipresent enameled bangle bracelets. Liz reaches across the table and places a hand on her wrist, stopping the action. That means it's been going on for a while. Angie brushes her brunette bangs out of her eyes and stares intently at her menu, one we all know by heart. Smart, Ang, keeping out of the middle. Or line of fire.

Ang's all-American attractiveness reminds me of a regular television date I had with my mother decades ago. *Charlie's Angels* had hit the airwaves and every week, without fail, Mom would sigh and say something wistful about Jaclyn Smith's "classic American beauty." (Farrah's blond locks were just too foreign.) As a teen, I had so wished for such compliments from my mother. Now I no longer need or expect her approval; however, in weak moments like this, I can't help but look at my friend with a bit of residual wistfulness.

The SUV lady checks over her shoulder and puts her monstrosity in reverse, then abruptly hits the brakes and glares at me. She obviously doesn't know her vehicle; I sigh and back up to give her even more room. No, that's not it. She's still staring, recognition in her eyes. I shudder. Great. Thus it begins. Maybe I should just go home. Too late. Rachel's long finger is pointing my way.

The urge to escape is replaced by a rush of guilt; it's Rachel I'm not keen to see. I've never felt as easy with her, but being included has meant overlooking minor misgivings. Overall it's been worth it; we've been a foursome since grad school.

Rachel Darby, Angela Blaylock, Jacqueline Kessler, and Elizabeth Samaras. Together, we are RAJE.

These women are the sisters I never had. However, in my parents' house, loving family members without actually liking them was a given. As our group coalesced I slid easily back into that old default setting. Of course, my frustrations with Rach probably say more about my own intolerance than her shortcomings.

The bracelets are, after all, my fault. When we started working with actual clients, Rach and I shared supervision in our graduate program. She and our supervisor helped save my butt with an early client, a mentally ill woman with a history of violence. The lady ended up on my caseload because the senior therapists at the agency I interned at were tired of playing hot potato with her. Rach, even more than our supervisor, helped me push beyond my own anxiety to understand the client's. Once the woman felt that shift, we made progress.

The bracelets were a thank you gift. There are three, each a primary color: blue for staying cool under pressure, red for the blood we sweat together, and yellow for our newly-forged friendship. That episode proved Rachel's fearlessness. I need some of it to rub off again.

To this day when I'm feeling unsure of myself, she says or does something to put me on the defensive. I hate that. At least the years of experience have taught me how to turn anger into something constructive. She knows it, takes credit for it. It's not wholly undeserved, but I resent being beholden. Okay, I admit it, that's my problem. Damn it, Rach, keep pointing.

Lorena, who runs the front of house, knows we consult on cases over lunch. She reserves this booth for us, tucked away from other customers. Today I especially appreciate the privacy. I drop heavily next to Rachel. She moves her raincoat to the other side, slides an arm over my shoulders.

Lorena steps up with fresh salsa and chips. "Hi, everyone. What'll it be?"

"Hi, Lorena." I hand over the unopened menu with a belabored flourish. "Pollo asado and a pomegranate margarita, if you please."

"A super grande coming up." A smidge of empathy adds to the underlying warmth in her smile. It's comforting that she knows me well enough to play along.

Rachel clutches my jacket sleeve, bangle bracelets chiming. "You can't do that. Aren't you going to the office after? You can't breathe tequila into your clients' faces."

Does she honestly think I was serious? I shake my sleeve loose. There's a metallic clink as Rachel makes a show of smoothing my now-crumpled linen. She pats me on the head to inject some feeble humor. "Not that we don't want to drink with you, Jax, but we do have our reputations to consider."

Liz stares at her, aghast; Angie's eyes are on me, alarmed. Okay, two out of four. Lorena hesitates; I try to telegraph the message that she read me right.

"Bucket-sized." My intended smile is more a grimace.

"Got it. And for you ladies?"

As they place their orders, I slowly and methodically snap pieces off a tortilla chip, let them fall onto my napkin. The others watch as I gather the sad collection and eat it. Lorena walks briskly away, and Liz leans in.

"So what'd he say?"

"He said," I pause to gather the strength to say it out loud, "I don't have much of a defense. He's pushing a settlement."

"That's crap," says Rachel. "A settlement's practically admitting your guilt. You gotta save yourself."

I think, And Amy, but can't get the words out of my mouth.

"Yeah, what kind of lawyering is that?" In spite of the regular precautions, Angie keeps her voice low and scans the neighboring tables to make sure we can't be overheard. "He's supposed to be on your side." She rubs at the condensation on her water glass. "Lawyers, insurance companies, and banks. I tell ya."

I contemplate the tortilla chip in my hand. "Wayne Lagergren. Ever heard of him?" They shake their heads. "Yeah, turns out we're not doing ourselves any favors keeping such lean notes. There's no way I can prove she wasn't suicidal or that I couldn't have known it if she was. There's only my say-so."

"And your, what, decade-plus history with her counts for nothing?"

"History, schmistory. The family's hurting and wants someone to blame. Why not me? Her parents were never keen on her getting therapy. They never made peace with her mental health issues."

"Mainly because they were major contributors."

We stop so Lorena can plunk three tall glasses of raspberry iced tea onto the table. She places an oversized margarita glass brimming with the same in front of me. I smile my acknowledgement and appreciation. Her mischievous wink fortifies me better than booze would have.

Angie stirs a packet of stevia into her drink until Lorena's again out of earshot. Rachel joins me in dismantling chips. I stop myself from stopping her.

"Imagine my surprise," she says, sweeping crumbs from her lap onto the floor, "hearing that my dear friend and esteemed colleague, Jacqueline Kessler, therapist extraordinaire, is being sued for malpractice." She waves an accusing chip in my face. "And you didn't tell us earlier because?"

"I was hoping the whole thing would disappear and we could have a laugh over it, after the fact. Didn't think it would hit the news." A rasp of bitterness sharpens my voice. I clear my throat to cover it.

"No. I meant that you were working with a celebrity all those years."

My jaw tightens. "She wasn't famous when we started."

Liz takes her glasses off, lays them beside her plate. "Rach, even if she was, we don't use names. Never have, never will." I appreciate her emphasis on the future. "Earl the Pearl Richmond. What a tool."

"As subtle as raw garlic." Angie uses a fork to transfer ice cubes from her water to her tea. I smile in spite of myself. When clients go through hard times I preach about the comfort of rituals. The truth of it lies in this oh so familiar event.

Rachel adds, "With him involved, you can kiss any remaining vestige of client confidentiality goodbye. By the way, how's your mom taking it?"

I feign a playful shiver. "She's into Korean soap operas, not the news. Best to let her live in ignorance."

"Are you kidding? You have to tell her. You can't let her hear from someone else, like we did. She'll flip out." There it is again, the pressure to do it their way. I have neither the energy nor the motivation to explain. Let *them* live in ignorance.

I press my lips together. Time to breathe deeply and count to ten. Eightnineten. Close enough. "Oh well," I say. "I'll cross that proverbial bridge whenever."

Liz redirects. "So what's the game plan?"

"Don't know yet. Wayne gave me some time to think things through. I want to fight back, but…"

"But what?" says Rachel. "Don't go all Asian on us. Now's no time to be meek and polite. There's no way you could have known she'd shoot herself."

Hmmm. Which part of that was the most hurtful? Don't think too hard, Jackie. Stay on subject.

"That's the point I'm trying to make. My client did not – I repeat – did *not* shoot herself."

Rachel nods. "That's the way, Jax. You'll need 'tude to play this game."

"Yes, coach," I say. Rachel pats my head. At least she took it as a compliment.

Angie chews the end of her straw. "Playin' devil's advocate here." The rest of us sigh. Angie's relentlessness is sometimes frustrating, but we've learned to hold our tongues because the ensuing debates usually yield irritatingly good results. She contemplates the teeth marks. "How can you know for sure? I mean, how well did you really know her as an adult?"

"I watched her evolve into that adult!" Once again, I am the Accused. I sweep my arm across the table to include them all. "We consulted on this case how many times? It took a while – all right, a long while – but my client –" I peek around the booth. All clear. Fuck it. She would've been on my case for not using her name. "*Amy* confided in me. I know how she would've done it if she had. Shoot herself? Never."

Liz reaches for my hand, squeezes it. Comfort or condescension? The former. There's love in her gesture.

"She tweaked her plan," I say, "refined it over the years. I knew every element of it. It may sound counterintuitive, but having that option was one of the ways Amy kept herself moving forward. When she didn't need it anymore she wrote a poem about it. Putting that poem to music was the sure sign she was safe. Suicidal? No way. The last time we saw each other, she was in a solid place." I scoop another load of chip bits into my mouth.

It'd been eight months since our last session. At twenty-nine Amy still didn't look old enough to buy beer. The major difference from our introduction fourteen years earlier was that her clothes actually fit. She removed the faded Mariners baseball cap and fluffed her trademark short, brilliantly dyed thatch. This time the natural black was streaked with magenta, indigo, and green.

She snatched the fuzzy old bunny rabbit from my collection of stuffed animals. "Missed you," she said, giving it a nuzzle.

I chuckled. "The boss is back. Speaking of which, I thought we said our goodbyes. What's up?"

Amy threw her head back with her yelp of a laugh. "Subtlety is still your middle name." She turned suddenly serious, gestured with the bunny. "I wanted one last check in with you to let you know I'm really okay. Better than okay – I'm doing great, and I wanted you to know."

"I appreciate that. You've worked at it – long and hard."

"Yeah, it was the only way to escape your constant nag, nag, nag. So thank you."

"You're … welcome?" I peered sideways at the young woman, assessing, constantly assessing. "I do have to say, I love seeing you smile."

"Yeah, I'll bet there were times you doubted my facial muscles were capable." She left space for a snide remark that didn't come, released a good-natured Ha! at my obvious self-restraint. "It helped that I could always call when I needed. I know we said *auf Wiedersehen*, but…" She reached into a jute shopping bag and pulled out a flat square package wrapped in plain white paper. In the center, drawn with a few bold strokes, was a brown Picassoesque rabbit. It was surrounded by smaller variations on the theme in a range of colors. All were created with Amy's implements of choice, fine-tipped Sharpies. "For you, IJ. A final token of appreciation."

I laughed and indicated the toy in her lap. "You gave him friends."

She lifted her chin toward the rest of the plush menagerie. "He already has family."

I carefully unwrapped the parcel, smoothed the paper, lay it aside. "Hey, ORB's new LP! 'Evolution.' Great title. This is terrific. Thank you, Amy." I flipped the album over and looked up, beaming. "And you signed it."

"Yeah, couldn't help myself." Amy smiled shyly. "It'll be released at the end of next week to coincide with the start of the tour. Everyone in the band contributed to the writing. The entire record is about our life journeys so far, how we got to where we are. We designed the cover together too."

The band members, three men and three women, were out-fitted in paint-spattered white overalls and caps. Holding cans of spray paint, they contemplated a high, broad wall illustrat-ed with the outline of a world map. Several seemingly random groups of letters in different hues were scattered across the continents. "This is our way of saying thanks to everyone who honestly gave a damn, and, well, here's you." She pointed to three letters in the northwest corner of the contiguous United States.

I took a closer look. "IJK. Are you ever gonna tell me what the 'I' stands for?"

"Nuh uh. You're educated. Figure it out."

"Oh, I've done a lot of speculation over the years: Insane, Impossible, Irritating. But my strongest hunch has always been Idiot."

Amy jabbed at the album. "Give it up and read the notes."

The liner notes included personalized thanks, arranged in alphabetical order. I read aloud: " 'To IJK, whose relentless searching for and telling of truths helped me breathe.'"

Amy's voice was quiet, quieter than I had ever heard it. "I originally had 'kept me breathing,' but your voice was in my head." She took on a shrill, schoolmarmish note. " 'It's your work. I'm just along for the ride.'"

I snickered to cover more vulnerable emotions. "You're scaring me. You do that a little too well."

"Heard it often enough." Amy sounded wistful. "Remember when we met? I was right out of the hospital, and hated even the idea of having to come see you." I nodded. "You said the hospital report said I didn't want to die anymore. You asked if I wanted to live. Rude, audacious question! Then you said something I've thought about a lot since then. We all commit to life every day. Sometimes we're just more aware of how hard that can be."

I was touched that she remembered.

Amy continued, "I want you to know that I've signed a long-term contract with myself, due to run for the next oh, sixty, seventy years." She waved a hand at my concerned expression. "I know, I know, it'll be up for regular renegotiation. God, you're such a killjoy." She sped up slightly and pushed the volume; her voice thinned and strained. "But I mean it. I'm happy, I'm healthy in all those ways we talked about. I've got good people around me now, people I love who love me back. I have my poetry, my music. All is good, IJ. No, all is better than good. All is fantastic!"

"Yeah, a solid place," I repeat, semi-hesitantly. "In my memory, up until now, Amy was relaxed and assured. But now I can't swear that's how it really was." I replay the end of that session in my head once more, searching for the truth.

Angie breaks the silence, her voice tentative. "Jax, I hate to say this, but people will often seem genuinely happy, even give their stuff away before –"

"Before they kill themselves because they've made up their minds, have a plan, and feel relief. You think I don't know that?" The others cringe. "I'm sorry. I don't mean to jump down your throats. Maybe I just don't want to believe it. No, I *don't* believe it. You had to have known her and how she communicated. Remember, she was Vietnamese. She and I went at things with an Asian spin, sideways, through the garden gate, not the front door. Otherwise it got too hot for her and she'd shut down."

Something snort-like escapes from Rachel. Liz jams her glasses back onto her face. The action barely covers the scowl. I don't know if it's in response to Rach or me. I guess the latter and plow onward. "Then she fell into poetry. She played with symbolism and metaphor; they became her new language. Her poetry and sketches, even her clothes…"

"Her clothes?"

"Amy got into shibori, an ancient Japanese tie-dye technique that illustrates wabi-sabi, the concept of beauty in imperfection. Embracing that philosophy freed her to be more herself, helped her to not give a damn what anyone thought about her."

She'd made several remarkable pieces of clothing for herself. She called them wearable reminders. Of what, I wasn't sure, and she wouldn't tell me. In any case, the gorgeous blue tunic she made for me is locked in my home office file cabinet. Many times I've been tempted to at least use it as household attire, but I can never get to that point. With its three-quarter sleeves and asymmetrical hem, it's like red shoes, something I aspire to but is a little too out there for me. Now I don't know that I'll ever be able to put it on.

"Back to the point." Rachel still sounds slightly insulted. "All this rock star stuff is new."

"We're therapists, not voyeurs." I think about other information I've withheld. Maybe I shouldn't have come after all.

Liz says, "So how did she make that shift? More specifically, what did *you* do to help her? And how does this connect to her calling you IJ?"

"It's a conspiracy! I don't know who to hate most, the witch or the wimp." Amy stopped, her chest heaving as she drew breath. "No, I do know. The witch started it. I know where she parks. I'll slash her tires. Follow her home and kill her stupid cat. You know she keeps a picture of her stupid, ugly cat on her desk? How pathetic."

In an exaggerated huff, I snatched my plush tabby cat from the top of the bookshelf and pulled its front paws over its ears. I glanced at the clock. Amy had been ranting for two minutes straight.

"Gimme." She pulled the kitty from my hands. "I'm sorry," she said, stroking its head and scratching it behind the ears. "I'd never hurt one of yours." She returned it to its fellows and looked at me pleadingly. "It's just fucking not fair!"

I was still caught by the sudden show of vulnerability when her eyes sparked; she was winding herself up again. To gain time, I reached out and touched her arm. She recoiled as if burned. She blinked, reached down, and pulled some crumpled papers from her backpack.

"Look at this!" She shoved her first semester pre-calculus final in front of my face. The math was a foreign language to me, but I did recognize the conspicuous red C defacing the margin. I'd never known Amy to get below a B+ on anything.

My shocked expression set her off on a new rant, her arms pinwheeling and her face as red as the grade. "Do you see?

How dare she flunk me! I've never flunked anything in my life. Doesn't she know I need a schol-ar-ship?" The last sentence was spoken slowly and carefully to ensure my comprehension.

It was her junior year; Amy carried a 3.9 grade point average and had scored disgustingly high on both the PSAT and ACT. She'd have her choice of schools and scholarships.

I said, "Slow down, Amy, you're working yourself into a froth. First of all, a C isn't a failing grade. Second, what makes you think she did this on purpose? Give me the whole story."

"This was a *partner* final. Macy Carmichael and I did this to-geth-er. We had the exact same answers. Macy got a B+ and I got –" she yanked the papers out of my hands, crumpled them, let them drop to the floor. I gave her my sternest look; she held her hands up in surrender. "Okay, okay. Long story short, I took the witch to arbitration with my school counselor, who got her to admit her *mistake*," she made air quotes with her fingers, "but she wouldn't give any points back because she said it would teach me to deal with frustration." Amy collapsed onto the floor. "That dropped my final grade. Now I've got a fuckin' undeserved B on my transcript."

I was about to say the last time I got a B in math was in sixth grade, that it was all downhill from there, but Amy's crumpled sense of self convinced me otherwise. I didn't want to be next on her hit list.

"That's ugly," says Angie. "But to repeat Liz's question, what's the point?"

Rachel's face puckers. "I didn't know she was a hoodlum."

"She wasn't. She was a kid born into poverty working her butt off, and here was this teacher standing in her way, one math problem at a time. Anyway, I convinced her stuff like that would only make things worse. Told her she could think all sorts of bad things, she just couldn't say them out loud or act on them."

Rachel pulls melted cheese from her refried beans and lays it over a bite of rice.

Angie again: "Teachers like that should be drawn and quartered."

"Symbolism and metaphor, please," says Rachel, eating the cheesy rice. She's bending, and I appreciate the effort.

"Okay, next session, she's happy as a clam. I ask what happened; she says she's taken her revenge. I'm thinking, Uh oh, time to call the cops. But no, thank goodness, she's been playing word games. Turns out the teacher's name was Sybil A. Blake. All second semester, Amy, in her head, called her SAB, aka Such A Bitch."

It feels good to laugh again. Rachel chokes as a gulp of iced tea goes down the wrong pipe. I bang on her back and everyone knows all is well again.

"After that, coming up with nicknames and playing with initials were regular things. It even spilled over into her songwriting."

"How?" asks Liz. She's been uncharacteristically quiet.

"Prime example? 'Enigma.' She uses her initials to make a statement about her self-identity. Every time she sings 'I am an,' it's A-N, Amy Nguyen."

"Never heard of it," says Rachel. "I don't listen to that kind of music." She focuses on her spinach enchilada.

Liz says what I'm thinking. "Maybe you should. It'd help you stay on top of what your kid clients are into."

I sigh deeply. Rachel's natural prickliness increases considerably whenever she's upset or worried. However, it's not helpful and can be contagious.

"Amy's song, 'Enigma.' It won ORB their first Grammy."

"One of my clients absolutely loves it," Angie interjects. "It was his class song." She relinquishes the floor with a wave of her knife.

"The first line of the chorus goes: 'I'm an enigma, an idea, a transient, roving thing.' See, Amy never felt understood, especially not by those closest to her, namely her family, so she's A-N, *an* enigma."

"Yes." Liz nods slowly. "Clever."

Encouraged, I speak faster. "She was supposed to fit *an* idea in her family's head, but she failed. And, not feeling like a Nguyen, she's plain Amy – *a* transient, roving thing."

Rachel's fork stops halfway to her mouth. "Oh my god, I get it."

"Through the garden gate?" says Angie. "More like sneaking down a dark alley, knocking at an unmarked door, and whispering the secret password. My client thought she spoke for all teendom. I don't think he picked up on this."

"How would he. Amy's poems helped her strip back and examine bits of her soul," I explain, "but you didn't know which bits unless you really knew her."

Liz reaches forward; her hand lands lightly on my forearm. "Stay on track. The IJ thing."

Crystal clear images of Amy spring to mind. The memory of her voice, sharp and sarcastic, brings a stab of pain, the burn of threatening tears. I suppress both. "Amy didn't address me by name. 'Doc' was as good as it got."

"You're not a PhD," says Ang.

"Yeah, that was her being a smart ass. Anyway, one day she slipped, called me 'IJ.' I bugged her until she admitted it's what she used when I ticked her off, which was usually when I caught her talking bullshit. It morphed into her way of telling me she got the point. By the end it was code for all is well."

I ramble on, no longer sure whom I need to convince, them or myself. "That last session it was IJ this, IJ that. Besides, why would she kill herself? She was happy in her personal life – okay, her Vietnamese Catholic parents were none too happy about her Somali Muslim boyfriend, but they were pleased with bragging rights about the rest."

We pause long enough to eat another mouthful or two. Liz, rolling prawns into a corn tortilla, says, "I think we can all agree that Amy Nguyen didn't shoot herself." Angie gives an affirming nod; Rachel chews. "But somehow she ended up dead. An accidental shooting was ruled out." Liz studies me. "You're implying she was murdered."

"Thank you. Now you're listening." I'm trembling. This is only the fourth time I've publically admitted to the thought. The first time was to Willem who, bless him, immediately agreed. But then I wouldn't expect otherwise from my husband of thirty one years. The second was to our kids, Natasha and Stefan, who wanted to rally the forces of justice then and there. The third was two hours ago to Wayne, who stopped just short of open ridicule.

"What?" Angie pales.

Rachel chokes, coughs, and swallows. "Are you serious?"

"Unfortunately. As far as that waste-of-space lawyer's concerned, there's nothing I can do, nowhere else to go, so he figures he'll eventually get his way with a settlement."

Liz clears her throat and tilts her head slowly downward and to the side. "I have a thought." She tilts her head to the other side.

"So tell us already!" Rachel fidgets in her seat and lifts a forkful of spinach in a threatening gesture.

"My nephew, Allan." We all know Allan Shaw, son of Liz's younger brother Don. Allan Shaw, the former cop.

"How's he doing?" Angie asks.

"Not well." Liz's voice is strained.

One morning the previous spring Allan's wife Zoe, a high school science teacher, had been standing on the sidewalk talking with a student as others arrived. Witnesses later reported seeing an old, beat up sedan crawl down the street. They heard what sounded like a car backfiring before it sped away. After the confusion cleared, two bodies lay on the ground, Zoe's and her student's.

The ensuing investigation revealed that the student victim had gang ties. Zoe had been next to the wrong person at the wrong time. The car, recorded in a smart phone video by a quick-thinking kid, was found the next day outside of Nooksack, a little town in northern Washington. There were no fingerprints. It was assumed that the perpetrator had escaped into Canada. Allan knew his colleagues on both sides of the border had followed every lead, handling the case as if Zoe had been one of their own. But every lead hit a dead end.

No recourse. No justice. Allan's sense of purpose was stripped from him and he spun out of control. He fell into a deep depression from which he was only beginning to emerge.

Liz rolls a cherry tomato between thumb and forefinger. "A couple weeks ago we got together for Don's sixtieth. I spent some time catching up with Allan. Frankly, I'm still really worried, and I told him so. He needs to work out his guilt feelings, but he doesn't know how."

"Why should he feel guilty?" says Ang. "There was absolutely nothing he could do."

"That's the problem, that sense of helplessness. The boy's living in a world of regret. Zoe had been after him to quit. Every time he left the house, her heart seized. He knew if they were ever going to have kids, he'd need to make a change. He'd just given notice when Zoe died. Now it's tearing him up that he put her through that for so long."

Rachel loudly sucks up the rest of her iced tea. "Is he getting help?"

"Since when is this that more perfect world?"

"What's your idea?" Rach asks. "Could he get some of his cop buddies to help Jackie?"

The muscles in Liz's neck tighten. It's my turn to gently close my hand over hers. "No, not exactly," she says. "When Allan and I talked, I suggested he find something worthwhile to do, a direction in which to turn his talents and attention. He did not disagree. So no, I wasn't thinking of his friends. Allan was a detective, a damn fine one. Maybe he could help you, Jax."

My hand retracts itself. "Help me how? You just described major depression. Rach is right; he needs more help than I do." That came out more cynical and dismissive than intended. I catch Angela and Rachel sharing a sideways glance. They agree with me.

"Has everyone turned stupid?" Liz shakes her head at us, wearing her patient look. "Jax, you need help proving your theory. The police and your lawyer have already shut you down. So what are your options? A private investigator? Sure, go for it. You'll probably shell out a whole lotta money for a whole lotta nothin'. On the other hand, there's Allan, an experienced criminal investigator who needs something to focus on and help him feel alive again. Sounds like a match to me."

I tap my fingertips against my thighs, turning the possibility over in my mind. An experienced detective would be a more capable ally than I ever imagined. Problem is, this particular detective would be both capable and tremendously damaged. How *able* would he be? Oh hell, rashness is the offspring of despair. Might as well keep it in the family.

"You think investigating a – what did Wayne call it – harebrained-idea-about-a-murder-that-no-one-else-thinks-was-actually-committed will help your nephew feel alive again?"

"Listen." Somehow my hand in now sandwiched between hers. "Ever since he was a kid, Allan's loved anything and everything about a mystery. He *thrives* on it. That's why he was such a good detective. That's what made it so hard for him to give it up. When Zoe was killed, not finding the solution almost destroyed him. The boy needs to know there's still some order and purpose in the world and that he can still contribute to it."

"He needs for you to stop calling him a boy," Rachel mutters.

Liz releases me. "I heard that," she spits. "And you're right."

"I don't know," I say. "It sounds like he needs help of a different kind first. Do you really think he'd want to help me? Do you really think he could? I mean, all the so-called experts are telling me it's pointless. And what if we *can't* find anything? I don't want to make things worse for him."

Liz pops another cherry tomato into her mouth and speaks around it. "I'll talk to him," she says, biting down. "He can decide for himself."

My turn on the sofa. It's a relief to let loose, let go

Back in grad school, I had looked for a professional community of local Asian American mental health clinicians. There was no community, but there was Mona Chen.

My mentor-turned-friend puts two mugs, each sporting a classic Far Side cartoon, on the coffee table between us. When Mona still worked with kids and adolescents her office décor was more rough and tumble, not unlike my own. Now, like so many colleagues, she sees only adults. The mugs are the only holdovers.

She says, "This is a fine mess you've gotten yourself into, isn't it, Grasshopper?"

"You're mixing pop-cultural metaphors. Mona, what'm I gonna do?"

"Looks like you're already doing everything you can. What tea do you want?"

"Chai, please. Make it a double."

"Oh my, you are in a bad way." She drops two tea bags into my favorite mug, the one with the world from a bird's eye view, and adds boiling water from her rickety electric kettle. "So tell me. What's really bugging you? Besides the public humiliation and threat to your reputation and livelihood, that is."

Time to fade away; I feel the veil descend.

"Oh no," she chides, "you can't hide from me, Jacqueline Kyung-hee Chol Kessler, so don't even try. Your Asian inscrutability works not at all on the likes of me."

I make a face at her.

She stirs the pepperminty contents of her own mug. "This is just a blip – yes, it's major and obnoxious; however, it remains but a blip in the grand scheme of your career. You *will* be vindicated. You *will* survive and continue to thrive as a professional." She offers sugar and milk. "There's something deeper here. What is it? Spill."

Of all the people walking the planet, only Willem knows me better. And there are things I've shared with Mona that I've never told Willem.

I take a deep swallow of tea, scalding my mouth. I relish the sting. "This is my legacy as much as Amy's. Since this started it's not only Amy and her family haunting me, it's my own. World War II, Korea, Vietnam. Three generations of female Asian war refugees from two families walk with me wherever I go, whispering in my ear to do more. I can't shake 'em." The pleading in my voice echoes the voices of those women, living and dead. "Amy deserves it, and by doing for her, I do for us all."

Mona's own shadows include ancestors that helped build the transcontinental railroad and others that fled the Chinese Revolution. "Quite the irritating shit show," she says, rubbing her chin. "Time to focus on yourself. Good thing your kids are grown. No need to protect them."

"Very good thing."

"How's Willem?"

"I'm not quite sure. This is absolutely the worst time for something like this to happen. Working on his recovery is exhausting enough; he shouldn't have to worry about me. And it's taking away from his time with Tash, bringing her up to speed. I feel so selfish."

Mona waves my self-pity away. "It's not as if you ordered this. As for Willem's stroke, at least Tash was able to come back and step into the business. True, it's earlier than you envisioned, but it was still part of the ultimate plan." She hands me a chocolate mint cookie. "Tell your mom?"

In a split second we're doubled over. Oh, Mona, I love you and your rhetoricals. It's so freeing to have someone who just plain knows.

When we're laughed out I ask, "What was it like for you, growing up in Duluth?" Freshly poached skin peels from the roof of my mouth. I encourage it with my tongue.

"Old territory, Jackie." She wipes her eyes. "I'm a psychologist. That tells you everything."

"Yeah, yeah, we're mental health professionals for a reason."

"And Amy turned to art for a reason. All three of us managed to transform the misery we inherited into something positive. Not easy to do."

"Nope, never is."

Suddenly, I feel proud. It's uncomfortable. And brings up an as yet unasked question. "Mona, back in the day, did you ever feel a blur between us?"

"What do you mean?"

"Like you didn't know where you ended and I began? Or vice versa?"

"Ah, the dreaded countertransference. You know, you weren't the only one feeling alone in this profession. When you came knocking, well…" She resets herself. "The answer is yes, fleetingly. But I was on top of it. Did you ever feel it get in our way?"

"No, but it feels better to hear you dealt with it too. I thought I was on top of it with Amy. Now I'm not so sure. I wonder if maybe I put Amy into my skin instead of the other way around. What was it like for you being in mine?"

"I never was," she says bluntly. "No need to feel insulted, Jackie. Ours was a very different relationship than the one you had with Amy. For one thing, I was your consultant, not your therapist. For another, you'd already done your heavy lifting."

"I saw Amy through hers, and by the end honestly believed she'd dealt with her shit like I dealt with mine, you dealt with yours. What if I was wrong?"

Mona raises her hand, palm facing me. "Stop. Move on. Now, if I remember correctly, she was initially referred to you because of the Asian connection, right?" She doesn't wait for confirmation. "What hat did you wear with her?"

"What do *you* mean?"

"When you worked with her, were you a Korean American therapist or a therapist who happens to be Korean American? Or did the distinction even matter?" Reluctant gears begin to turn in my head. "How much did she activate the second-generation refugee in you?"

I wince.

"Eureka! I know for a fact she's not the only client of color – kid or adult – you felt akin to. What was it about this particular client that got to you in that particular way?"

I blow on my chai; piquant steam bathes my face. Deciding against further injury, I place the mug on the table and tear a paper napkin into thin strips.

"I'd gotten comfortable before Amy crossed my threshold. Her trauma definitely meshed with mine. What she had to deal with was insane. It woke me up, reopened my eyes to the institutionalized racism in my backyard."

She says, "It's a hard thing to fight."

"One of my teenaged Black clients nearly got assaulted on the bus a while back. Another passenger, a White man, told him to move to the back, got ugly when my client refused."

"Damn."

"Thank goodness for the driver. She pulled the bus over and threatened to have the guy arrested if he didn't back off. According to my client, the other passengers didn't lift a finger, didn't say a word."

"I read that the number of hate crimes is skyrocketing. We have the nation's second highest increase after California. What the fuck is going on?"

"See, that doesn't surprise me at all. Western Washington and California may pride themselves on being liberal strongholds, but there's a yin to that yang. A lot of people in both places learned to fake political correctness. They didn't say what they actually thought and felt for fear of being labeled racist or misogynist or homophobic or whatever. Now things are different. With some of our so-called leaders modeling the very worst of human nature, everything that's been pent up for who knows how long can finally be released. It's pouring out with added interest."

Mona's smile has been widening throughout my rant. "Feel better?" I respond with a sheepish nod. "I agree," she says. "And in the intervening years, we've forgotten how to have the hard conversations. They're out there, hanging in the void, waiting for us to gather the courage. But very few are willing to go there anymore."

"Yup."

"And Amy went there with you?"

"Yup."

"No wonder she got to you. I'd have loved her, too."

I stare at her, mouth slightly agape. I'd never thought of those words to describe my relationship with Amy. Not with any client. Damn that Mona, stripping me to the core. But it's true.

"I did love her." I feel so much better, lighter even, now that the words have left my mouth. "I keep picturing her when she was a kid, fighting tears, not able to admit to feeling alone and afraid, wondering whom she could trust. Finally daring to trust me." I take a huge swig of tea. The roof of my mouth stings sharply; tears spring to my eyes. "No way in the world I'm going to let her down." I take a deep breath and ask, "So now what do I do?"

"Hard conversations are comin' down the pike." Mona mimes a matador egging on an enraged bull. "Toro!"

The hardest conversations with Amy were about family, family, always family. Even at the age of twenty four, despite her public successes, she couldn't get past what she considered her private failures.

"For the first time, I feel like I can do it. Before, after I admitted to myself that she doesn't really love me, doesn't really care…" Amy squeezed the stuffed bunny. "I survived out of pure, unremitting spite. Now I want to see for myself what I can do. People say we've got something going, and I'm starting to believe them."

"It's about time. You have a lot of important things to say, and your audience is growing. This morning I heard 'See Me' on the radio. And I love your cover of 'True Colors.'"

Amy sighed. "Every color has its meaning." Her wistful smile brightened. "Don't tell anyone, but Cyndi Lauper's one of my idols."

"That secret's out. It was in the *Rolling Stone* interview."

She stared at me with mock amazement. "You read *Rolling Stone*? You're cooler than you look."

"I read it when ORB is on the cover. Your scowling face caught my eye in the grocery store check-out line."

She flipped me the bird. "So you read it once."

"Get on the cover again, I'll read it again."

She nodded; the deal was done. Her parents hadn't seen the article. As far as she was concerned, they couldn't be bothered. Even so, Amy had bought them a house and continued to financially support them. She was putting her brother Bill through university; he'd just been accepted to law school. According to Amy, he'd already set himself a target date for passing the bar exam. There was no disputing the family resemblance; he sounded just as determined as his big sister.

When I praised her love and loyalty, she said, "Yeah, well, family is family. No matter how much you can't stand each other. But the joke's still on me. Now the woman's resentful because the heft of her wallet depends on me. No matter what I do, I can't win."

"But you are winning. Everything you just said is proof thereof. Maybe she only calls you the crazy one to keep from feeling so crazy herself."

"Don't start going all soft on me." The acid in her voice made my mouth pucker.

"Amy, she may never be able to love you the way you want. And if that's the case, you have to decide how you're going to let it affect you."

Amy's voice grew wispy and far away. Tears began to slowly slide down her cheeks. "Other than the money, I'm poison. Why? She's treated me like that my whole life. Why am I toxic? Why can't she love me?"

"You might never know." I knelt on the floor beside her and squeezed her hand. "But she's the one missing out. Amy, you are not toxic. You're a wonderful, loving, lovable human being. Don't let your mother's hurt take away from you. You can't fix it for her."

Amy cried silently. "Why can't I let it go?"

Being no expert, I had no answer for her. All I could do was pat her hand ineffectually and offer her a tissue.

Note to self: There are many things in life over which we have no control and limited influence. When this happens, we can only control our reactions.

This irritating shit show of a lawsuit is nothing compared to what my family and I have already survived. In less than three weeks, I'll know how this episode will play out and I'll be able to let it go. Or will I? The old poison has been reactivated, more potent than before. I feel it seeping through my system, feeding long-festering questions, doubts.

It's raising some in other people as well. Since the story broke, I've lost one client after another. Can't blame 'em. But now I dread checking messages. The positive? The empty blocks in my schedule let me stop by the house and check on Willem. Even though our daughter's back, I'm uneasy being away for more than a few hours at a time. Willem's new alarm button will alert both me and Natasha, but there's always the chance he won't be able to activate it.

That thought keeps me up at night. I watch him, listening to the gentle puff of his breath, trying to stifle images of this bedroom, this house, this life, without him. It came so close.

When I arrive, the effort of kneading pieces of Kalamata olive into a yeasty bread dough is making him sweat.

"Hey, Schätzli," I say. "How's the PT going?"

"Savory this time." His recipe choices reflect his moods. Last week it was walnut bread.

I brush a smudge of flour off Willem's chin. He steadies himself and stoops low while I stand on tiptoe so we can kiss.

"Who would have thought this would be so good for me," he says. He concentrates on making a fist, gives the dough a final punch.

"You'll hear no complaints from me." I stow my box of leftovers in the fridge.

"What did you think of the lawyer?" he asks, carefully forming two loaves.

I tell him.

"What do you want to do?"

Before I can answer, Tasha walks in with Bonkers, a short-haired, gray-striped fluffball. The tiny cat winds her way around my ankles; I untangle myself from her leash. Tasha inspects her father's handiwork, opens the fridge, peeks into the pollo asado. She shakes her head at Willem, who looks at me with dismay. I shrug and pick up Bonkers, who rubs her forehead against my cheek with a blood pressure lowering rumble of a purr. It's still delightfully surprising to hear that much sound emanating from such a compact creature.

Willem loses his grip on the pastry brush; it drops into the shallow bowl of olive oil that stands ready. Oil splashes onto the countertop. I reach for a paper towel.

"Stop," he says. I pull my hand away, take a step back. Now I feel even worse. More than thirty years we've been together and I still don't know how to give him what he needs. So much for being a therapist.

He covers my awkwardness by asking, "How'd it go with RAJE?"

"Liz thinks her nephew might help."

"Allan? The cop?" says Natasha. "How's he doing?" We watch Willem slowly and deliberately brush a light coat of oil over the plump loaves.

"Better, but Liz thinks he needs something useful to do. Helping me might be it."

"That wouldn't be bad. He always seemed pretty sharp." Tasha takes an orange from the fruit bowl. "Man, it's been years since I've seen him."

"Well, if it works out, he'll probably be around. You both okay with that?"

Tasha's 'sure' choruses with Willem's 'of course.'

I watch our daughter's receding back. Willem carefully places the baking sheet in the oven. "When are you home to-night?"

"A new prospect's coming at six. Adding that hour to my schedule is paying off."

"Yes," he says, "that's prime client time." After Willem's architecture firm was on solid ground and the kids were out of the house, I cut that six o'clock slot. It used to be our prime time.

He stands and stretches, camouflaging a sigh. This is defi-nitely not what we'd pictured. Back when we were the frus-trated parents of two pigheaded adolescents, we'd nudge each other back into good humor with reminders of the good times yet to come. These were supposed to be them.

Oh, well. Only fools believe there are guarantees in life.

Willem dries his hands and comes to hold me. I wish I were taller. Even a couple inches would make it easier for him. He laughs it off, says reaching down to hug me means he can still touch his toes. Add my lack of height to the list of things to grouse about today. If I don't watch myself, my mother's dire prediction will come true: I'll end up just like her.

"What about dinner?" Willem leans away from me, uses the kitchen counter for support.

"Plenty of snacks at the office."

"You're not taking good care of yourself," he says. "I don't like it. Why don't you take some time off? At least until this mess is cleared up."

I think, We need the money, but say, "I need something to take my mind off this mess."

"Schätzli, I'm glad you're talking with RAJE, but you have to do more than that. Let them – please let *everyone* who loves you help you more than you do."

"How? What can you do that you aren't already? Willem, I should be doing more for you."

"If I let you, you'd be wiping my ass for me."

"Thank you for that lovely image."

"Seriously, Schätzli, did you ever consider I could use a distraction too? The thinking part of my brain still works." He cautiously knocks himself on the noggin. "Liz's idea. I like it."

"It has possibilities." I give him a we've-been-together-thirty-years-but-you're-still-holding-back-on-me look. "You didn't seem at all surprised when you heard it was Amy Nguyen."

In answer, he takes his cane and leads me to my home office. He stops at my record collection in the bookcase, flips past Ray Charles, Yes, ELO, and Edith Piaf. His look of concentration eases as he pulls an ORB album from the shelf. He taps the brilliant blue signature scrawled across the ORB logo, a stylized teardrop cradling the earth in its bulb. Beneath Amy's autograph is a tiny, hand-drawn bunny rabbit.

I expect, How dense do you think I am. It's a surprise when he asks, "How committed are you?"

"I am, but Wayne's right. I have no idea what to do, where to start, even. I need someone like Allan. It's up to him now."

"Don't make him your excuse. I know you. I know what you're thinking. You need to do this for both you and her. I say then do it."

I can't breathe. RAJE, Mona, now Willem. They're all behind me, and the pressure is unbearable. I should've kept my stupid mouth shut, kept my doubts about Amy's death to myself. It's like when parents spout off and threaten a misbehaving child with some type of kneejerk consequence, only to find that the required follow-through inconveniences them even more than the youngster. I always warn parents to think first, and think big picture. If they don't follow through, they're sunk. I've got that sinking feeling.

Willem slowly strokes the back of my head, says, "We're with you, Jackie. We're all with you."

That's right. They love me. I am not alone anymore. No one's behind me, pushing. No. My people are with me, beside me, holding me up. It's what we do for each other, what we've always done. As Mona said, this is just a blip. We've all survived worse. And we've gotten through a lot of it together.

I nod and check the clock. Time to go to work.

At the door Willem wears the sly smile that's made only rare appearances lately. "Drive carefully," he says, "and watch out for weirdos."

I crunch across the gravel parking lot toward the mid-century Craftsman Willem and I bought during the 2007 real estate slump. We'd repurposed it to house my office and those of three colleagues. A splash of unruly green at the roofline catches my attention. Time to get the gutters cleaned again. But then, why bother. The building belongs to my practice, so losing the lawsuit means kissing this retirement income stream goodbye.

I unlock the back door and, as I step across the threshold, take on the camouflage of my professional persona.

Taneesha is the daughter of an Indonesian mother and Black father. Her mom called soon after their move from Oklahoma, looking for someone to help a young adolescent with a first-class case of culture shock. Taneesha is unnervingly bright and unremittingly motivated; info on local kid culture and a few coping strategies did the trick. For the next few years we saw each other whenever, as she said, life happened. Now, as a high school junior looking ahead, she comes in weekly to talk with a grown-up who isn't Mom or Dad.

Today she's in the armchair on my left, tilted forward at the waist, palms pressed together between her thighs. Her parents, Murni and Neil, are on the sofa across from me. Murni's face is to the window, but her eyes shift toward me. Neil's arms are crossed, his expression grim. We all like each other. That's what makes this even harder.

Neil says, "Taneesha, this is your therapy. You're in charge here."

I wonder how much he means it.

Murni cuts in: "But you know how we feel. You and Jackie accomplished a lot, but you've got college apps to think about, a lot of decisions coming up. Maybe it's time for something new."

Now we know. Poker face time.

Taneesha looks from me to them and back again. "It's the Amy Nguyen thing," she says.

I don't envy her parents. Our kids put Willem and me under pressure plenty of times but, luckily for us, not with the intensity of this shimmering young woman.

"You don't need to put it out there like that," says Neil.

"Does she have a point?" I ask.

"What'd we say back at the house, T? Jackie's got to be hurting enough as it is."

I say, "Thanks for your thoughtfulness, Dad."

He looks at me uneasily. I give him a supportive smile.

They kept their daughter safe through some turbulent years and events. What they're doing now is even more courageous. It's one thing to say she's earned the right to set her own course; it's another to actually drop the reins.

"Given the accusation against me," I say, "you have good reason to wonder if this is the right place for your daughter." Murni gives her daughter a see-she-agrees-with-us look. "Your parents say it's your decision, Taneesha, so you need to be as fully informed as possible."

Murni looks apologetic. "We really want everything to go well for you, Jackie, and I hate to ask, but what do you think the chances are that this will …"

"Go well for me?" I finish her thought with an exaggerated shrug. I consider, My ass is grass and a culturally ignorant legal system is the lawnmower. Yeah, that'd be smart. Instead, I opt for honesty. "I have no idea. This is a first – and hopefully last – for me." I turn to face Taneesha. As far as I'm concerned, from now on she's the only other person in the room. "Where are you with this?"

A spot on the floor has her attention. "They don't want you putting weird ideas in my head. Mom, especially."

"All I can say is, I do my best with all my clients. I follow my profession's code of ethics and my own set of values. We've known each other a longish while and it's fair to say you know me … pretty well." My smile is answered by hers. "Tell me. What're *you* worried about?"

"She was here before she made it big?"

I nod.

"They called you a Svengali. I looked it up."

"Amy was tremendously talented. Her accomplishments were her own."

Now she looks me in the eye. "You said I could be president."

"You've been a very involved, effective member of student council since freshman year."

"We were talking about the White House."

Ignoring, or maybe because of, Murni's sharp intake of breath, I continue. "I've never met anyone your age who cares more or is more politically astute. I stand by what I said: I'd vote for you."

Neil's voice, sotto voce: "So would I." There's a rustle, as if someone's getting elbowed. "Well, I would." That was a little louder.

"What about Columbia?" Taneesha says. "My school counselor said I should play it safe, stick with second tier schools. That would guarantee me a spot somewhere, and it'd save time, effort, and money."

That woman's incompetent and/or racist. Maybe related to Amy's old pre-cal teacher. Nope, can't say that either.

Instead I nod again and say, "I agree." She gives me a shocked look. "Who wouldn't want an acceptance letter from a solid school in their pocket? But do you want to limit yourself? Columbia's your number one choice. Sure, it's super-competitive and odds are you won't get in; however, what chance do you have if you don't give it your best shot? You'd be shutting a door in your own face. How much do you want to live with the coulda-shoulda?"

"Yeah, yeah," she says with her patented Taneesha twinkle, "and let's not forget the what-ifs and if-onlys."

"Maybe it *is* time for a change," I say. "It's a bad sign when you start quoting me."

We smile at each other for a long moment. She scuffs the carpet with the toe of her shoe.

"They don't know if we can trust you anymore."

I feel very much on the defensive, want to confess, but to what? I'm not sure. I just know I don't want to lose another client, especially not Taneesha. "What do you need?"

"I like you, Jackie. I really do…"

Nope, we're not going there. Sentiment right now would slay me. This is about you, Taneesha.

"Leaving the decision up to you shows how much your parents trust your judgment. Don't base your decision on how much you like me. If staying means you or your parents will be worried about what I'm doing, that's not good. The only thing that matters is you, where you're at, and where you want to go next. Are we clear?"

Her turn to nod. "I still don't know what to do."

"What do you need from me to help you decide?"

"Tell me what to do?"

"Yeah, right." I take a moment to breathe and think. Time to act on what I've said. "Taneesha, I'm going to ask you some questions. They're for you to answer in your own way and time. And it'll be important for you to be totally honest with yourself. Agreed?"

"Yes." She has her look of resolve.

"Okay, here's the first question: How have things changed for you since we started working together?"

"Wait a sec." She pulls out her cell phone. Her mother reaches for it; Taneesha pushes the intrusion away and quickly types a message to herself. She looks up. "Okay."

"What has helped and what hasn't?"

"Yup."

"What do you still want to work on? And here's the last and most important question: How much do you trust me to help you do that?"

I massage my scalp and check the clock. There's time for my daily meditation, embracing a positive. Looking down at my feet, I wiggle my toes. Comfortable shoes are a definite positive. An even bigger positive than these wide slides are my clients. Once, when my mother complained about my choice of profession, I claimed to only work with people I find lovable. At the time I was being flip, but there was truth in it. Go figure.

I wonder who, out of those lovable people still left, will stick with me. If Taneesha's parents had been able to find another therapist with my multicultural chops, we'd have already said our farewells.

Thank goodness there are still people who don't know or care about my legal woes. Based on the intake forms he filled out on-line, tonight's prospective client works at a tech start-up. Here's a plus: he comes with excellent health insurance. Maybe he has colleagues who are thinking about therapy. Word of mouth is my most dependable referral source. Time to make a good impression. I plump the sofa pillows and brush my hair.

Beneath his day's growth of beard, Tim's face has a ruddy glow. His wide smile exudes confidence, openness. I warm to the young man.

"I'm glad this worked out," he says. "A lot of therapists I've called aren't taking new patients." I clench my teeth; ordinarily I wouldn't be either. "I've been thinking about this for a while," he continues, "looking for the right person. I've been stressed out and can really use the help." He takes a seat on the sofa, casually drapes an arm across the back.

His forthrightness is refreshing. "Glad to be of service, Tim. So you've been stressed out lately. Please say more about that."

"I've got money problems, right?"

"That must be rough." I take note of his official Seahawks jersey and new high-end running shoes. "How can I be of help?"

He lifts my crocodile puppet off the bookcase, zips the teeth open and shut. He reopens the crocodile's jaws and squeezes the head of my plush tabby cat into it. Any warmth I harbored for him evaporates.

"You're the one getting sued, right? For killing that singer?"

A second warning light flares in my gut. So this is life with the Amy Nguyen thing. Lilac, honeysuckle, rose. I force my shoulders back, take a slow breath, keep my voice flat. "You got it wrong."

"I just moved into this great apartment in Belltown but I've got massive student loans. My salary's decent but it doesn't cover my expenses and, like, let me have a life. This is the perfect solution."

My chest constricts. I grip the armrests of my chair. "I appreciate you coming to meet me and apologize for any inconvenience, but we're not a good match after all."

"I heard how you screwed her up and now her family's suing you for millions."

Teneleventwelve. I stand. "Thanks for taking the time."

"I looked it up – you gotta have insurance to cover this stuff." His ingratiating smile is in jarring contrast to the rest of him. "I'm your patient, my health insurance pays you – you're happy. You mess with my head a while, maybe a couple months, I sue you, your malpractice pays me – I'm happy. Win-win."

"You need to leave." I stand and open the door. He looks at me uncomprehendingly, so I add, "Now."

"What?" he says. "This is bullshit!" He leans forward, eyes hardening, body tensing.

The toys fall to the floor. I'll disinfect them.

"I agree. That's why you need to leave." The weight of my cell phone and keys in my jacket pockets is reassuring. I usher the sputtering man down the hall and out onto the porch, lock the front door behind him. I lean with my back against the wall and hug myself, hot tears forming. My breath catches in my chest.

"What the hell was that?" Erica, the therapist in the office next to mine, stands in her open doorway, briefcase in hand.

"Sorry." I quickly wipe my brow, feigning tiredness, and motion with my head toward the porch. "A nutcase wanting to see ... hey, there's something –"

"We know, Jackie," she says, indicating her fellow tenants, "and we support you. I'm so sorry you have to deal with this crap. If there's anything I can do to help."

"Thanks, but no, there's nothing. I hope there's no fallout on you or the others, no guilt by association."

"We can take care of ourselves." She and I walk toward the kitchen. "Don't worry, Jackie. You'll be okay."

"Yeah, I'm fine."

I watch her drive away then double-check the deadbolt on the back door.

"I'm fine," I say to the empty air. "Desperate and disgusted, but fine."

Halfway to my office the unexpected sound of tires on gravel sets my heart racing. I scurry to the kitchen. Is the weirdo back? A surreptitious peep out the window brings a sigh of relief. Liz, Rach, and Angie arm themselves with bulging bags from the trunk of Liz's car.

"Honey, we're home!" Rachel calls as I unbolt the door. "We brought dinner."

They bustle inside and deposit their loads. Angie is quick to explain. "We figure we need to meet as often as possible until this clusterfuck blows over." Before I can argue, she hugs me, says, "We need it as much as you do, Jax."

Rachel rummages through the cupboards and sets the table. I ready my phone to call Willem but drop it back into my pocket. Liz is slicing a hefty loaf of kalamata olive bread. She waves the bread knife at me. "We're under orders to see that you actually eat. To that end, Theo cooked." I smile, picturing Willem with Liz's Greek husband, sharing this same excellent meal. Time to let everyone who loves me help me more than I do.

Theo's vegetarian moussaka is worth subjecting the roof of my mouth to more suffering. Afterward I'm very aware of the tender spots as the four of us, glasses of wine and hunks of raspberry cheesecake before us, dissect my encounter with Tim.

"Safety is a definite concern." Liz's face is set in a concentrated scowl. "Your name's out there now, and so are a lot of creeps."

"I'm pretty good at weeding them out during an initial phone call, but there's no way to screen with on-line scheduling. I've decided to take Willem's advice and lighten my client load until this is all over."

"But eventually you'll be back full time," says Angie. "And you'll still have to deal with weirdos. I only let established clients schedule themselves on-line. You can't ever let hunger for new clients trump common sense, pardon my

French. If another dirtbag slips past, you need to be prepared. Do you guys have a safety protocol?"

"Emergency numbers programmed into our phones. And we can always yell for help."

"Lotta good that'll do if you're here alone." Rachel bites the last word off. I'm often the last one here, and they know it.

I say, "Don't worry, I've got moves. PE, senior year of high school." Liz and Angie watch expectantly; Rachel eats cheesecake. "We girls had two teachers. They seemed really old at the time. Strange to think they were probably the ages we are now."

Rachel swallows, says, "Get to the point, Jax."

"Anyway," I say, forgiving her brand of concern, "they brought in a couple female police officers to teach a unit on self-defense."

I stand, abruptly lift my comfortably-shod foot and kick down at an angle. "Knee!" I almost lose a shoe. Rachel guffaws. Angie elbows her. I bring my knee up sharply. "Groin!" Now I grab at something unseen and snap my hands up and away. "If someone holds you from behind, break their thumbs to break their grip." I attack the air with the heel of my hand. "Nose!" And finally shape my hand into a duckbill, and jab. "Eyes and face."

Rachel takes another forkful. "Geez, the most exciting thing we did was a daily warm-up to 'Goodbye, Yellow Brick Road.'"

I ignore her. "They also recommended rape whistles." I pull my keyring from my jacket and isolate a slim metal tube. "And keeping your keys on you at all times." I display my fist, metal points bristling from between my fingers, and punch a phantom assailant in the gut.

"Okay," says Angie, "keys out of the desk drawer, into the pocket. That's a no-brainer."

Rachel scrapes the last crumbs from her plate. "That's your security measure? Pointy keys or no, faced with a six-foot tall, two hundred pound guy with long arms, you're still dead meat."

DAY TWO

• •

Sharp sunlight glints off the sidewalk, reflecting an oppressive heat. I walk up the hill toward my office; a familiar form approaches from the opposite direction. I remove my sunglasses, squint to focus. I can't believe it.

Amy strolls casually toward me, her head tilted down and away, eyes up, that sardonic grin on her face. My heart quickens. As we near each other, I open my arms in supplication. "What happened?"

"I know, I know," she answers blithely, her hands outstretched, shoulders raised in that characteristic shrug.

Before we can embrace, Amy is gone.

"What time is he coming?" Willem asks.

"Nine." I brush my shorts to remove detritus from my ongoing campaign against the boxwood hedge lining our property. Its destruction and removal has haunted my to-do list for years. The stress of the lawsuit finally pushed me into action.

I kick off my muck-caked sneakers and step into the house. It takes a couple tries for Willem to pluck the stray twigs and leaves from my tangled hair. I take care to hold still.

The dream has been running through my head all morning.

"I wish I could help you with that monster."

The regret in his voice stings. He doesn't often allude to the things he can no longer do.

"This is personal, a matter of honor." I display a bicep and fist. "Only one shall emerge victorious. Besides, I'm getting all my aggressions out."

"What happened there?" Willem points to a line of red trickling its way down my left shin. Neither of us mentions the healthy bruise beginning to color my right knee.

I lick a finger and swipe at the scrape. "I hate that hedge. I'm winning, but the damn thing bites back. What's in the oven? Smells good."

"Nice try." He hands me a damp paper towel; I wipe my shin, blinking away the glaze of tears before he sees it. "Are you sure about this?" he asks.

"What? You're asking now? You said it was the right thing to do. I thought we were in this together."

"It is," he says with the slightest hesitation, "and we are. But I know you, Schätzli." He leans down, touches the blood still oozing from my leg. "You worked long and hard at putting them to rest, but bad habits and worse memories are emerging from the shadows. Suicide…"

"I know," I sigh. "I'm dreaming about Matt again."

"Is that what's keeping you up? I wondered."

No need to mention the dream about Amy. The Matt dreams provide enough wretchedness to share. Willem takes my shoulders in his still unreliable grip. "Remember, you couldn't save your brother. It wasn't your job to save him. And as you yourself say, you are responsible to, not for, your clients."

I turn away. "Sometimes that's hard to remember."

Willem's gray eyes cloud. "I don't know how else to help you. I hope this detective can."

"We'll figure that out soon enough." I undo what's left of my wayward ponytail, shake my hair loose. "Now back to what's truly important," I say, a little too breezily. "Whatever you're baking smells super."

"How's *Mandelkuchen*?" he says, playing along.

"Perfect, Schätzli. Thank you." I take Willem's hand, turn it over, touch my lips to the base of his palm. "Shower time."

I used to see Allan Shaw every year at Liz and Theo's Labor Day barbecue bashes. For several years, RAJE kept our collective eyes on him. At Liz's request. Allan kept to the edge of the festivities, never made an effort with the other kids. Whenever I encouraged, or ordered, my two to eat with him, they returned defeated. Stefan attributed it to the age difference, Allan being a few years older than the RAJE kid crowd. Natasha called him weird.

I tried to explain that he was sad because his mom died when he was really young. Being around other kids who still had both parents fussing over them must be hard. Knowing that didn't matter. As Tasha said more than once, making friends means both sides have to try.

There was a gap of almost a decade during which Allan avoided the annual festivities. He turned up again after his marriage, but his and his wife's attendance was spotty because they spent part of every July with her folks.

I liked Zoe. She was smart lady with a light, easy presence and an infectious belly laugh. When Allan and Zoe bought a fixer upper, Zoe asked me for design advice. The guided tour was the last time I had seen Allan. The therapist in me couldn't help but notice their joy in being together. Allan had been a contented, happy man.

The loss of his wife is in the set of Allan's jaw, the way his feet hit the floor. I feel the chip balanced precariously on his shoulder and wonder which way it will fall.

"Welcome, Allan. Good to see you." He delivers a firm, though slightly moist handshake.

"Good to see you, too, Mrs. Kessler. Sorry I'm late."

"That's okay. Thanks for coming. And please, call me Jackie." He smiles tightly in response. From the moment we met, Zoe and I were on a first name basis.

I shepherd him down the hall to my home office. There's a fragility about him; he moves cautiously, as though unsure where his body is in space. It reminds me of Willem.

Once seated, I search his features for a resemblance to his aunt Liz, hoping to find some sense of familiarity and comfort. His face is gaunt, his frame thin and angular, a contrast to Liz's robust physique.

"Liz must've given you the lowdown on my predicament," I blurt.

"Yes, although I'm not quite sure what kind of help you want. She was vague on that."

"What do you know so far?"

He twitches forward in his seat. Is this irritation or a hint of the detective Liz described? "A former client of yours died of what was determined to be a self-inflicted gunshot wound. You're being sued by the family."

"Right. Bottom line, I think she was murdered. If I don't prove it in the next eighteen days, I'm toast."

Allan cocks his head, his expression diplomatically neutral. There it is, a patented Liz move. "Look, you should know," he says, "I was late because I was circling the block trying to decide if this is a good idea or not."

"I appreciate your honesty," I reply. "What do you think? Thumb up or down?"

"I don't know what I can do for you. I'm no longer on the force. You'd be better off with a private detective. I can't —"

Time to interrupt. "I'm Korean, a collectivist by nature. I depend on my tribe. If I have to choose between working with a stranger and someone who comes highly recommended by someone I love, who do you think it'll be? Your aunt says we'd make a good team; I trust her judgment. The fact that you're no longer on the force means you have more flexibility in what you can do and how you do it, doesn't it?"

"There *is* something called the law."

"I'm not asking you to break the law or even bend your ethics. What I am asking for is a degree of creativity, maybe even foolhardiness. It'll take a certain … verve to see this through. To be blunt, I need all the help I can get, and Liz said you could use something to focus on."

Allan's shoulders tense and his face flushes. "So much for privacy."

Damn. Pushed the chip the wrong direction. Oh well. No coulda-shouldas for me either.

Outwardly, I smile. "Liz is like a sister to me. We don't have many secrets. And you're her family so, like it or not, you're an automatic member of the aforementioned tribe."

"I was in narcotics, not homicide."

"It takes certain skills to be any kind of detective, right? You have to be a critical thinker, a good problem solver."

"Get an engineer."

The man's face immediately turns an even darker red, and he looks as if he wants to bite his tongue off. I recognize the signs of depression, but can't hide my chagrin.

"I'm sorry," he says. "Didn't mean to be rude."

"Sure you did, and I deserved it. I apologize for being so pushy. I can only imagine what an impossible time this has been for you." His stillness guides me. "I'm surrounded by people who're doing what they can, but this has us all spinning. I need someone who knows crime to at least steer us in the right directions."

Allan draws a slow breath deep into his diaphragm, holds it, and releases a long, loud exhale. His shoulders relax and the high color in his face recedes. Liz was wrong; he picked up at least one self-care tip.

"All right," he says. "Give me the details and we'll see if there's a case."

"I'm being sued by the family of Amy Nguyen."

"Amy Nguyen?" Allan looks stunned. "I wasn't paying much attention to the news at the time, but this did penetrate. I was sad to hear about her. Local girl made very, very good."

"What do you know about her and ORB?"

"Not much," he admits. "I always figured their music would be more ethnic than I'm into." He looks embarrassed. I let him wallow in it. "I did see her once, though, downtown at the convention center. She delivered the keynote at a symposium on refugee families. She was very effective."

"I'll bet."

"She talked about ethnocentrism and how it's part of being human, that we develop preferences based on what we know. There's a thin line between preference and prejudice, a line that's easy to cross. She dared us to identify the stereotypes we hold, the assumptions we make about people. She said doing that was the first step in counteracting -isms of every kind, not just racism. It really got me thinking."

There's a relief; his memory for detail is still excellent. "Good," I say. "She was right." Amy's words got him thinking. She would have been disappointed; she wanted people to feel and act as well.

"Amy Nguyen." He regards the two bulging files on the desk, the same documentation I shared with my lawyer, Wayne. "Who would've thought."

I'm tired of that reaction. I want to say, Her celebrity shouldn't matter. But, as with Wayne, I can't afford to alienate Allan and don't know him well enough to take chances. What comes out is: "I sure didn't. Still don't."

"That's why we're here," he says. "I know this must be hard for you." He doesn't know how hard or for what reasons. "Start from the beginning, but watch yourself. If you feel protective of her, you'll leave things out. It's often the smallest details that warrant the most attention."

I give him the rundown of Amy's therapy from the age of fifteen, her long slog out of depression, how she struggled to tame her overpowering anxiety.

Throughout the recital, his body has been tightening. He's restless, practically squirming in the chair. What's it like for him hearing how someone else worked their way through pain? He was barely four when cancer claimed his mother. Then to lose his wife.

"It's obvious you helped her," Allan says. "But by your own admission, Amy Nguyen's suicide was all over the news. You still haven't told me why you're so convinced she didn't kill herself."

I look toward the ceiling and mutter, "This is harder than I thought."

Amy and I reviewed progress at least every six months. To mark the five years of teamwork behind us, we did a broader overview, back from the beginning. As trust grew Amy had revealed more of herself. She'd started sharing her poetry in therapy sessions. From there she'd progressed to local poetry slams, first at high school events, then at local clubs. With each recitation and round of applause, she'd gained more confidence and a stronger, clearer voice.

It was natural for her to fuse her magic with words with magic at the keyboard. The results were haunting, provocative songs and a full ride from the University of Washington.

Since starting classes, Amy was coming in once every couple of months. She'd been doing well, had more outside support in friends she'd made within the music department. They were an eclectic, international group of students with similar backgrounds who traded thoughts, ideas, and dreams. Now the inevitable had happened; they'd formed a band.

"Rehearsals are going really well." She tossed the toy bunny up and down. "We're working on a sound, a style. Three of us are songwriters, so we've got original material." She shook the bunny playfully. "Some of it might even be good."

I savored the hope in that statement. "Sounds like you mesh really well."

Amy's forehead wrinkled. "Sometimes it feels a little too easy."

"Oh?"

I smiled inwardly as she struggled for a response, could practically hear her inner dialogue. I wondered which it would be, being told I was nosy or dense.

She gave me a welcome jolt instead. "It's like we get each other without having to explain ourselves, like we've all been there, y'know? In different ways, but also the same. It's such a — " She searched for a word.

"Relief?"

"Yeah" she agreed. "I finally feel like I belong." She exuded joy, contentment. And surprise.

"That's huge, Amy. I'm happy for you." I left her another second of peace. "Okay, it's killjoy time."

"Oh, gods. Must you?"

I shrugged. "It's my job."

"All right. Go ahead."

"Be honest with me. How weird does it feel?"

"Really weird." Her eyes clung to the vine maple framed in the window. "I don't trust it."

"That's actually a good sign. It's a natural way to feel. I'd be worried if you said there were no red flags." Her right palm found its way to the inside of her left forearm. "This is an enormous change. You're learning to see and experience yourself in a whole new way. That's bound to feel freakish. Watch yourself, Amy. There may come a time when that distrust hits your system and fights to get things to go back to the way they were. You might not even know it's happening until you catch yourself in a what-the-hell situation."

She closed her eyes, slouched back in the chair, arms dangling. "I think that's already happened. A couple times. It's weird to feel more foreign in your own family than anywhere else. Now I've got the band. *They're* my family, my home. But I've done things to piss everyone off and I don't even know why." She opened her eyes and sat up. "I always regret it and apologize, but I don't even know where that shit comes from."

"You just described it. After all your hard work, things are coming together in a big way. You're making your own destiny. You're not used to that. And according to your parents, that's not how life is supposed to work." She shakes her head. "Your system's triggering the *that's disloyal* alarm, and it's bound to up your anxiety. Remember, for most minorities, anxiety is a lifetime companion. Hell, it's practically our middle name. But you know the signs to look for, you have the tools. Use 'em."

She absorbed this, looked at me slyly. "Thanks, IJ. Don't let it go to your head, but today was actually helpful." She laughed when I stuck my tongue out at her. "We have a name." I didn't budge. "What's this? LMN has left the building?"

"No, Little Miss Nosy figures you'll tell her when you're ready."

She sighed and wound the bunny's ear around her forefinger. It was loose enough not to cut off her blood circulation, but the long, furry ear still maintained a tight curl. "Okay, you win." She dropped the mysterious tone. "It's ORB. O-R-B, all caps. It's sharp that way, commands attention," she said, anticipating my question.

I sat back and considered. "ORB. I like it. What does it stand for?"

"Nothing. It's just ORB. Wanna see our logo?" She dropped the toy and headed for the art supplies, not waiting for an answer.

"O-R-B," I said while she sketched. "How about Our Refugee Band? That makes ORB." I gave myself a mental pat on the back for cleverness while her face puckered.

"No."

"Why not? It's perfect. You're all from refugee families."

"Geez, IJ, just how old are you?" She held a hand parallel to the floor, palm up. "ORB? Cool. Like a circle, no beginning or end, like the earth cradling all the countries we come from. Our Refugee Band?" She flipped her hand over. "Totally uncool." Her expression was patient, laced with pity.

"You could be vague about it, like W.A.S.P.."

Amy ignored my attempt to impress with knowledge of heavy metal bands, courtesy of another young client. "Picture this. Someone comes along who's perfect for us and we turn her away because she's not a refugee. Who're we hurting then? And wouldn't that be discriminatory? You're the one who pushes inclusiveness all the time."

She handed me her drawing. I ran my fingertips over the image, the Earth cradled within the bulb of an elongated teardrop.

Leaving no space for further reaction, she said, "I have a new one. It's called 'Way To Go.'"

Amy drummed a light rhythm on her thigh, the rest of her body following the beat. She broke into a song-poem, her young voice at first tremulous and self-doubting. As she progressed, her voice grew in clarity and strength until the recitation came to a close:

"I knew from the start I should hide my heart
But my fatal flaw made me lose it
Fallen high to low, just one way to go

You must see we can't refuse it
The love has all drained, there's been too much pain
Our secrets coalescing
There is peace to come, tomorrow's not done
Trust in love's convalescing."

I was reluctant to break the lingering hush. "Beautiful, Amy. There's so much of you in it. Here's to you and your new one." Deadpan face, pause for effect. "Well done."

She turned her head, aimed a small smile at a spot near my feet, inhaled and exhaled deeply. She was satisfied, maybe even relieved, that I'd gotten the point. So I wasn't the only one constantly assessing. Fair enough.

Her head jerked up, the sign of something snide in the works. This time, another surprise. "It's a living thing, IJ. Easiest thing ever." She swiveled the chair to face me directly, but her attention was still on that spot on the floor. Her left forefinger was wrapped with the rabbit's right ear, this time pulled tighter. "I was never in charge – it just flowed. Once it was on paper I never changed a word."

"If I didn't know you better, I'd almost think you're finally giving yourself a break."

A catcher's mitt would've come in handy as the bunny came flying past. "Doc," she laughed, "you should give yourself a break and not think so much."

I push the stop button on my old boombox as 'Way To Go' ends on a keening, yet somehow victorious note.

"Yes, and?" Allan asks.

"It's all there," I say. "Did you pay attention to the lyrics? Want to hear it again?"

"It's a love gone wrong song."

"Yes and no. You missed the point."

He shrugs, still mystified. "What *is* the point?"

Allan's face reflects his own conflicting emotions, but I'm not about to spoon feed it to him unless I absolutely have to. When he speaks, his face is calm, his voice controlled and steady. "Jackie, you did fine giving me the facts. Now I need your interpretation of them. Tell me about Amy's state of mind."

Damn. I absolutely have to.

"See, that goes against my grain. I've spent my entire professional life keeping that stuff confidential." I lift a faded brown plush toy from the bookcase. I hold the bunny close, protectively. "This was Amy's special friend," I say. "I can't remember a single session where she didn't have him in her hands. I brought him home the day I learned of her death. I like to imagine he misses her as much as I do."

There's a sudden gush of tears. Allan watches anxiously before retrieving a tissue box from the desk. He places it on the floor at my feet, and gives voice to my internal debate. "To find Amy's killer, someone has to tell her story. Amy can't do it herself. Do you think she'd want you to?"

Did I hear right? Did he say, Amy's killer? I'd worried about having another Wayne on my hands. Maybe Allan's more sensitive and intuitive than I thought. I'm now weeping openly, beyond embarrassment. I yank out a fistful of tissues to wipe my streaming face. "What right do I have?" I ask. "After all this time, how can I be sure I even have it straight?"

"Jackie, I need to know what the public doesn't know, what I can't get by reading back issues of *Rolling Stone* and *People*." He looks relieved when I nod and blow my nose. "Go back to the song. You said it's all there. Show me."

To buy time to regroup, I offer him a slice of the previously neglected Mandelkuchen. At least it's something concrete.

"You were right to call 'Way To Go' a love song. It was Amy's love letter to herself. But it's a love gone *right* song. It's about learning to forgive and accept yourself. Most people think it's a goodbye song like you said, healing from an ended love affair. That's like thinking 'Every Breath You Take' is a romantic little ditty when it's really a nasty stalker song."

Something catches in Allan's throat and his eyes lose focus. "I had that same argument with my wife while we were dating. She thought it was one of the most romantic songs ever recorded."

"It's so easy to lead people astray with the right tenor and attitude." I stop at the sudden change in Allan's expression. "Are you all right?"

"I just realized something," he says, still looking surprised. "That's the first time I've thought of Zoe since she died that I haven't wanted to put my fist through a wall."

I can't tell if he'd rather laugh or cry. Maybe both. If so, I'm right there with him. We look at each other, caught in this moment until he self-consciously gestures for me to continue.

My engine's revving again. "In 'Way to Go' Amy is the rope in a tug-of-war between the angels of life and death. She ultimately allows herself to embrace her suffering and transcend it by submitting to the angel of death."

Allan gasps. "So she *was* suicidal."

"The operative word being 'was.' Amy would work at something from every imaginable angle until it made sense to her and became ingrained. Then she could let it go and move on. Even as a teenager she was clear she never wanted to die, but she so wanted the excruciating emotional pain she was living with to end. Through this poem she realized that giving herself permission to die meant simultaneously giving herself permission to live. That was her personal paradox, and it became her safety harness whenever she got close to the edge."

"How can you know that for sure? Did she tell you as much?"

"She didn't have to. She knew I knew."

He studies my face as closely as I study his. C'mon, Allan.

Amy's keynote address stuck with you – make the connection. Nope, I guess not. Time to plow forward.

"What Amy said at that symposium plays here too. Understanding her family's history and multiculturalism is vital. The way I figure it, that's what the police missed in their investigation. They looked at it through their lens, not the victim's. They ignored the importance of context."

Allan picks up the CD cover and concentrates on the photo of the band.

"Amy's parents and older sister were Vietnam War refugees, boat people," I say. "They lived for years in a Thai refugee camp before coming to the States. Amy was the first member of the family to be born on US soil. People take it for granted that because she was born and raised here and spoke English without an accent, she was one hundred percent American. Nothing could be further from the truth. They don't understand what it is to be a second generation immigrant, especially in a refugee family."

"You're losing me."

I put my hands to my head, tears forgotten. "When I think about Amy, I automatically go into Asian mode. That's how we communicated. We used to joke about it, called it Asian-speak. I warn new clients up front that I tend to talk in circles, and ask them to haul me in if I'm being too obtuse." I put on a comically bad John Wayne imitation. "I can speak Western, really direct and to the point, if I wanna." I drop the accent. "But I usually don't. Asian-style English is my first language, American-style English is my second."

He trades the CD cover for the stuffed bunny, gently rotates it in his hands, absent-mindedly straightens the curious curl in the right ear.

I continue: "Amy's message, her art, is all about her struggles with acculturation and identity, being in-between, belonging nowhere with nobody. She came from a collectivist culture. To put it simply, collectivists absorb basic societal rules in utero. The finer points we get by watching and imitating our elders." I check to see he's still with me. "The US has an individualistic culture; the rules are spelled out in minutest detail, from a fifty-page manual for a new toaster to huge placards listing dos and don'ts in a parking lot."

He says, "I've seen those."

"Okay, so picture this. In immigrant families like Amy's, the parents don't know how to raise their kids in a new alien environment, and there's no one to learn from. The elders don't have elders. And the kids are caught in the middle, too American to please their parents and too foreign to fit in with their majority culture peers. It's a common dilemma."

Allan's head swivels, taking note of the international hodgepodge that is my office décor. Larch wood floors and ceilings. Upholstery and curtains with a distinctly Swiss accent. Korean wall scrolls, the celadon vase and Korean lacquered box nestled in the bookcase below the over-sized cow bell with the edelweiss painted on it. He must be used to it. Liz and Theo's home is furnished in what RAJE dubbed Arizona-Greek chic.

"Amy was too smart, too aware for her own good. She felt every gram of those cultural differences and blamed it on her supposed inadequacies. Collectivists are also big on keeping the peace, no matter the cost. Loyal daughter that she was, she followed family rules and didn't tell anyone about her problems, her fears, or failures. She was supposed to figure it all out by herself, and if she couldn't she was supposed to buck up, deal with it, and suffer, suffer, suffer. That eventually landed her in the hospital."

"Is that how you two connected?"

"Yes. Before we met, she'd fired her share of therapists, thought they were useless because, as she said, they didn't get her. But deep inside, she blamed herself for that too."

"Let me guess. It was further proof that her mother was right and she really was crazy."

"Yes."

"And those therapists were White."

"Bingo. Mind you, being White wasn't the problem, lack of cultural awareness was."

Allan's quiet. He puts the rabbit down. I wonder how personally this middle-class White man takes my sentiments, so I check by saying, "You must think I'm a flake."

He waits half a beat too long. "On the contrary," he says. "I'm just taking everything in."

I sigh. At least we're both trying. "Like I said, Amy's issues with culture were camouflaged in her music. Her language of choice was that of metaphor. The first verse of the song lays out how she would kill herself: 'Don't waste time reminiscing/There will always be something missing/Sleep it away and avoid another day/You can't just wish this end away.'"

He smacks the back of his right hand into his left palm. "She would have OD'd."

"Yes! Her plan was sleeping pills and alcohol. We talked about this at length. She wanted to keep things as peaceful, for herself and her family, as possible. No pain and especially no mess. She was from a tight-knit Vietnamese immigrant community. Everyone knew and watched everyone else. And the family has deep Confucian roots while also being devoutly Catholic. On the one hand they venerated their ancestors, on the other, her mother and sister attended daily mass. Rules of society, rules of the church. Bottom line, whatever Amy did would reflect on them all. She saw overdosing as a mellow way out. Most importantly, her family could spin it, call it a heart attack, embolism, whatever. The community would buy it because they'd want to."

"And her family would save face."

"Right again."

Allan stands and stretches, takes his slice of Mandelkuchen, watches a squirrel argue with a Steller's jay on the lawn outside the window.

"This is a lot to ask of you," I say. "You came as a favor to your aunt. And to me."

"Don't worry about it," he replies, returning to his seat. "I'm ready. Let's continue."

I swallow a chunk of cake without chewing; almond slices scrape their way down my gullet. "Amy wrote 'Way to Go' before anyone ever heard of her. You think a person who was so reluctant to heap shame on her family when she was a nobody would bring this type of notoriety to them when she was famous? No way."

"When's the last time you saw her?"

"Two weeks before she died." I pick a record album from the bookcase and hand it to Allan. "This was a final thank you before the kickoff of the ORBit tour, the one she never finished. It was her first trip to Europe. She was so excited, full of plans for the future. ORB was set to be goodwill ambassadors for the United Nations, working on behalf of refugees."

"How appropriate."

"Yeah, right? When Amy talked about this she was ... vivid! Does this sound like someone who wanted to end her life?"

"The police didn't interview you?"

"No, and I never got to ask my question."

"What question?"

"In Amy's opinion, war, violence destroyed her family. She was the ultimate pacifist and hated guns with a passion. What in the world would she be doing with one?"

Allan leans back in his chair, the LP on his lap, and looks me in the eye. "To answer that, all we have to do is figure out who killed Amy Nguyen, and why."

Why, indeed. Lately there are too many whys to count. If I let myself, I could follow a string of unanswered whys back to childhood. String of whys. String of pearls. Pearls of wisdom. Pearls before swine. I shake my head vigorously to stop the nonsense but stay stuck.

Time to detoxify.

Halfway across the metal foot bridge that leads to the beach I stop and turn ninety degrees to face north. A woman and two young children follow, chattering about the salmon-shaped slide at the playground they've just left.

The girl halts a few paces away. "Mommy, what's she looking at?"

The mother quietly shushes her, moves to hustle her brood past me.

"It's okay," I say, giving mom a wink. She smiles apologetically.

I crouch to be at eye-level with the kids and point to a freight train emerging, centipede-like, from a distant coastline-hugging curve. I say, "D'you like trains?" In answer, the boy grabs hold of the chain link enclosing us, his dimples deepening with anticipation. I grab hold too. "Be ready when it comes."

Happily, the engineer spots us and gives a cheery wave. The kids wave back with their entire bodies. The long freight train rumbles beneath us, rattling the bridge. The boy covers his ears. The girl giggles as the whoosh from below sets her hair aswirl.

"It's our first time here," the mom yells over the noise. "This is a wonderful park."

"Indeed," I yell back. When Tash and Stef were kids, the combination of playground, meadow, wooded trails and beach made Carkeek Park one of our family's happy places. It's still a personal refuge. "Keep an eye out," I tell them before moving on. "Cool things live in the sand and hide under the rocks."

Down at water's edge I claim a solitary corner and stand, arms and face lifted, encouraging the combined forces of water, wind and sun to wash, blow and burn the negativity from my system. Spears of afternoon sunshine draw my eyes across the water, beyond the Kitsap Peninsula, to the snow-covered peaks of the Olympic Mountains.

"I love the blue and green." A male voice, lightly accented, comes from behind. Young-sounding and at the same time full, rich, mellifluous. "There's so much water here."

A long, slender shadow falls across the damp sand as the owner of the voice moves to my side. I look up, up, and up. My body knows the angle required by Willem's six feet seven inches. This man is close to seven feet tall.

"I can only imagine what a change this was after the Kenyan refugee camp," I say.

"Yes, it was quite a shock," he says. There's a longish pause. "So you know me."

"Well, Mr. Ahmad, let's say I feel I already know you." I'd heard and read about him for years. Mohamed Ahmad, Amy's closest friend, the co-founder of ORB.

"Please. Just Mohamed. I feel I know you as well, Mrs. Kessler."

"Thank you. I'm Jackie."

He extends a hand; I take it. "This can't be a chance meeting," I say. "How did you find me here?"

His head tips toward a stern-looking man standing nearby. "Our security company was helpful." What the fuck? He's having me scoped out? Followed? I wouldn't have put that past my legal opposition, but this? It must show because he adds, "Please don't worry. He's here for me, not against you."

What a curious turn of phrase. But dude, put me at ease you did not, thank you very much.

He leads me a couple steps further away from Mr. Congeniality before bending slightly at the waist. "I have a request," he says quietly. "I wanted to make it in person, not over the phone."

Better. And to be fair, I know from Amy that English is this man's fourth language. I'm willing to play nice, Mr. Ahmad. For now.

"I see. What can I do for you?"

He shifts his weight. "We ORBers are still having a very difficult time with Amy's death. We miss her very much. I hoped you would be able to help us."

His forehead is wrinkled and his hands are clenched at his sides. Seems he doesn't have much experience making an emotional request like this. It tugs at me; this is something I'd ordinarily say yes to. I clear my throat. "I'm sorry. I can only imagine what you're going through, but I'm not the appropriate person."

"Not appropriate? I don't understand. We need someone who knew and loved her. I know she felt loved by you. That makes you the *most* appropriate person."

"I'm sorry, Mohamed." I step back to ease the crick in my neck. "This is a difficult time for us all. I'm in a complicated position and don't want to make things awkward for you."

"I know of your position," he says, gently yet persistently. "It does not affect our wishes."

"There's another, even more important reason I wouldn't be of use to you. I'm mourning her too. I'm willing to meet with you, and only you, because I know what you meant to her. But I wouldn't be there as a therapist. I'd be there like you said, as someone who misses Amy."

His demeanor is contemplative, turned inward. Decisions, decisions. Take all the time you need, buddy.

Finally, his eyebrows rise. "What you can offer must be enough. But perhaps there is more we can share."

The tension in his body relays a sense of a man literally holding himself together. I try to tap into his emotions. Hurt, even desperation. No, there's something more.

"What do you mean, Mohamed?"

"I cannot make peace with what has been said."

Uh oh, hot potato. My turn to decide. Let's follow his lead. "I can't either." Ah, hell. Let's go for broke. "Knowing her the way you did, do you think it could be true?"

"No. I do not." There it is. The hard clip of his voice, the slow burn in his eyes. Rage. He turns away.

"Neither do I."

I know from Amy that Mohamed is an extremely private person, one whose Somali culture discourages the open show of deep feeling. It's happened before that prospective clients don't follow through after an initial phone call. Having held so much in for so long, they spill their guts only to regret having revealed so much to a stranger. He's probably rethinking the in-person option.

I park myself on the smooth top of an otherwise barnacle-encrusted boulder and rub my thumb against the faint, jagged scar on the inside of my left thigh, just above the knee. When the wound was fresh, I'd claimed to have fallen from my bike. My mother was so ready to believe it. Even after all these years I can still feel the reassuring scratch of the paper clip as I ripped it through my flesh.

The young man seats himself on a sun-bleached log. We watch in silence as gleaming white ferries headed out of Kingston and Edmonds seemingly meet in the middle of Puget Sound. Mohamed's long fingers pick at one of the many rounded pebbles embedded in the soft wood. It must have taken a lot of pressure, being rolled and pounded in the surf and thrust onto shore, for those little rocks to implant themselves.

I pick half of an empty mussel shell out of the sand, angle it so the pearly insides catch the sunlight. "Mohamed, I get the feeling there's more. Is there anything else you want from me?"

He keeps working at the rock, manages to extract it. He inspects it then flicks it away. When he looks at me again, his expression is fascinatingly enigmatic. How'd he learn to do that? More importantly, why'd he have to? This is different from Allan's blank expression and my own therapist face; those are waiting for responses without wanting to influence. Here there's something beyond the blankness; I sense opposing forces pulling at him. I've met this before. Here's a man who's seen bad things happen.

"I would like to know how you intend to fight the lawsuit." Now he's committed.

I pull in a breath between closed teeth. "How do you know I will?"

He smiles cautiously, recognizing that I just committed myself. He starts working another pebble loose. "Amy always said you stood up for her. I trusted you would do so again. And for yourself."

I've never had a panic attack before, but this pushes the right button. It's unnerving to hear how Amy talked about me, that she portrayed me as having the fortitude I envied in her. I wrap myself in bravado and will myself to make it real.

Another deep breath, a forced smile. "Amy knew me pretty well." Oh brother, I wonder if that sounded as stilted to him as it felt to me. But he's right. If I go through with this, I'll be standing up for Amy too. Keeping her in front of me might be enough. But what would that make her, an inspiration or a shield?

Amy was a suspicious, cynical little soul, a similarity to myself I found both frustrating and endearing. Getting her to open up was as hard as shucking an oyster with a splintered mussel shell, yet she trusted Mohamed Ahmad. I throw the shell I'd been cracking onto the sand.

Oh hell. I have nothing to lose. "I have a theory about how she died, and I'm going to explore it."

He speaks slowly, carefully. "In other words, you will look for the person who killed her?"

Ah, what a relief. Another person who speaks my language. "Yes."

"Alone?"

"No, with helpers."

A pause to watch the two ferries sail steadily away from each other, toward their respective destinations.

"You will then bring that person to justice?"

"That's the hope. No, that's the plan."

The air is ripe with salt and seaweed. The surf lapping at the rocky beach is rhythmic, hypnotic. All of a sudden, I realize I'm calm.

Mohamed is quiet. The muscles in his face relax and he rolls his shoulders back. He carefully places the newly liberated rock on the log next to him, pats it reassuringly with a forefinger as if it's a precious thing.

He says, "I understand about meeting with the band. But there is one who will not take no for an answer. She said to tell you that Kick is asking."

When I hear that, I change my mind. He takes in my change of demeanor and adds, "But before you meet her, there is something you must know."

The cloud cover is a dull slab of gray; it looks as cold and hard as the concrete beneath my rear, as harsh and unrelenting as Mohamed's news sitting in my craw. In my profession I've found there are few things I must know. Rather, there are things people must offload. My job is to help them figure out what those are so they can problem-solve and find new ways to deal with them. But this is my private life Mohamed has invaded.

Something I must know, indeed. As opposed to something I want to know. But when it comes to someone else's offload, I seldom get the chance to choose. What was Amy's most common complaint? Ah yes, mysteries and secrets, and lies, lies, lies.

I was stupid to agree to this so soon. The panic attack that wasn't is pushing on me again. More deep breaths, Jackie. Reclaim the *calm*. Forget the gray above. I focus on the earthbound and warm myself with the view from our seats, halfway up the Green Lake grandstand. In spite of drab skies, spring in Seattle is sublime. This afternoon, color blooms high and low, and the seemingly infinite shades of green soothe and refresh my soul. Ducks and the occasional Canada goose dot the water, and there's a general air of good cheer among the weekend walkers, bikers, joggers and skaters. Another Kessler happy place. Way back when, we'd rent pedal boats or a canoe and circle Duck Island, ending the excursion with ice cream from the vendor near the Boathouse.

Isha "Kick" Dorji sits rigidly, her hands beneath her thighs. Her long black hair hangs loose over her narrow shoulders, framing a pleasant, round face which today is clouded by upset.

Mohamed had quickly arranged this same-day meeting before I could change my mind. He needn't have feared; I want to make up my own mind about her before … hell, there's no way to know what'll come next.

As Kick begins to speak, she splutters and coughs, turns an alarming shade of red.

"Are you all right?" I ask, aware and wary of the impulse to smack her on the back.

"Yes." It's a raspy reply. Her breath comes in gulps, her eyes are streaming. "I'm fine. I swallowed wrong. I'm so sorry. This is very embarrassing. It's just… I'm very nervous. Thank you for meeting with me. I know you didn't want to."

"That's not true. Well, you're right," I admit. "Not initially. But you knew I'd want to meet Kick."

At the sound of the nickname, the young woman flinches.

"I'm sorry, Isha. I didn't mean –"

"No, it just caught me by surprise. Amy was the only one who called me that. I've missed it. Please, call me Kick. And yes, I hoped you would recognize the name."

"Kick, what do you want from me?" No need to share what I want from her.

A crow flaps down to plague an abandoned Spud Fish and Chips bag two rows down. Kick begins abruptly. "Every once in a while Amy would tell me what you talked about. She said she told you about me." I remain non-committal, allowing her to fill the space. "I feel I know you. Amy liked you, and that's good enough for me."

The weight of her statement adds to that of Mohamed's and settles firmly in my consciousness. We're skipping close to professional boundaries. Maybe I should have talked this through with RAJE first. Maybe there's a graceful way to bow out of this conversation.

She continues: "When I was a kid, we lived in a building next to the farmers' market. I liked to sit by the window and watch. I especially liked the buskers, the man who played the violin, the kazoo trio. It's how I first heard bluegrass and bagpipes." Her face lights with enthusiasm. "The piano was a surprise. At first I thought someone was playing a CD extra loud. I mean, how could there be a piano at the market? But there she was, three stories below, pounding on that little thing and singing with a voice so strong it sounded like it was coming from next door. I had to go down."

Good. If she does all the talking, we're in the clear.

"How old were you?"

"Just out of middle school. The first few times I kept my distance. I was embarrassed and didn't want her to see me.

After a while I pretended I was shopping so I could follow her when she took a break. I had such a crush on her. She was beautiful and talented and seemed so grown up. I wanted to be her so bad." Kick pauses, remembering. "Then one day she stopped at a bakery stand and bought a rhubarb tart. I was at the next stand pretending to look at tomatoes. All of a sudden, she turned around and took my picture with her cellphone. Then she put the tart in front of my face and said, 'Here – if you're going to follow me around like a puppy, I might as well feed you.'"

The two of us share in bittersweet laughter. Amy had proudly shown me that photo of her first groupie.

"My favorite dessert is still rhubarb tart," the young woman confides. "Amy was very patient. It couldn't have been pleasant to have me hanging around. That's why she called me Kick, you know, because she wanted to kick me in the pants." She sees my surprise. "Yes, she told me. Once when I annoyed her, she said she was going to talk to her therapist about me." A shy smile emerges. "I didn't tell her, but I didn't know what a therapist was. Anyway, that was the first time I ever heard about you. I wasn't sure if it was good or bad that she talked to you about me."

"It was a good thing. I remember the first time she mentioned you." Boundaries? Bye-bye. "She wasn't used to having admirers and didn't know what to make of you at first. Over time she learned to enjoy it. That's the other reason she called you Kick; she thought it was a kick to have such a faithful fan. And friend."

She nods slowly, clearly relishing those last words. "Friend. Yes. Amy was my best friend."

Kick's story gushes out of her like a waterfall. They were Lhotsampas, ethnic Nepali who lived in Bhutan without the protection of citizenship. Her parents' opposition to the government's prejudicial rules led to their exile. The family was sent to a refugee camp before being accepted into the United States.

A year after their arrival, Kick's father died. The official diagnosis was a heart attack; Kick claimed it was of a broken heart. Her mother, Dawa, worked hard to maintain the family. She had little time or energy for her children. As the eldest, Kick was in charge of her siblings.

"My only break was on Saturday mornings." She hugs her body with her arms, a gesture reminiscent of Amy. "It was hard to stay on top of my studies. I thought I should drop out and get a job, but Amy said I couldn't give up my education. She gave me good advice about life. I asked her once how she learned so much. She said someone helped her; now she was helping me. So you see I had to meet you, to thank you."

This time it's me swallowing hard. I feel my heart simultaneously expand and constrict.

Amy mentored her young fan over the years, encouraging her interest in music and the performing arts. This smacked of rebellion to Kick's traditional mother, who was thoroughly against her daughter spending time on trivialities.

However, Dawa Dorji tolerated her daughter's relationship with Amy because it meant someone was looking out for her. Fellow hotel housekeepers, many of them also refugees, warned that teenaged girls in America, especially those from poor families, often dropped out of school and even became pregnant. Dawa did not want this for her daughter.

ORB had already established itself as an invigorating force in the Pacific Northwest music scene when Dawa was laid off from her job. Kick, then a student at Seattle Central College, again planned to quit school when Amy stepped in to help. She hired Dawa as her personal housekeeper. These wages, plus financial aid, covered Kick's tuition.

The girl had a voice, so Amy and Mohamed promised her a place in ORB, but only after graduation. They were adamant that all band members live their values of perseverance, determination, and education. That way, if the band ever failed or broke up, each member would have a college degree to fall back on.

Kick sheds quiet tears. "My sister is finishing nursing school. My brothers are in college. And my youngest sister is a national merit scholar. None of this would have been possible without Amy."

I picture Amy's keen mind studying, digesting, seeking understanding and a way forward, and wonder anew at the way her flip manner and nonchalance camouflaged her caring.

As the words and tears dry, Kick and I reach an unspoken agreement to leave things be, our shared grief too painful to touch for now. But both of us feel the bond that has been forged, delicate yet abiding. The door is open for future connection, with no need to specify what or when this will be.

I don't know Kick Dorji's mother, but I've met and heard the stories of many like her. All of them were frightened and protective, none had murderous intent. No, Mohamed. I'm not about to ask this young woman if she thinks her mother killed her best friend. Allan and I will have to find another way.

Amy violently scrubbed her hands back and forth through her hair, this time tipped with virulent shades of blue and magenta. Her back to me, she lifted her face to the warmth of the afternoon sun. Midway through her sophomore year at the U, she was still skittish, but stretching.

"I like the new blue," I said. "Purply, like a sunset."

She turned and shook a finger at me. "*Indigo* to be precise. Deeper than the old blue." She turned to the window again. "You can really feel it, can't you?"

"Feel what?"

"The healing power of the sun. Ahhh. A day can be total crap, but then the sun comes out and everything's better."

"Yeah, a little bit goes a long way. And we get little enough as it is, so soak it up while you can."

"Little Mary Sunshine today, are we?" Amy said humorlessly as she turned, the stuffed bunny dangling from her left hand.

"Familiar tactics, Amy. When you talk about the weather, you're stalling. What's up?"

"Blah blah blah blah blah." She turned back to the light. "Can't a body appreciate nature's marvels? Why does anything have to be up?"

" 'Nature's marvels?' Now you're really pushing it." I couldn't hide my smile. "Whatever. Marvel away." I leaned back into the sofa, my eye on the clock.

Two minutes, three, four passed with neither of us speaking.

"I read this magazine article," Amy began, still facing away. "It was about how old-time Hollywood movie studios protected their stars' privacy. If secrets came out, it could ruin careers. Like it said the public only found out Rock Hudson was gay after he died."

"I remember. That secret had been locked up tight for decades. Women around the world were devastated." My mother included.

"You remember that?" Amy said with mock surprise. "Just how old are you, Doc?"

"Old enough to remember when homosexuality was not okay anywhere. It wasn't talked about. Heterosexuality was automatically assumed. For instance, I grew up watching a pianist named Liberace on TV. No one even suspected."

"Liberace." She nodded. "I read about him too, saw photos, some videos. How could people not know? I mean, really."

"Eh." I shrugged. "Back in the day, he was considered the consummate showman. He was a huge draw in Vegas, where people expected flash and sequins. Think about it – he set stepping stones for the likes of Elton and Freddie."

"Yeah, I guess," she said, twirling the rabbit by its hind foot. "More celebrities are coming out now. Actors, athletes, writers, singers."

"Yeah. It takes a lot of courage."

"Yeah. Some are even people of color. That must be even harder."

"Yeah. It's a double whammy."

One minute, two, three minutes passed as she paced, throwing the stuffed bunny into the air and catching it. She missed and stooped to retrieve it.

"What do you need, Amy?"

"If I knew that, I'd know something, but I don't know nothin'." She shook her rainbow locks. "I'm cursed."

"How so?"

"They have it hard. Just imagine if *you* were gay. Being gay and Korean would *not* necessarily mix."

"No. That's a hard combo. On par with being gay and Vietnamese. But it's not impossible. And if it happened, we wouldn't be the only ones."

"I know that," she spat, tapping her temple. "I have a friend. He has to hide it from his family, said they'd kick him out if they knew." She shot me a sideways glance.

"I assume you mean out of the family, let alone the house."

She lifts her chin approvingly. "Not the only ones? How many gay Vietnamese people do you know? I don't know any."

"I'll bet you do; you just don't know you know. I've worked with a few, have known others on a personal basis."

She took a seat in the swivel chair, stroked the stuffed bunny. "Just think if it was me and my mom found out."

"She'd definitely flip her lid." I nudged a little. "How much would you care?"

"Enough to want to keep her from knowing." She picked at her healing cuticles, caught herself, absentmindedly yanked out a few strands of hair, shook them from her fingers. We watched them drift lazily to the floor. My fingertips rested on that familiar spot above my left knee.

"How would you do that? Keep her from knowing, that is."

"Easy enough. Like you said, Doc, people expect everyone else to be straight. It'd be like the studios protecting those stars."

Her face closed, closing the topic as well. I contemplated the next step. "When you said 'secret' just now, it sounded like 'sacred.'"

"You're going all weird on me, IJ." The sarcastic note was back.

"Maybe so." At least she stopped pulling her hair out. "Maybe it's because I think of our sexuality as something mystical, a sacred gift so to speak. It's up to the individual, celebrity or not, to decide what to share with whom."

Amy nodded, satisfied. "Okay," she said.

"Okay," I answered.

DAY THREE

●●●●●●●●●●●●●●●●●●●●●●●●●●●●

llan arrived early and we're killing time over coffee until the group assembles. The reasons for meeting weigh heavily, making it more awkward for Allan, Willem and Natasha to get reacquainted. As the linchpin, it's only fair the conversation goes through me.

"Why did you become a therapist?" Allan asks, trying to sound casual.

"Why do you ask?" I fight the fidgets by playing with a teaspoon. My tone is lighter than what I feel.

"Liz says people become therapists for a reason. I know hers; I was curious about yours."

"Ah, yes," I say. "I became a therapist because the family I was born into was batshit crazy." I open my eyes wide and menacingly. Natasha snorts, Willem shakes his head.

Tasha responds to Allan's perplexed state. "Don't mind us. We're members of that batshit crazy family too." She gathers Bonkers, attaches a leash to the tiny cat's collar.

My standard story queues itself up. "When I was a kid…" Hmmm. How much to reveal. Ah, what the hell. Allan knows more about my business than I ever would have wanted anyway. "No. It goes further back, before I was born, before the Korean War. Keep in mind that Korea was under Japanese occupation from 1910 to the end of World War II. My parents were born and raised in a country under siege. Both witnessed atrocities during this time. Then there were just a handful of years before the communist invasion and civil war."

I sit stiffly upright and my voice takes on a protective, cynical edge. "Both my parents lost friends and family members. The Korean War ended, they met, married, and lo and behold, somehow got tickets to the Promised Land, aka student visas to the U-S-of-A. They and their families were saved.

"Dad had it all planned out. After Mom graduated she'd support him while he earned a PhD, which was, in his opinion, the epitome of achievement. Both of them worked while they were in school. But then Mom got pregnant. This was back when pregnant women couldn't remain students or members of the workforce."

"Couldn't or didn't?" Allan asks.

I bop my spoon in the air, keeping time to the rhythm of my family's misery. "Couldn't. Mom was both kicked out of school and fired. Dad's dream was dead and, as far as he was concerned, it was his wife's fault. They couldn't live on what Dad made, so he quit school and took a job managing an apartment building in North Seattle. My brother was born, Mom babysat the tenants' kids, and it looked like they were the only ethnic minorities for miles around. No fun, but a rent-free two-bedroom apartment was part of the deal, so they sucked it up and made it work."

The spoon stops of its own accord. Tasha pets the impatient cat, listens intently. She's heard the story dozens of times, in all its – and my – moods, yet never tires of it.

"Dad had studied engineering and was pretty handy. He saved the building owner a ton of money by being the resident fix-it man. Imagine the come-down. Even though he was proud to have a son, every traditional Korean parent's goal, my father remained resentful for the rest of his life.

"By the time I was born five years later, Dad had an appliance repair business. As a sideline, he specialized in extracting the joy from his family without anesthetic. You see, the only thing my parents knew was work, and neither of them had ever learned to trust. For them, the only way to survive was to maintain strict control. That did not for a happy childhood make, but it did result in one family therapist."

Allan is sweating. Hey, buddy, you wanted to know. I end the narrative here, but the story plays on in my head.

The business evolved into an appliance store, and my parents bought a house in the burbs. The American dream. In high school my brother Matt looked into becoming an electrician or plumber in order to make some serious green, but our father said no. With Matt's intelligence and potential, not going to a top tier university was not an option. The son would earn the prestigious degree the father was forced to forego.

Matt headed for the East Coast to be a continent away from dear old Dad. Our mother was hurt because her son hadn't chosen Stanford, so much closer to home; I felt abandoned and alone; Matt was miserable in his pre-med program. Only our father was satisfied.

Matt told us about Euro-American dormmates ranting against the injustice of affirmative action. They accused Matt and others like him of supplanting truly qualified students. Matt couldn't stand it and asked permission to come home and transfer to the University of Washington. Dad said the UDub wasn't good enough. He ordered Matt to do his duty and make the best of it, just as he had.

After that, Matt ceased contact. I was entangled in my own pubescent concerns and paid little attention. Suddenly my parents announced they were flying to upstate New York. The university had informed them that Matt was on academic probation; his scholarship was in jeopardy. They had to go and clear things up, set their son straight. They didn't know how long it would take, so I was pulled from school and sent to relatives in Illinois.

My older cousin, the first-born male of our generation, told me the truth. A hiker had found Matt in the woods. My parents didn't bring my brother home. Instead they had his body cremated and scattered his ashes in those same woods.

I raged at them when they returned. How could they lie to me? How could they not give me a chance to say goodbye? At first they denied it, saying Matt had run away; they were still looking for him. Then my father did an about-face and accused my cousin, aunt, and uncle of breaking their promise of secrecy. All connection with them was cut off from that day forward.

Seven months later, on what would have been Matt's twentieth birthday, my father had a massive heart attack and dropped dead in the store. Oh, the irony. Maybe the old bastard had loved his son after all. Afterward it was just my mother and me, saying nothing about what happened or anything else of substance. I spent the rest of my adolescence and a large portion of my young adulthood trying to make sense of it all. And oh, that luscious guilt. At my selfishness, my anger, my resentment at Matt for having left me behind. Twice.

I take a gulp from my mug, gently replace it on the table, and offer an empty smile.

"Thank you," says Allan. "I don't take it lightly."

I bow to accept the honor. "I blame war. Trauma. Poverty. Of course culture and my parents' personalities were factors too, but I can't help wondering what life would have – what my parents could have been like if they'd grown up in peace, without fear. Healthy, with enough to eat. Would they have met and married? Would my brother and I even have been born?" I shrug. "That's what Amy and I had in common. She asked the same questions about her own history."

A car with darkened windows moves slowly up the street. It must be Mohamed. I honestly didn't know where the conversation at Carkeek Park would lead, never imagined he'd want to join the team. Based on the info he shared, I wasn't about to say no. Willem's on board, of course. Tasha volunteered, too, but I asked her to step back until we need her. With RAJE practically frothing at the mouth, it's a matter of too many minds and bodies.

Oh my. Mrs. Dobbs is watching from across the street. If need be, I can dash outside. Poor ol' xenophobe had a conniption fit when we moved in. That was over twenty years ago, and her opinion hasn't changed.

Amy once showed me a sketch she had done, a proposal for an early album cover. The ORBers, in a classic Cadillac convertible, approached a sign on a country road leading to a cliché of a small, all-American town. Rather than informing passersby of the fire danger level, an arrow indicated *Very High* on a racial alert scale. The band's record label had nixed it without comment or discussion.

I know from Muslim clients that they're exposed to hatred and suspicion on a daily basis. And I know from personal experience how being on perpetual high alert wears on your psyche. I wonder what Mohamed's radar tells him about the danger level in my neighborhood today.

Tasha's at the front door. There's the buzz of introductions. She says, "We ask everyone to take their shoes off. Do you mind?"

That rich baritone answers, "Not at all. We do the same."

Shake of the head and shoulders to loosen up. I go to greet my guest.

Mohamed tries to look several directions at once. I'm approaching from behind, the cat's face is buried in his left shoe, and Tasha's having difficulty extricating the stubborn bundle of fur.

"Bonkers, where are your manners?" Tasha turns to Mohamed. "She has a shoe fetish. Better go home before we both regret it."

Mohamed turns to face me. "I have never seen a cat on a lead," he says with wonder.

"Neither had I," I reply. "Natasha found her at the animal shelter. She'd had a head injury. We don't know what she was like before she was hurt, but now she doesn't have a lick of sense."

"Ah, Bonkers." Mohamed smiles approvingly.

"Yes. She loves to go outside, so the only way to keep her safe is to keep her on a line. We were surprised she took to it. But then Tasha has a way with cats."

We watch Natasha carry Bonkers into the house next door. "Your daughter lives there?"

"Yes, it was originally for my mother. When she moved into a retirement community, my husband Willem turned it into his workspace. Tasha came back from Los Angeles not long ago to join his firm. She's living there until she finds her own place."

I feel refreshingly at ease with Mohamed. He'd told me he hadn't expected me to accept his involvement, was thankful I'd said yes. I'd been clear in expressing my doubts, was thankful he'd stuck with it. Since both disclosures we're able to talk on a different level.

I lead him down the refreshingly sunlit hall to the back of the house. "I hope you don't mind so many people being here," I say. "We don't want to intrude upon your privacy."

"No, no, I'm happy to be included."

We pass the entrance to the dining room, the center of which is dominated by a long table. Today the worn blond planks are sprinkled with sheets of paper covered in handwritten notes. On the left is our open kitchen, also on my list of happy places. Willem and Allan stand at the large butcher block island in the center. The younger man studiously pumps the stainless steel handle of a manual milk frother. My husband expresses approval as he pours steaming water into a French press coffee maker.

Mohamed is maybe three inches taller than Willem. They literally measure each other up. When we first met, Willem was the tallest man I'd ever seen close up who wasn't a professional basketball player. The two smile warmly at each other; I imagine a bond immediately forged based on going through life with everyone else looking up their nostrils. They joke at their differently accented English; that seems to seal the mutual deal.

The motion of Willem's handshake looks smoother, delivered with more strength and assurance. It's comforting to see. Allan and Mohamed introduce themselves. Their handshake seems more tentative.

We move across the hall to sit at the dining table. While Willem studiously pours coffee, I set out the fluffy, fragrant orange rolls he and Natasha baked earlier.

"I am so glad to be here." Mohamed accepts coffee, ignores the pastry. "We must ensure that justice is done."

"Here's to that." I raise my cup in response.

"Justice." The word oozes out of Allan's mouth as if it has a bitter taste.

Mohamed's attention flicks from him to me. "He is our investigator and he is not convinced?"

"No, I'm convinced," Allan counters. "I'm just not that trusting in justice being done."

I look at him with concern. Mohamed, however, shows a mixture of relief and hopefulness. "I never thought I would hear a former police officer say this," he blurts. "Perhaps we truly are on the same side."

I bite off a laugh. Now I understand the hesitant handshake.

"Being on the same side doesn't guarantee the results we want," says Allan.

"Then we need to ensure that it happens." Mohamed balls a fist for emphasis.

"That's why we're here," I say. "Go ahead and tell them what you told me."

He takes a seat, stands, sits again. He sets his coffee on the table and rubs his hands together. "Isha Dorji," he says. He sees Allan's look of sharp interest, and quickly dispels any doubts. "No, she would never hurt Amy. But there is history that cannot be ignored." He shakes his head. "We ORBers are from different countries and have all had our hardships. It may have looked easy to outsiders, but we had to work hard to understand each other and bond as a unit.

"Being Amy's protégé did not make this easy for Isha. Her own mother was against it. She wanted her daughter to finish school, get a respectable job, and take care of her. After all her struggles, she felt she had earned this. You see, being Amy's housekeeper made the mother very bitter. But Isha was not yet earning enough, and they still depended on the income from Amy." Mohamed stretches his shoulders and neck. He looks searchingly at me. "You know what my relationship with Amy truly was?"

"Yes, I do."

Mohamed turns away again. I don't know if it's out of relief or shame. He tells us that shortly before the ORBit tour began, Mrs. Dorji arrived at Amy's early and discovered her with a woman. That night, Isha and her mother had another terrible fight. Mrs. Dorji accused Isha of secretly seeing someone; she was afraid her daughter's relationship with Amy was more than it was.

Mohamed's hands are raised in consternation. "She threatened to expose Amy. Isha offered to quit but Amy would not allow it. Instead, she tried to convince Isha to make up with her mother. She said if it would help, she would talk to her. After Amy's death, Isha was out of control. She was afraid this was why Amy returned to Seattle."

Willem says, "It was reported that the housekeeper found Amy's body. That was Isha's mother?"

"Yes."

"Do you think she could have done it?" asks Allan.

Mohamed shrugs. "I don't know what to think. I pray it wasn't her and that we will find whoever did, insha'Allah."

"Amy and mothers," I say. "First her own, then Kick's."

Allan stands at the large whiteboard mounted on a tripod next to the table. He swipes a dry erase pen down the center to create two columns. He labels one *Suspects*, the other *Motives*. *Mrs. Dorji* and *protecting daughter* are the first entries.

We're interrupted by the arrival of RAJE. I make the introductions; Mohamed bows slightly, politely to each.

I make an impulsive executive decision to move on, keeping RAJE out of certain loops. Amy hadn't come out before her death, and I'm not about to do it for her. I say, "You're just in time. Mohamed was about to go over the last days he spent with Amy." He gives me a relieved, grateful look.

He describes the start of the ORBit tour. The London gigs sparked a flurry of fan mail. "In Paris the story was the same. Amy spent the free night between the last two shows reading her letters. Her goal was always to handwrite her replies."

Angie whispers, "That's dedication."

Mohamed holds his hand to his cheek as if he has a toothache. "The next morning Amy was quiet and withdrawn. I teased her about not being able to stop, about applause going to her head." He sounds regretful. "She said she had indeed stayed up too late and felt a little under the weather. She said she needed some time alone and would go for a walk. I urged her to take a bodyguard, but she refused. She said she wanted to be a normal person for the day."

Rachel releases a gasp of surprise. She's probably wondering why anyone would want to be out of the limelight, even for a day.

Mohamed says that after her return several hours later, Amy was irritable and short-tempered. She blamed it on stage fright – she wanted that show to be particularly good, so her nerves were particularly bad.

"It went well," he says, "but Amy did not have her same energy or life. The next day as we were packing, she told us she had to return to Seattle. A matter had come up unexpectedly. It was not terribly serious, but she could only take care of it at home, and we were not to worry."

"Do you have any hint if it was personal or professional?" asks Liz.

Mohamed shoots me a nervous glance. He'd agreed to share his concerns about Mrs. Dorji with Allan and my family, no one else. I hadn't prepped him for these questions; I should've anticipated them. RAJE wouldn't let details like this slip.

He clears his throat. "If it were professional, she would have discussed it with me. The timing made it seem not too great an emergency." Well done. He's quick. His voice holds more confidence: "We had the next week off to rest and be tourists before our Munich gigs. Amy said her trip would not disturb our performance schedule. We were touring Neuschwanstein Castle at the same time her body was discovered." Remorse and shame are written in his face.

"It was after the funeral that Sam Reyes, the head of our security, spoke with me. He's a good man. Tough. Very experienced. Very observant." Mohamed's face lights with fresh enthusiasm.

This is news to me. We didn't get this far in our previous discussion. But then, maybe he didn't want to mention his head security guy with one of his men so close.

According to Mohamed, on that strange day in Paris, Reyes had finished checking with his people and was at an outdoor café about a mile from the hotel. He'd seen Amy emerge from the Métro and look around. "Furtive" was the word he'd used. He'd watched as she got into a private car, not a taxi.

"How can we get in touch with Mr. Reyes?" asks Allan.

"His contact information is here." Mohamed pulls a business card from a pocket and offers it to Allan. He removes a cell phone from another pocket and says, "He's based in London. It's still early there. We can call him now, yes?"

I'm tentative. "We?"

"Of course. I loved Amy. This is as much my journey as yours."

Allan hands the card back to Mohamed. "Call him."

"Celebrity takes a toll." Sam Reyes's voice is deep, authoritative. "I only work for people who hire my team because they have to, not because they're into flaunting their fame. That only invites trouble. We keep as far in the background as possible, but even the ideal client needs space every once in a while. I don't like it but I get it. I thought it was that type of day for Amy."

"Is there a way to find that car?"

For some reason Mohamed's question hits me hard. There's something, something. I reach for it in my memory, but it slips away when Sam says, "It shouldn't be hard to track down. Even though I understand a client's wish for privacy, I don't necessarily grant it. I have the license number."

"How did you think to do that?" I ask.

"My job is to protect the band," Sam says quickly. "Little details are the easiest to overlook and are often the most important. It pays to be proactive."

Echoes of Allan. I say, "Now what do you suggest?"

"A physical presence in Paris, sooner rather than later. But not me; I'm not an investigator."

Mohamed and I instinctively turn toward Allan. He's been disturbingly absent from this conversation.

"Allan," I say, "you're the only one qualified to make this trip. Please, will you go?"

"No."

Willem lays a hand on my shoulder. I stop clawing at my elbow. I hadn't even noticed.

Liz goes into Aunt-mode. "Allan, you have to."

"No," he growls. "I have things to handle here."

Reyes sounds impatient. "Who can I expect?"

"We'll get back to you as soon as we can," says Allan.

"All right." It's clear to us all that it's not. "Keep me informed. In the meanwhile, I'll see about tracking down the owner of that vehicle."

"I am so sorry," Liz had said, as if she was the one who'd let us down.

What the hell was I thinking? Liz had warned me that since Zoe's death, Allan no longer trusts his instincts. I hold mine suspect too. Well, we both have good reason. Pure hubris, thinking I could give Allan – what was it Liz said – something to focus on and help him feel alive again.

I had to get out, and said so. We gave ourselves an hour to cool off and think. Everyone wandered off to neutral corners, coffee and orange rolls in hand. Last I saw of him, Allan was in my study, fiddling with his phone after having added *Paris meeting* and *?* to the whiteboard. Shit. What a start. No telling how many unanswered question marks will end up there.

Sackcloth and ashes time. I can go back to Wayne on my knees, mea culpa-ing all the way up to the twenty-seventh floor.

Well, this is scary. I know I drove here, but I have no recollection of it. One thing to be thankful for: the threat of rain is keeping people away. Either that or the excitement's dimmed. News articles at the time identified Horizons Cemetery as the last repose of many Vietnamese refugees. They commented on how appropriate it was for Amy Nguyen to spend eternity among her people. Even at a distance the spot is easy to identify. Mementos spread over its surface form a colorful collage. The brass marker, only recently installed, contains the pertinent dates and reads simply: *Amy Nguyen, Poet.*

I've been coming on a semi-regular basis. The first time, a month after Amy's death, I arrived hoping for a quiet moment with the girl-woman I knew and admired. Instead I felt jarred in the company of young people, come to pay tribute to their idol. They left hand-written notes, drawings, and photos downloaded from the internet with messages of grief or gratitude scrawled across them. Yet others were there to feed their morbid curiosity about another Seattle rock icon who had died too young. Their cameras and smart phones clicked away as they tsk-tsked, making none too subtle comments about the inevitable outcome of sex, drugs, and rock 'n' roll.

What the hell did they know.

Since then I aim to arrive early, as the gates are unlocked. Today I'm soothed by the solitude, the birdsong, the breeze. A tug-of-war between cloud and sun is reflected in the mirrored behemoths of downtown Seattle. It's a dramatic canvas, one Amy would have appreciated.

Standing at the foot of her grave, eyes closed, I ask, "Now what?"

I can almost hear her: *Why're you asking me, Doc? Aren't you the oracle?*

Fuck it, I know nothing and this is all my fault. As an intellectual exercise over a casual cup of coffee, a murder investigation had seemed so reasonable.

Another echo: *Don't make me call you a hypocrite, Doc. All that stuff about being your own advocate – was it just a load of crap?*

It wasn't, Amy, and you're the proof. However, you were, without a doubt, way more courageous than I've ever been called to be. Now I look to you. I re-conjure the dream figure on the sidewalk. Once again I appeal to the young woman with the red and indigo streaks in her hair. "What happened?"

The sound of a faltering step on the gravel path. My heart catches in my throat then releases as I open my eyes. A slight, middle-aged Asian woman with a handful of daisies and a watering can stops at the grave next to Amy's. The marker identifies it, in English and Vietnamese, as the final resting place of a faithful and beloved wife and mother.

We nod respectfully. We've come across each other before yet have never spoken.

"I'm sorry," the woman says hesitantly, a guttural quality in her pronunciation. "I don't want to bother you."

"It's no bother," I answer.

"Did you know her," the woman asks, "or are you a fan?"

"She made amazing music and did a lot of good in the community. I like to pay my respects."

She pours water into the flower receptacle at her mother's grave and arranges the bouquet.

I say, "They're beautiful."

"Yes. Her favorite." The woman bows her head a few moments then moves to stand beside me. She regards the of- ferings from fans and shakes her head. "Such a waste."

I don't respond, not knowing if she means the gifts or Amy. I send one last silent message to Amy before turning to go.

"You can stay."

"No," I answer. "I have to go."

"Jackie, you're not going alone." This is as close to pleading as Willem gets.

I try to say this as gently as possible, for both our sakes. "Schätzli, you can't travel yet, and you need Tasha here. I'll ask Stefan to meet me." He's in Switzerland converting the Kessler family's one hundred-thirty-year-old farm into an ecofriendly B&B.

"Don't," says Willem. "He's still buried in bureaucratic bullshit."

Rachel waves a hand with the last orange roll in it. "Sign me up." She looks slightly defensive in response to our silence. "Oh come on. It makes sense, doesn't it? It's RAJE to the rescue and, of the three of us, who can take time off the easiest?" Neither of the others can easily afford mass cancellations at this busy time of year. "And don't you worry, Jax. I'll pay my own way."

She doesn't often mention it, but her husband Stan was a firm believer in life insurance. When the shock from his death wore off, Rachel cleared her debts and her sons' student loans. Another chunk was invested, and the rest became a cushion for emergencies. I don't know that she had other people's emergencies in mind.

Willem shoots me a telepathic message of concern. Rach and I have never traveled as a twosome. It's always been the full quartet attending conferences or us, plus our spouses, on our roots trips. This time there will be no buffer, and we know from experience that traveling in close quarters can make or break a relationship.

"Thanks, Rach." I am truly grateful, but still have to hide a gulp. "We're partners. Only you're coming to help me, so I'm paying."

"Okay." She turns to my husband. "Willem?" Good lord. As if I need his permission. With a hint of a smirk he motions for us to carry on.

There's a non-stop from Sea-Tac that'll spit us out at Charles De Gaulle Airport at a decent hour two days hence. I produce my credit card to complete the ticket purchase when Mohamed gently stops me.

"No," he insists. "The costs of the investigation will be paid by ORB. Amy was ORB's mother as I am its father. This is a family matter."

I argue; it's ethically and morally wrong to abdicate my financial responsibility. It's my name on the lawsuit, my professional reputation and future on the line. We wrangle a bit before reaching a compromise: ORB will pay for our airfare and Sam's time; I will cover food, lodging, and Allan's wages. I feel a pang, but it's bearable. Mohamed's pockets are a lot deeper than mine.

Everything's being arranged remarkably smoothly and quickly. Willem and his fluent French are calmly booking a room at the Hotel Monique, a family-run place in the Latin Quarter where Sam sometimes books accommodations for lesser-known clients. He said it's well-situated and the management is cooperative and discreet, qualities which make his team's duties easier to fulfill.

I tell Rachel, "There's not much time for planning."

Angie says, "Since we can't go, can we help with that?"

"Sure, I guess."

"RAJE dinner. My place. Potluck. Come help." She pulls Rach out of her seat; they scurry off to prepare.

Allan warns, "Keep in mind this might not lead to anything."

I put a hand on his, hoping to settle the insecurity coursing through us both. "If it's a dead end, we'll accept it. But Amy wouldn't take off like that without a reason. Right now, we have no other direction."

No other direction, indeed. I feel like a cow making its blind, panicked way down a crowded cattle chute. Forced onward, no thought possible, only the mad press of the other animals, their frantic mooing in my ear.

I treasure all the help and support, but need more time to think, get a moo in edgewise. I make my excuses and retreat to my home office and pull the old brown bunny off his shelf. I flinch at the sound of the door opening.

"Why're you hiding?" asks Liz.

"I understand Amy's need to take off," I say. "That was her MO, assign herself a mission and establish a goal without worrying about the consequences. I've been handed an assignment, equally nebulous. Major difference? This isn't of my choosing. And I long ago learned the meaning of fear. I worry about consequences all the time."

My breath is quick, shallow; my whole body is pulsing. Deep breath in, hold it. Long, slow exhale.

"What're you thinking?"

"I'm thinking there's no chance. I'm thinking I need to fire my lawyer and find someone I can trust."

"What about us?"

"Of course I trust you."

"But," she says. I can't disagree. She takes the bunny away and holds my hands in hers. "You know how we've all had those clients where we don't know what the hell is going on, have no idea what to do?"

"Yeah, sure."

"When we get stuck it's because we're missing an angle. Sometimes not knowing is our best advantage. It can force a new way to see everything."

I squeeze her hands in appreciation. Liz is right. Experience has taught me that floundering can lead me in directions never before considered. Many's the time I've found myself in a session, clouded in frustration, cursing the murky world of thought, emotion, relationship. Then the forces of the universe come together to suddenly reveal an unexpected cross-road.

Time for a change of perspective, Jackie. You have history with that.

It was a few months after her sixteenth birthday. Amy had been spinning like a weather vane in a tornado. Of particular concern was the fact that she could now drive. Two weeks earlier we'd updated her safety plan.

During that day's risk assessment she'd reluctantly shown me the most recent results of her ongoing feud with herself. The shallow, curved wounds on the inside of her right forearm were mostly healed. I was relieved; it had been a half-hearted attempt, and she was ready to talk about it.

I held her right wrist loosely, rotated her arm to see the shape from different angles. "What was it going to be?"

"A dove. You ever seen Picasso's?"

"Yes. Spartan, powerful images." I dropped her arm. "How did you stop yourself this time?"

"I'm right-handed." She mimed the act. "Didn't have enough control to get what I wanted."

Time to test her tolerance. "You're a pianist. Don't you have to be kind of ambidextrous?"

Her expression hinted at either disgust or pity. Maybe both.

I scratched the old itch above my left knee. I'm right-handed too.

"What did you do instead?"

"Followed the plan, Doc. Went to my happy place."

The public library.

I kept my voice matter-of-fact, my expression neutral. "You can always call me. That's on your list too."

"When do I ever call you?" The question was clearly rhetorical. "Your voice is in my head enough as it is."

"Oh, that's not so good."

"Tell me about it."

"Since you brought it up, have you ever considered changing therapists?" Testing, testing, one, two, three. "You're still not stuck with me, y'know. There are plenty of good people out there who'd be happy to work with you." It was my duty to remind her of her rights, although I wasn't sure about the veracity of that last statement.

I was relieved when she ignored the question and went to the bookshelf, examined the volumes, one by one.

I looped back around. "What set it off?"

"Thinking too much, I guess. All that sweet sixteen crap is just that – crap."

Thank you, Amy! Instead of closing down, she created more room to maneuver. I knew her well enough to recognize my turn on the hot seat. To hell with boundaries.

"I remember. Luckily, it's survivable."

She pulled out a book that was stashed behind the others. "*Harry Potter und der Gefangene von Askaban?*"

"German's my second language and I like to practice. It's true what they say about foreign language: use it or lose it."

"Hmm." She thumbed through the pages. "I'm taking German."

"Yeah, you told me. How do you like it?"

"It feels good in my mouth." Amy read a passage out loud. Her pronunciation was more than respectable. She glanced in my direction, said casually, "How'd you survive it? What did you do to forget?"

"I just told you I remember it. In nauseating detail. It's permanently etched here," I pointed to the center of my forehead, "and here." I tapped the center of my chest. And pictured the scar on my knee.

"Bad times, huh?" She looked almost pleased. "No forgive and forget?"

"That's another load of crap. Forgiving's vital, but forgetting gives us permission to keep repeating the same mistakes. I'm into forgive and learn."

She replaced *Harry*, continued to inspect the other titles. I was curious to discover which ones would attract her attention.

"What the hell is this?" She delicately extracted a paperback and held it at arm's length, the corner pinched between her thumb and forefinger. The cover featured several gnarly-looking blue-skinned men hanging onto the wool surrounding a sheep's bewildered face.

"Good choice! Terry Pratchett – he's a master. That one's about a kick-ass girl who saves her obnoxious little brother from some evil fairies with the help of those little blue guys."

She cracked the cover. "Wow, he wrote a lot of books. There are, like, dozens of titles."

"Yeah, he wrote mostly snarky, satiric fantasy novels. They're pretty entertaining, also surprisingly philosophical and deeply humanistic."

She made her sour now-we're-being-pretentious face. "Whatever floats your boat. What else've you got?"

There were a few professional tomes, some classic self-help books, but the bookcase was, and still is, mostly stocked with works I enjoy: my second grade reader, *Harriet the Spy*, other novels my younger clients had recommended over the years. There's more truth and wisdom in kid lit than in the undecipherable blah-blah written by clinical researchers. If I get stuck with a client, I bypass the heaping pile of professional journals gathering cobwebs in my basement and reach for *Percy Jackson*. When in doubt, read fairytales.

Amy took a slim, dog-eared volume to the swivel chair, thumbed through it, frowning with concentration. I held my breath. It was one of my favorites, a holdover from high school.

Her face tight, she held the book up accusingly, looking as if she'd been pranked. "Is this even English?"

"Better than English. It's E. E. Cummings. Poetry." That last was in answer to her blank stare.

"No, we did poetry. Longfellow, Dickinson, Plath. This ain't poetry, this be trippin'. There's no capitalization and the punctuation's fried." She squinted at the page. "Huh?"

"Don't think so hard. Concentrate on the rhythm, the feel."

She closed her eyes and slowly repeated the lines she'd just read, rolling them around with her tongue, tasting them. I was amazed at how quickly she had memorized them.

"It starts out jagged, harsh." She took some deep breaths. "Then it spins, gets lyrical, kinda sexy." One more breath. "The words paint pictures." Her eyes flew open. "He? She?"

"He."

"He still alive?" Amy asked.

"No."

"Too bad." A sorry shake of her head. "He must've been one crazy dude. White?"

"White, yes. Crazy, I don't know. Definitely gifted. Either way, I agree with you. He pushed and pulled at language and got some fascinating results. Check out number sixty one."

She flicked to the right page. A quick glance and her head shot up. "He must've been on some really good shit when he wrote this one. *Who* lived in a *what*?"

"Come on, smartass, give it a chance."

She flipped me the bird and proceeded to read silently to herself. By the third stanza, she was reading aloud. Not even a flinch as my voice merged with hers.

As our duet ended, she closed the book, ceremoniously splayed her hand across the cover. "Lonesome."

"Yes. But even in the midst of that anonymous void, there was love. And that was enough for them. Even if only one person sees you, really sees you, it can be enough."

She stroked the book the way she stroked the stuffed rabbit. "This is weird shit. You understand it?"

"To be honest, only bits and pieces. But it's fun to read out loud. Kind of like German; I like the feel."

I wove as many thematic threads as I could, wondering how far she'd take it if I left her be.

"Uh huh," she said. "Can I borrow this?"

"Sure." A casual shrug camouflaged my relief and pleasure. She'd taken the seat I'd offered at the loom.

She reopened the book, was instantly absorbed. I was sorry to have to call her back, but there was one more challenge to throw at her.

"You could do it."

"What?"

"Mess with words to make pictures. You already do that with your drawings."

"No." She looked up with a frown. "Ask anyone. I'm no good with words."

"I beg to differ. My experience of you is that you're so good with words other people can't keep up. When that happens they turn it around and make it your problem. Don't believe 'em. Your words paint pictures too. If you wrote 'em down I'd keep 'em on my bookshelf."

"At least it would add some color to your collection."

"Diversity wasn't a thing when I was in school. Thank goodness that's changing."

She turned back to Cummings. "This dude is impossible."

"Meaning?"

"He totally makes stuff up. I defy you to find a dictionary with 'undying' in it."

I smiled. "Undying love."

"Oh. Yeah. But that's not the way he uses it. Well, it is. But it isn't. Shit. Okay." There was a longish pause as she stretched her entire body and closed her eyes. "Undying, unliving. Unlying, untruthing. Unhating, unloving." I felt her new, impossible words throb in her mouth, her head, her heart. She sat up, riffled the satiny edges of the book's pages with her thumb. "Interesting." Another pause, then: "You see me, don't you, Jackie."

My system went on high alert. Until now she'd only referred to me as Doc or something equally sarcastic. This was the first time she'd ever called me by my real name.

"Yes, Amy, I do."

"Right," she said. "Good. You oughta know – I see you too."

Before I could respond she brightened and leaped from the chair, stuffing the book of poems into her backpack. "Time's up, Doc. See you next week."

"I'll hold you to that," I said as she walked out the door with a wave.

Angie's back door is open. As Liz and I approach, we hear Angie say, "… name's Nick."

"Who's Nick?" I add our crackers and cheeses to the cold cuts, crudités, breads, and dips already laid out.

Liz inspects the fruit salad. "Short on grapes." Her eyes flick to Rachel. She looks as sour as I feel. Our previous burst of optimism had drained away on the silent drive over.

As Angela dispenses glasses of her homemade high-octane sangria, Rach says coyly, "Someone went on a date last night."

"What?" The grape shortage is forgotten.

Angie enunciates slowly and clearly. "Date. Last night. Me. Went on."

"Oh my god," I splutter. "Hooray! How was it?"

"You walked in mid-report," says Rach. "Now spill. Who is he, how'd you meet him, what does he do for a living, and are you going to see him again?"

"As I was saying, his name is Nick, he's an old college buddy of my cousin Dorothy, and I don't know if I'll see him again."

"Why? What's wrong with him?" Rachel blurts.

"Nothing's *wrong* with him," Angie says testily. "It was just really weird. Dating again, y'know? After Richard left, I kind of took it for granted I'd be single the rest of my life. But now the boys are on their own, I'm getting lonely. But it was hard. I felt kind of disloyal."

"There's no need for that," says Liz. "You really tried."

"I know; maybe that's the wrong word. Maybe not so much disloyal as confused and stupid. It's been a long time. I don't like feeling so awkward."

"Are you gonna tell us? How'd it go, Ang?" The longer the attention's on someone else, the happier I'll be.

"Oh it was fine, I guess. I wasn't sure what to expect. I mean, he's a family law attorney. Dorothy warned me, said he has a heart of gold, the rest is pure asshole. Makes for a good lawyer, I guess. He was nice enough. Courteous, friendly, smart. A gentleman – he held doors open for me. Scoff if you must; I liked it. But I don't know if we're a match. Our tastes are kind of different."

"What do you mean?"

"He took me to Ray's Boathouse. The restaurant, not the café. Richard and I only ever went to the café; we couldn't afford the restaurant proper, not with the boys' appetites. Anyway we're in the restaurant talking about food, right? And what we like to eat? He says *langoustines*. I didn't know what he was talking about. I pretended I did, but I really didn't. Googled it when I got home." She shakes her head. "He has expensive tastes."

Rach asks, "What's a langoustine?"

Liz's voice layers over mine. "Saltwater crayfish." "Mini-lobster."

Rachel's forehead wrinkles. "Okay, some of us have had more extravagant lives."

"Mine's definitely been more limited," says Angie. "I think that's what got to me. Nick said he'd like to see me again, but I'm afraid spending time with him will just show me all the things I've missed out on and then I'll feel bad."

"It could also be your opportunity to have more fun. You deserve it. Have a langoustine or two." I tease to prolong the diversion.

Angie sticks her tongue out at me. "Maybe" comes a split second later.

"Indubitably," says Liz.

"In any case, give it a think," says Rach. "There's no hurry, is there? At least you're out there again. More than I can say for myself. Nick sounds like a stand-up guy, not a creep, so that's in your favor. Heck, if you don't want to date him, you can give him my number."

"He loves to travel." Angie continues her own train of thought. "I told him about our roots trips. He thought that was a great idea." RAJE and our spouses had travelled together since discovering our shared interest in tracing family history. Starting within the United States, we'd crisscrossed five states exploring our families' post-immigration migration routes. The death of Rach's husband and Angie's divorce put things on hold, but we're back on track, currently saving for a trip to Germany and Switzerland. The unspoken question is how Willem's stroke will affect our plans.

"Like-minded," says Liz. "Good sign."

"Yeah, but then I got self-conscious and things sort of petered out. At one point I felt so desperate I told him the weasel poop story."

"You didn't!" Rachel splutters.

"I did," Angie says shyly. "He laughed. Nearly choked on his sablefish."

"Sense of humor," says Liz. "Another point in his favor."

Rach mouths *sablefish* at me.

Angie sweeps a carrot stick through a bowl of hummus, points the stub at me. Damn. My turn. Being singled out rankles. I stop myself: *Rein yourself in, girl. These are your dearest friends. It's empathy, not pity. Soak up the goodness.* A big part of me would rather reject it.

Angie says, "Let's remember we're not here to talk about my as yet non-existent love life. We're actually here for you. I did ask if he knew anything about Wayne the Wonderful. Apparently, the guy has a good reputation. You could do a lot worse, Jax."

Rachel says, "Yeah. Don't do something else you'll regret by giving up on him too soon."

I sigh and turn to Liz. "What else did you tell 'em, eh?"

Rachel shakes herself like a dog. "I've always wanted to see Notre Dame. Too bad about the fire." She reaches into the bowl of fruit salad, nabs a few red globes. Liz gives her the evil eye. "I read once how there are water taxis on the Seine. We can get on and off wherever we want."

"Rach, this will not be a pleasure trip." I pinch off bits of French bread and roll them into spongy pellets.

"I know, but there's bound to be some down time, right? We don't have to go to the Louvre or anything that takes all day, but geez, let's at least go to the Eiffel Tower."

I eat the spoonful of bread bits with a chunk of deep-throated Irish cheddar.

"Listen, Jax." Liz places a warm palm on my shoulder, gives a strong squeeze. "But for the grace of the therapy gods, it could just as easily have been me or Rach or Ang. This particular load of steaming crapola just happened to land on you. We are RAJE," she says firmly. "No one goes under during our watch." She raises her glass; Rachel and Angie match the salute. Angie nudges my elbow until I participate.

I say, "Let's stay real. There's a whole lot that's out of our control." I sip at my sangria. It refuses to go down without a fight.

"Your point being?"

"Is Macy's hiring?"

Angie punches me in the arm. "Listen to you, talking yourself into defeat."

"Yeah, lighten up, Jackie," says Rach. "You always do such a number on yourself. Up till now we'd always thought your warpedness was fairly harmless. But now we know different. You inscrutable Asians."

I tense from this one-two punch. First, more instruction on how to get it right. And now this. I consider a rebuff but, as so often before, let it pass. Over the years, there have been many comments that tugged in a hurtful way. This is just one more misdirected, seemingly playful jibe. My mother's quiet yet emphatic voice echoes in my ear: *Don't say anything. These people don't understand. If you want to have friends, if you want to have success, don't cause trouble.*

I got plenty of instruction on what not to do. It was a manual on developing other options that was thoroughly lacking.

"Liz is right," says Angie. "You're not alone in this. How can we help?"

"That's the hard part. I don't know."

"Then let's take a look at it." Angie raps her fist on the table. "We're mental health professionals. Damn fine ones, to boot. The ultimate goal is to prove you correct, correct? There are two ways to do that." She extends her left forefinger. "Either prove it wasn't suicide." She extends the right. "Or prove it was murder."

I hook my forefingers together. "They're connected."

"We need a new way to look at it," says Rachel. "It's like when we get stuck with a client." Ah, that's what else Liz told them.

In proof, Liz slaps her thigh. "Right. Things evolve for reasons. Murder happens in relationship."

"What if it was a random killing?" Angie's in devil's advocate mode.

Liz rolls a cherry tomato between thumb and forefinger. "How can there be such a thing? Even in a so-called random killing there's the killer's relationship with him- or herself, with their environment, society, whatever. Murder doesn't develop in a void."

"Murders evolve," I whisper. So do suicides. I disassemble a cracker. "Wayne's having me go through my notes with a fine-tooth comb. He's right. There's nothing specific. Memories get sparked, but I don't know how much to trust 'em. Emphasis on this word or that syllable changes the whole meaning. A smile or a smirk marks the difference between sincerity and sarcasm. After so long, how can I be sure what was which?"

"Things get misinterpreted all the time. We're only human. The best you can do is go with your very dependable gut." Rachel pokes me in the stomach. The sangria gone, she uncorks a bottle of wine. "Forget the Eiffel Tower. Bring the case notes with. We'll give 'em the once over." I reach over and give Rachel's forearm a gentle shake; the thank-you bangles sing.

Liz says, "You two will be plenty busy figuring out what sent Amy barreling back home into harm's way. You don't know what or who is out there, or whether they'll have your best interest in mind." Rachel looks as stunned as I feel. I don't think either of us thought there could be any danger involved. "We can take the non-suicide route and go through the files while you're gone. Up for it, Ang?"

She rubs her palms together. "You bet."

"Okay," I say. "It'll help to have fresh eyes on. Wayne told me to cross-reference my notes with the things Amy gave me to find evidence of progress over time. It's hard, though. The more famous she got, the more complicated things got."

"Quite the web." Liz eases the cherry tomato into her mouth. "I mean there couldn't have been much in Amy's background to prep her for fame and fortune."

"Yeah," Rachel takes a deep swallow from her glass. "Not like some lucky people who have their whole lives laid out for them from the get-go. No surprises that way."

"You call that lucky?" says Angie. "My future was all planned out practically from the day I was born. My parents programmed us: Dream big, work hard, and the world is your cornfield." Her face scrunches. "They didn't know what dreams I was capable of. Got the shock of their lives when I got the heck out of South Dakota."

I say, "There's a twist to that for refugees. They leave home because they have to, not because they want to, and their traditional rules and regs go with them. Problem is, what worked in the old country usually doesn't translate well in the new. That means trouble."

"Come on," says Angie. "Not all immigrants have it so bad. My clients from India and China do really well."

I feel my face flush; we've consulted on them many times too. I say, "Of course, on the surface. They're educated and have the clout of their high tech jobs. But as I've said before, you have to be aware that what they say to you and what they say to someone like me can be vastly different."

"And as I've said, they're all really open with me."

"I'm sure they are, but odds are it's in an I'm-sitting-with-a-White-woman way. If they let on how difficult things really are, the prospect of shame pops up for both sides, and that's not allowed."

"What?"

Here we go again. Lecture mode. "Cultural differences, and we're not just talking skin color, can get in the way of our work. However, it's a hard subject to broach. If I, the client, tell you, the therapist, about my hardships in this culture I shame myself in not being able to cope. I also shame you, a member of the culture that's causing me pain."

Angie sits back, simultaneously defiant and deflated.

"Every client has their own story and we only hear selected parts," says Liz.

"And I'm not exempt," I say. "I know full well I get the we're-all-minorities-together version. But bottom line? If you're a minority who's struggling, you're seen as a drain on society and are resented. If you're a success, you're taking more than your share and are resented. Members of the majority culture – "

"You mean us *White folks*?" Rachel laughs uncomfortably.

"Yeah, you *White folks* are often too far removed from your own family's migration stories to relate." I wave away the wine glass. None of her sidetracking. Besides, the last thing I need tomorrow is a hangover. "Think of all the Euro-Americans whose ancestors emigrated because of the clearances or the potato famine." Both Liz and Rachel raise their hands.

"Or war, political or religious persecution," says Angie, ticking these off on her fingers.

I nod at her. "How hard was it for *those* refugees, *your* ancestors, their children and grandchildren? It's easy to forget we share that because our families came from different parts of the world during different eras under different circumstances. What all our ancestors had in common was hope for better times. But when life yanks you off your feet and everything changes –"

"– everyone's screwed," Liz says, completing the thought.

"Yes, unless or until we find other ways to learn and adapt. That's where resilience comes in. That's a personal trait, to be sure, but it's also part of a family's culture around survival."

Rachel's eyes have glazed over. She issues a deep, patient sigh and shakes her head. "Is the sermon over? Jax, I love you dearly, but sometimes you get so wrapped up in the culture and acculturation stuff, you maybe miss the point."

I stiffen. Should I smack her now or later? "Oh, yeah? What point, pray tell, am I missing?"

"Maybe Amy was just an extremely depressed, maybe even mentally ill person who wanted the unhappiness to end. Maybe her family history had nothing to do with her emotional state." She waves her hand as if shooing a fly. "People are people, families are families. We all grow up with our own brand of misery. And plenty of people who come from shitty environments end up doing just fine. It's called free will."

Fuck. There it is, shoved into my face. Thank you, Rach. You're such a pal. I feel light-headed. A familiar refrain runs through my head: *Anger is poison. It hurts only myself. Remember what it did to Dad and Matt.* I squeeze my knees so hard I can feel bruises forming. *Anger turned inward...* My inner eye turns toward the scar on my left thigh. Where's a goddamn paper clip when you need one.

I take a multigrain cracker, spread it with Brie, and hold it out to Rachel. What I want to say is, This is me adjusting to you and your culture. Do you remember that potluck at the beginning of grad school? We each had to bring something typical of our heritage. You said it felt like being in third grade again and brought snickerdoodles. I brought roasted seaweed, rice, and kimchi. Someone asked what stinks and opened the windows. You laughed.

What I do say is, "Here. It's the good stuff from Trader Joe's."

Rachel takes the peace offering, pops the whole thing into her mouth. "I mean, let's be honest," she says as she chews, "playing the culture card over and over again can be considered kind of racist."

I regret the cracker. I prepare another and bite into it myself. "Okay," I say, "I see your point. You see it as a crutch. It skews my perspective." Rachel raises her glass in confirmation. "The problem is, it is and always has been my reality. What's your excuse? How about your blind spots? I've never asked, Rach, but I've wondered. How come you don't work with minorities? You always send them to me."

Angie's desperate voice says, "We're getting off track."

Rachel ignores her. "We each have our specialties. You're the best when it comes to multicultural stuff."

"So you admit multicultural stuff is an issue?"

"Sure, but not for everyone. That's your bag; mine is addiction and eating disorders."

"People of color have addictions and eating disorders too, but you're clearly not interested. Why not?"

"Who are you, and what've you done with my friend Jax?" She washes another cracker down with a quick swallow of Shiraz.

I run my hand over my face. So many years of camouflaging my feelings. I can't do it anymore.

"Jax is just a sliver of me. This is the whole me, Jacqueline Kyung-hee Chol Kessler. There's a lot of me that you don't know, and you've never shown one goddamn bit of interest."

"And whose fault is that? You could've said something."

"Oh, lord," I exclaim, slapping my palm against my forehead. "What a fool I've been all this time! So many wasted opportunities."

"Like I was saying." Her voice holds more than a sliver of ice.

"Hey, you two –"

"No." I cut Liz off, my hand raised in warning. "Tell me, Rachel. What do you see when you look at me?"

"I see my friend Jackie."

"Peel the fuckin' onion. *What* do you see?"

"Uh, you're basically White."

I sit back and throw my arms into the air. Our supposed friendship of over twenty years has been built on this, my basic Whiteness?

"And there we have it, "I say. "I grew up watching the people around me. I learned how to do the White thing, rearranged myself to fit into your world. Do you know how exhausting that is? I've tried to open the subject with you, Rach, and you shut me down every single time. But if you think culture and race – oh, how I hate that word – aren't important, you're being naïve. Look around you." I sweep my arm in a circle. "The world is changing. Fascism's on the rise, both here and abroad. We're being split down the middle by the hatred and fear being force-fed to us by our so-called leaders. Good grief, we're therapists! Acknowledging this and knowing how to help people deal with it – no matter which side they're on – is a moral and ethical imperative for us."

Rachel takes a thin slice of baguette. It tears beneath the pressure of the cheese knife, leaving a smear of Brie on her palm. "No. I'll be in practice another ten, fifteen years. I'll retire before it's an issue."

"Rachel. It is already an issue. It killed Amy Nguyen."

"How do you know, huh? Just how the hell do you know?" Rachel tosses the knife and bread onto the table. I smell the alcohol on her breath, see the unnatural ruddiness in her cheeks. "For you it always boils down to culture, culture, culture. Did you ever stop to consider this lawsuit might be all about you and *your* culture? Maybe you were so focused on finding something else to blame culture for that you totally missed what was really going on with your client, and now she's dead."

I lower myself into a chair and slowly crumble a cracker. The broken pieces miss my plate. Rachel looks beseechingly from Angie to Liz and back again.

"Nothin' from you, huh? Well I'm done with this," she mutters. "I am so done." She gulps the remainder of her wine and wipes her hand with a napkin. Then she carefully places her glass and plate in the sink, gathers her belongings, and walks out.

The click of the front door breaks the spell.

"What the fuck just happened?" Angie's mouth hangs open. "We can't let her drive." She jumps up to follow Rachel.

Liz sighs and pulls me out of my chair into a bear hug. "Honey, she had one glass too many. We're all stressed out about this. She didn't mean it."

I shake my head. "*In vino veritas*. At least she was being honest."

"What do you mean? Are you implying we're not?"

"Rachel didn't say anything I haven't already thought. Haven't you thought it?"

"No," she says, a fraction of a second too late. "Never entered into the realm of possibility."

"Maybe you're the naïve one." I deposit my dirty dishes on top of Rachel's and leave by the back door.

I slam into the house from the garage. Willem looks up in surprise. "I'll be on the treadmill," I call over my shoulder, heading for the staircase.

Forty minutes later I hear Willem stop at the door to gauge the treadmill's speed. I'm walking. Slowly. He knocks and enters.

"Want to talk about it?"

"No."

"Whenever you're ready." He waits patiently.

I stop the machine, wipe sweat off my face and neck with a hand towel. Willem takes my hand, turns it over to kiss the center of my palm.

"Rachel and I …" I stop and search Willem's face. "Good thing you're not a poker player, Schätzli. Who called, Liz or Angie?"

"They were on the line together," he replies, "both talking so fast I could barely understand what they were saying."

"It looks like you understood enough."

"Sometimes friendship is hard work. When do the efforts outweigh the benefits?"

The challenge slides over and around me, threatens to pull me under.

"I let Rachel get under my skin. She's pretty sick of me on my soapbox, and I'm just as sick of being there, but she can't understand that her lousy attitude forces me back up."

"Can't, doesn't, or won't?"

"Please don't therapize me." One of our kids' standard retorts. Only they usually left out the please.

He smiles. "We've lived together a long time. It rubbed off."

"I'm not ready to call her a racist, but I can't and won't ignore ethnocentric crap when I see or hear it, especially when it comes from RAJE." I drop the towel to the floor. "But I think I'm mostly pissed because she might be right. She may be a pain in the ass, but she's a really smart pain in the ass."

He looks pointedly at my carry-on bag propped in the corner. "What do you want to do?"

I have no answer. Even though I expect it, I shudder when he says, "What do you think she'll do?"

DAY FOUR

•••••••••••••••••••••••••

A furry face emerges next to my elbow. "Eat your own breakfast." I nudge Bonkers away from my bowl of oatmeal. "I'm not keen on leaving."

Willem sighs. "When are you ever?"

"Yeah, well, especially not now. I should be here with you. You're top priority."

"So are you. There's something you have to do, so go do it. I'm not helpless."

"You're the one said I couldn't go alone."

"I was wrong. It's better this way, less side-trouble."

He's right. Can't use Rach as an excuse anymore. My greatest fear forces its way out of my mouth. "What if something happens while I'm gone?"

Tasha jumps in: "I'll stay in my old room till you're back. Besides, Papa and I have plans. After we drop you at the airport, we'll visit Grandma, and dinner's with Mohamed and Allan at Liz and Theo's tonight."

Before I ask about what happens after today, Willem says, "It'll be one constant party. I'm more worried about you. You're looking for excuses, and that's never good."

I blow a raspberry in his direction. He knows me too well.

He asks, "Have you heard anything from Rachel?"

"No, and I don't expect to. If she were still coming, she'd have been in touch."

Liz and Angie are under orders to steer clear. If Rachel calls one of them, okay, but there is to be no pressure of any kind. Ultimately, she has to talk with me. She has to make up her own mind.

The doorbell rings. I push out of my chair.

There are another five hours before I head to Sea-Tac airport; no reason to waste them. Allan, Mohamed and I are sequestered in the dining room. I'm no longer bitter about Allan refusing the trip, but time is moving ever more slowly as the morning progresses.

"What exactly are the things you have to handle here, Allan?" Okay, so maybe just a tad bitter.

"I have some questions."

You have some questions? So do I, buddy. We don't even know for sure that Amy was murdered. I could be flying halfway around the world to expose what turns out to be my delusions. You're the smart one, staying home.

"It's all happening so fast." I wave my boarding pass, hot off the printer, in the air. Allan looks at it like it's an eviction notice. Judging from the tremor as he pours himself more coffee, I'm not the only one having second, third, maybe even fourth thoughts. I hope none of us come to regret this.

Mohamed pours with a remarkably steady hand. I anchor myself to his certainty and ask, "What questions, Allan?"

"Mohamed," he says abruptly, "I was at the symposium Amy spoke at a few years ago. The one on refugee families."

There's a minute adjustment in Mohamed's posture, a tiny shift in facial musculature. For a fraction of a second he looks delicate, brittle, before that empty look takes over.

Allan continues: "If I remember correctly, she mentioned racially motivated attacks against ORB." He waits for Mohamed to absorb this. "What can you tell us?"

Mohamed moves as if to speak, stops. He begins again, this time addressing me. "I think it's important for you to know that it was not always the way I portrayed it." He must see my puzzlement. "The public has not always been so kind and accepting of ORB."

This I already know. "'What do you see when you look in my face?/Do you really see me or do you just see my race?'"

"'See Me.'"

I nod. "An early draft. I came across it the other day." I explain for Allan's benefit that there had been an on-line smear campaign after ORB won their first Grammys. Oh, how it had pissed Amy off. I reach into memory and compose myself to recite:

> "'What do you see when you look
>   in my face
> Do you really see me or do you just
>   see my race
> You're showing your hand;
>   it's a goddamned disgrace
> I'm holding a deuce and you've got the ace
> Don't let your hate be a federal case
> We both want our peace;
>   we want equal space
> I want reason for hope when we stand
>   face to face'"

Mohamed leans back, rubs his forehead, tells us of ORB's increasing political activism as they became more successful. They ardently supported Barack Obama's second run for the presidency, sponsored voter registration drives before gigs, and advocated for social justice.

"Not everyone appreciated our efforts," he says. "We received threats."

There's a familiar pressure on my chest. Shit. That damn car. I riffle through the fat file folder on my desk.

Amy had arrived incognito: baggy clothes, baseball hat pulled low. It was like she was fifteen again. Only now she was twenty-five, a popular local celebrity and recent Grammy winner. She didn't go out of her way to call attention to her presence, but it wasn't like her to try to disappear altogether.

She was on the floor, sketchbook on her lap, sorting through my art supplies. "No decent colors left." She held up a fistful of washable felt tip pens. "And I must reinstate my protest at the dearth of Sharpies."

"I work with kids," I said, handing her a semi-new box of colored pencils and a manual pencil sharpener. "You know what kind of damage can be done with permanent ink? My landlord would have a cow." No need to reveal that the land-lord, c'est moi.

She outlined a shape with a charcoal gray pencil, filled it with yellow. More details were added in black, more gray, some red. After thorough evaluation, a section was erased and carefully redrawn. "Here." She turned the picture my way. It was a scrubby yellow car. Instead of a front grille, it had the jaws of a shark. It was not at all cute or cartoonish.

"What's this?"

"It spoke to me." Her voice had a weird edge to it.

"Must've said something significant." Amy was not a cas-ual in-session doodler. If she drew something, there was a reason, and this was not her usual quick sketch. I tried again. "What is it?"

"A major piece of nasty."

I waited. No response. I added a scowl.

Her laugh was a sharp yip. "Lighten up, Doc." Two beats. "It followed me home the other day."

"One of the admiring horde?"

Her forehead creased. "Nope. The vibe was all wrong. For sure a nasty." She heard my inadvertent intake of breath. "Don't worry. You're probably right. Must've been a fan." Her body slouched and she smirked.

"A mad dog fan by the looks of it."

Her laugh was false this time; she looked concerned at my concern. I wished I could redo the last ten seconds.

"Good thing I didn't feed it," she said. "Wouldn't want that hound to stick around."

I turn to Mohamed. "She told me about your meetings at that coffeehouse on Capitol Hill."

"Yes. Beancounters. It was our favorite place." He sighs and his shoulders come down. "Before people began to recognize us, we had coffee there every Monday morning."

"That's right. She told me about Beancounters while she drew that." I shake off my cowardice of that day, point to the picture. "She said it followed her home, then clammed up. When she was evasive like that, I would usually circle back at a later session and try to get more out of her. It didn't work with this, though. Amy insisted she never saw it again."

Mohamed crosses his arms. "I remember the day. It was the first time we realized we were true public figures. We were recognized and she was followed."

"Followed?" Allan's been listening intently.

"Yes. We always drove separately. When I got home, Amy called to ask if I had arrived safely. I said of course and asked after her worry. She said a car, an old yellow Honda, a small sedan, had followed her. When she stopped at her place the car drove on. When it didn't happen again, we decided we were getting paranoid. But the next week the same car went past my house. Two days later the first letter arrived at my home."

"Letter?" Allan's starting to look pissed.

"ORB originally hired Sam and Co. because they were getting nasty mail," I reply.

Allan says to me, "These are the types of details I want to know about, sooner rather than later." He turns to Mohamed. "Did you ever see that car again?"

"No, but I didn't look for it. You see, I was determined not to live in fear. I still am."

"So the driver knew where you both lived."

"Yes. Some letters were mailed to us directly, but they stopped quickly."

I guess where Allan's going with this and ask a classic therapy question. "What happened that was different?"

Mohamed looks at his hands in his lap. When his head rises, his brow lifts. He tells us that he and Amy's next trip to Beancounters was in the company of one of Sam's crew. Again, they were recognized. Autographs weren't enough, and the other customers refused to keep their distance. The bodyguard took care of it. Afterward, they bowed to Sam's recommendation of a private meeting place.

"I'm so sorry that happened to you." The words feel empty even as they leave my mouth. I'm more than sorry. I'm livid. "Amy talked about racism but never mentioned threats. How serious were they?"

"She probably said nothing because we tried not to be overly concerned. The messages were more 'the Grammys are American awards and you are undeserving because you aren't Americans' and 'go back to where you came from, or else.' But then Trump took office and everything became much worse, so we fought back even stronger."

"How did the threats change?" Allan asks. I run that through my head again. From the way he asked, he already knows the answer.

"The letters sent to our homes threatened our lives. Our manager informed the police, and the FBI investigated."

"Sent to your homes." Allan leans back, considering.

"Yes, and they were always the same."

"What do you mean?"

"The same font, my name was misspelled the same way every time. And the letters always arrived on a Thursday."

This news makes me shiver. As does the fact that Amy never told me. The little twerp. What else did she choose to omit? Did she do it to please or shelter me?

"What did the FBI find?"

The sneer on Mohamed's face looks unnatural. "They called it bark without bite, the price of celebrity and our outspokenness. As far as I am concerned, in any form of hatred there is bite."

Allan steps to the whiteboard. *Letters* goes under *Suspects* and *hate crime* becomes the newest motive.

I say, "I wonder if they'd have said the same thing if all the ORBers were White."

"This was our thought, exactly. The FBI did not build our confidence in them. Sam's team has been providing security for us ever since. The letters stopped when we hired him." He turns to me. "Jackie, you will be our ears and eyes and voice with Sam."

I stretch my legs in guilty pleasure. That Mohamed. Over my objections, he'd booked us seats in business class. His argument? On such short notice, adjoining seats in coach weren't available. I wouldn't have minded sitting separately, maybe would've preferred it. Moot point. Rachel decided, damn her. No word equals no show. I'll reimburse Mohamed for her ticket. At least I'll save on food and lodging. And there'll be peace and quiet.

Noise-cancelling earphones in place, I shut my eyes to further block out the boarding hubbub. Something hard bumps my elbow.

"I'm in there."

I open my eyes. Rachel points beyond me to the window seat. She heaves her offending roller bag into the overhead compartment, those damn bracelets clanging. "No need to move," she says. As if I would. "There's plenty of space." I stay put; she pushes past.

As she gets settled, I put my reading glasses on, open a copy of the in-flight magazine. The flight attendant comes by, asks if we'd like orange juice or champagne.

"Can I have one of each, please?" asks Rachel.

"Sure. And you, Ma'am?"

"Could I possibly have a mimosa, please?"

"Oh, that's what I want," says Rachel. "I didn't know you could order it that way."

The young man aims an energetic smile at us. "I'll be right back with your drinks."

Rachel says, "He's cute." She experiments with her seat until it's fully reclined. "This is posh."

I put the magazine aside, take my glasses off, look at her as blandly as possible. "That's how you want to start this?"

"Damn it, Jax, how else do we do this? I'm here, aren't I?"

I pick up the magazine again. "You said it yourself; it's a free trip to Paris." I hold back my next remark: You can take the Eiffel Tower and shove it. Here's to my self-restraint.

I accept my drink, choose a bag of lightly buttered popcorn to accompany it. Rachel's mimosa is gone in two gulps. She nervously starts on some deluxe salted mixed nuts. She couldn't have made a more fitting choice.

"Jackie, I'm … forget the Eiffel Tower." How'd she read my mind? "I'm here because I'm your friend. You have to decide if you still want to be friends with me. But remember, if you're willing to throw a quarter of a century's worth of whatever we have out the window, it better be for a damn good reason."

Who coached her, Liz or Angie?

Takeoff provides a welcome respite. I need every second of it. Once the plane clears the clouds, there's no way to ignore her.

"If we do this, Rachel, we do it properly. Ground rules: honesty, respect, good intentions."

She adds, "Openness to each other's opinions and willingness to admit mistakes."

I'm very aware of the Kleenex balled in my jacket pocket. My fingers yearn to shred it. Instead, I ask, "How are you?"

"Angry," she says, her voice weary. "Sad. Frustrated." She grips the bangles to stop their music. We both wince as metal grates on metal. "Mostly angry. You?"

"The same."

"I'm not sorry for what I said. I *am* sorry for how I said it."

"I'm also not sorry for what I said. I'm sorry for what I *didn't* say. For all those years."

We look past each other's ears.

"Why didn't you?" Rach demands.

"From early on, I felt it wasn't allowed, that it made you all uncomfortable. I figured it wasn't worth the bother. We all get more than enough heavy stuff at work and during consult. Who needs it in our personal time? You know how Ang always says the best part of RAJE is that we laugh so much."

"She's not wrong."

"No. But that puts the brakes on anything serious."

She contemplates a cashew. "I know. It stops me too."

"Stops you from what?"

Rachel's face is flushed. "Do you really think I'm racist?"

"Sometimes you say things without realizing how they hit."

"All you have to do is tell me."

"It's that simple, eh?" I do my best impression of her, including the extravagant hand movements. " 'Jeez, Jax, it was just a joke.' 'Don't take things so personally, Jax.' 'I didn't know Asians could be so sensitive. What happened to the model minority?'" I drop my hands. "I mean, what the fuck?"

"Okay, okay." Rachel puts her hands up in self-defense. "But what about you?"

"What about me?"

Rachel empties the last of the nuts into her mouth. "I listen to you guys breathe fire about your political views all the time. Because I keep my mouth shut, you *assume* I think the same. Did you ever bother to consider what it meant to grow up in Ritzville? Most everyone I knew lived below the poverty line. The hoity toity Democrats never paid any attention to us, never did anything for us. There are good reasons my family's voted a straight Republican ticket for as long as I can remember. Of course, that turned out to be a nightmare with Trump and his toadies, but that's because my party changed; my values haven't."

Damn. I never had a clue. No, if I'm honest, the clues were there. It was easier to ignore them. I cringe at my holier-than-thou speech in Mona's office. Was it only three days ago? I had it all figured out in my head but never saw it in front of me. In one of my closest friends.

We sit facing forward, staring holes into the seatbacks in front of us.

"So, Ms. Business-Class-Mimosa," she says tentatively, "now that you know my deepest, darkest secret, are we still allowed to sit together?"

"Only if you brought your cloth coat, Ms. Hardcore-Republican."

"A fleece isn't enough?" she whines. "I checked the forecast."

Oh, wurra, wurra. I look at her with alarm. So much for her deep Republican roots.

"Did you bring your fur?" she asks with a hopeful twinkle.

Damn, caught in it again. Only this time I laugh. Yes, we're therapists for reasons.

It was early on in Amy's treatment. She was still coming. And still talking. Sort of. It depended on her mood. This day's mood was particularly foul. I suggested we play a game, trading random questions. It was Amy's turn to ask; she was taking her time. I watched two squirrels chase each other around the maple tree outside the window.

"What's one of the weirdest things you ever ate?" Amy's arms were folded tightly across her chest, driving in the message of what a colossal waste of time this was.

I quickly sorted through my mental Rolodex of food-related memories. "I can't pinpoint one thing, per se." She scrunched her face. "It'd have to be a whole meal, a Thanksgiving dinner that was a combo of Korean and American. We had the traditional meal, turkey with all the fixin's, plus kimchi and a bunch of other Korean stuff on the side."

No reaction.

"The weirdest part of it was these little dried snack fish that you ate whole, tails and heads still attached. They'd stick in your teeth worse than caramel. Anyway, as we're filling our plates my brother points at the fish with their bulgy eyes and says, 'Hey, Jackie, our lunch is looking back at us.'"

Got her. She smiled in spite of herself.

"Your turn on the hot seat," I said. "What do you like and not like about being in two cultures?"

She turned away. I marked the time.

Almost a minute passed before she swiveled back to face me. "Sometimes it's okay, but mostly it sucks."

"What's the okay part?"

"We're probably not as boring as a lot of other people."

Was she referring to her family or including me? Made no difference; a tiny door of opportunity just opened a sliver. I stuck a toe in, wiggled it around to test the maneuvering space: "I grant you that. The sucky part?"

"Sometimes I'd rather be boring."

"Like when?"

"Do I really have to do this?"

"You're not being graded."

Another face-scrunch, another out-the-window stare. She whispered, "I don't fit in anywhere."

"What was that?" C'mon, Amy. There's space for two.

Obnoxiously loud this time. "I. Don't. Fit. In. Anywhere."

"I bet you don't."

"What's that supposed to mean?" She sounded torn between insult and intrigue.

Time to decide, Amy – toe in or out? Perhaps a little shove would help.

"Look, I grew up in a very White suburban neighborhood. I can still feel that squeeze in my chest that came from the funny looks, the stupid comments, the crap that goes with not fitting in. You know what I mean?" Her stillness showed that she did. "I've met lots of people like us; some have been clients but most haven't been. And there was something we all – literally all – had in common."

She turned back to me, sour-faced. "Such as?" Petulance teetering toward desperation. There she was. Toe in.

"Being totally and constantly stressed out just trying to live our lives as peacefully as possible. Figuring out how to be in unfriendly surroundings, the costs involved, and if the effort would be worth it. All the while comparing ourselves to others and feeling like we don't measure up, even being told so to our faces. That can make us not like ourselves as much as we could." I paused. "Any of that sound familiar?"

"Are you telling me I'm supposed to feel like shit?"

"No. I'm saying that if you *do* feel like shit, there are solid reasons for it. And the feeling doesn't have to be permanent."

Her face went blank. I hoped I hadn't lost her. One minute, two minutes. She pulled the stuffed brown bunny from the top of the bookcase, wound the right ear tightly around her left forefinger, let it loose when her finger turned purple.

I said, "What're you thinking, Amy?"

"You're a therapist."

"Yeah, and?"

"You've been at this a lot longer than me."

"Yeah, and?"

"If you're as fucked up as you sound, maybe there's hope for me."

The Hotel Monique is housed in a compact building on a narrow side street. Even so, it's an eyeful of weathered, golden-hued stone, black wrought iron railings, and planters overflowing with enthusiastic red geraniums. Each balcony has just enough space to comfortably hold a small round wrought iron table and two matching chairs.

As the cab pulls to the curb, Rachel comes to giddy attention. "Just like a picture postcard. Nope. Better because this is real and we're actually here."

The elaborately carved wooden front desk, the murals of Parisian landmarks on the thick stone walls, and the cordial reception by the staff have her gasping with downright glee.

"I've always heard Parisians are snobby and hate Americans," she says, a little too loudly, as we follow a porter up the stairs. "But they're super friendly. Sam was right – this place is great!"

Our narrow room quickly changes her opinion. The heavy antique furnishings leave only a cramped margin down which to walk.

"What a gyp," says Rachel, fists on her hips. "I saw what this costs. For that much money, they should give us something bigger."

"Quit with the slurs," I say. She looks at me, uncomprehending, then smiles faintly. I'm too tired to explain it's not a joke. "And this is old-school Europe. If you want something bigger, go find a Best Western."

For a split second, she looks hopeful. Then, thankfully, the message penetrates. As she stows her underwear in the armoire, she mutters, "Not even a mini-fridge."

Half an hour later she's wrapped in a bath towel, pulling a comb through her wet hair, yawning. "Oh, I need a nap."

I say, "Jetlag is for sissies. The way around it is through your stomach. C'mon, get dressed. Time for lunch and a walk."

"Too. Tired." She moves to lie down. "Go without me."

"Too. Bad. You're coming with." She groans as I haul her onto her feet.

She's making a huge effort by being here; it's time for me to reply in kind. Besides, until we meet with Sam Reyes there's nothing else to do. While she dresses, I go downstairs to the concierge desk, walking map of Paris in hand.

From the Café de Flore it's only a ten-minute stroll to Notre Dame. Rachel is delightedly snapping pictures, texting them to her kids. My shoulders sag. The whole of the edifice is still magnificent, but it's easy and tragic to imagine the devastation within.

Rachel comes up beside me, also contemplating the blackened walls and empty spaces. "How depressing." She shakes my shoulder. "Don't take it as a bad omen."

At the Batobus station, Rachel shakes my shoulder again, this time with unabashed excitement and joy.

"This is why I love you!" she gushes. "I didn't think we'd be able to."

Jetlag forgotten, she's practically dancing as the boat approaches the Eiffel Tower. My friend-duty is done. It's a relief and more. This time we're both taking photos.

Back at the hotel we kick our shoes off and sit at the balcony table. A sleek gray-striped tabby cat, a bigger, obviously more capable version of Bonkers, slips out of an open skylight across the street. This leads my thoughts home, to Tash and Stef, to Willem.

Rachel's voice cuts through. "They didn't come back."

I startle, thinking she means my family. "What?"

"None of 'em," she says. "None of 'em came back."

"Who're you talking about?"

"You asked why I don't work with minorities." Her eyes are riveted on the cat's dainty progress across the tile rooftops. "I was assigned minority clients during my internship. One, maybe two sessions. After that they didn't come back. I did everything my agency supervisor told me, but nothing worked."

"How come you never brought it to our supervision? You helped me with Crazy Lady; I could've helped you."

"Well, here's the thing. I shared supervision with the only person of color in our cohort. I didn't want to look totally incompetent. At least my agency supervisor didn't know anything either, so I didn't feel so stupid."

I believe her. The first agency I applied at for an internship scooped me up. Unbeknownst to me, as soon as the paperwork was signed, I was appointed the staff's ethnic minority mental health specialist. The other therapists, some with more than twenty years in the biz, couldn't transfer their clients of color fast enough. It was disgusting. And overwhelming. The office manager later let slip they'd been desperate for an infusion of color.

"I did fine with White clients," says Rachel, "so that's what I ended up with, and that's what I stick with. I mean, why fight it? I don't click with people of color."

"Is that why we can be friends? Because you consider me White?"

The camaraderie of the afternoon is punctured by her sudden stiffness. I'm thrown back to the pain and humiliation of that night at Angie's.

"You may see me a certain way," I say, "but I'm so not White. Remember the trip to Huron?"

On a roots road trip a few years earlier RAJE, with our husbands, had rented a large van and made our meandering way from Seattle to Huron, South Dakota where Angie's forebears had homesteaded. First it was being followed through the aisles of an Idaho drugstore. Then it was stopping at a self-identified "Friendly Family Restaurant" off the I-90 in Wyoming. It didn't take a genius to notice the ethnic rainbow in the dingy back room where we'd been seated, whereas the cheerful, half-empty front room had only White diners.

"You take everything personally," Rachel says, pulling from a plastic half-liter bottle of mineral water. "We were with you, for goodness' sake. It happened to us too and we're White, so it wasn't on purpose. It could've happened to anyone."

"It happened to you because you had the misfortune of being with me. Remember the guy at the frozen yogurt place who called me a stupid Indian when I caught him trying to short-change me?"

"Yeah, you and Willem shouldn't have complained. I didn't tell you at the time, but it was embarrassing."

I feel like I've been slapped, only the sting goes far deeper than my face. "You could have spared yourself by going back to the van."

"I wanted my huckleberry fro-yo," she says plaintively. "Come on. The kid wasn't out to get you. There was that huge long line, the register was down, and he couldn't do the math. I felt for him. Education must suck out there in the sticks."

"Yeah, you felt for him, the poor, uneducated White kid. What happened when I helped him out, told him the amount I was due? He refused to believe me. Did he do that to Angie? Or Liz? You may see a White woman when you look at me, but no one else does, and they treat me accordingly. Did you see how the manager shrugged me off until Willem came over?"

Rachel looks at me accusingly. "You think you're the only one? You know nothing about that guy, what he probably had to put up with from know-it-all tourists, no matter what color. My sister and I grew up being called white trash to our faces. Our parents sent us to the food bank every week because they were too proud and too hungover to go themselves. I was fourteen when my crummy excuse of a father left. I thought things would get better after that, but they only got worse. Mom sucked herself into any bottle she could find. Booze, pills, whatever was easy and available. You have no idea what it was like, starting every morning afraid we'd find our mother dead on the floor. You have to give it to her, though. She stuck it out till Sandy and I finished high school."

"I thought she died of lung cancer. You told us secondhand smoke."

"No, you assumed it was cancer. My mother died of secondhand smoke caused by attaching a garden hose to the tailpipe of an ancient Chevy and sucking up exhaust for all it was worth. Do you know what happens to a body that dies that way? It ain't peaceful and it ain't pretty. And all Sandy and I were left with was a boatload of hate and regret."

I've never felt such a void in my friend, not even when her husband died. She contemplates the empty bottle in her hand. "Not one day goes by I don't live in mortal fear of becoming like either of my parents. You know, my dear old dad whipped me once when I was eight because instead of coming straight home from school I went to play at a new girl's house. A girl named Elsa Sanchez. I never dared talk to her again, even though we were in school together another ten years. She was a really nice girl, too. *She* had *friends*." Rachel wipes the back of her hand against her eyes. "And here you are, calling me a racist. Well fuck that and fuck you. Sometimes you're the one with no clue."

"You're right," I say, stunned. "I'm sorry."

I want to say more, but what is there? I'm guilty of everything I accused her of. She passes the bottle from one hand to another, as if she'd like to heave it into the street.

"I know I had too much that night." She carefully stands the bottle on the table. "I just got scared, y'know?" She looks at me pleadingly. "At first I thought coming here would be fun, an adventure, just you and me. And my first time in Europe, with a pro to show me the ropes. Then I got to thinking about what we were actually coming for, what you're going through, and it scared the shit outta me."

"It scares the shit outta me, too."

She stretches out her hand. "Jackie, I am so, so sorry." Tears are running into the corners of her mouth. "Please, please, please…"

I squeeze her hand hard, feel tears drip off the end of my chin. "I will. Will you?"

"Done deal."

I don't know how long we sit, grasping hands.

Suddenly, she seizes my forearm with her free hand and says, "What's the equivalent of makeup sex between friends?"

I blink at her dumbly. "Eclairs?"

DAY FIVE

•••••••••••••••••••••••••

Sam Reyes has a warm, inviting manner. The cool distance I'd originally expected in a security expert was first put to question at Monday's send-off. Allan pulled me aside to privately share the results of his research into the man. "He's legit, but be careful. He has a reputation for bending standard security protocols."

In a separate moment, Mohamed also filled me in. "Sam is great. He gives custom-tailored services. It was exactly this which convinced us to hire him."

The same message from different angles: Sam gets more personal with clients than Allan, a man who respects boundaries, appreciates. Sound like collectivism in action.

As soon as we're seated Sam asks about our flight, whether either of us has been in Paris before. Charming way to seize the initiative. We'll see about that, sir.

The first time Willem took me to Switzerland, we walked down to the stream that cuts through the family farm. His mother had ordered trout for that night's dinner. I had no interest in holding a pole, still don't, but was curious at the way Willem chose his spot, checked the speed and temperature of the water's flow, then patiently, repeatedly cast his line. He said, "The trick is to think like a fish in order to lead it to you.

135

You must become one with the surroundings. If your shadow falls across the water or you frighten it in some other way, you'll end up hungry."

That concept has come in handy with people too.

Rachel cheerfully describes the previous day's sightseeing. I ask about Sam's history with Paris. Cast number one.

Our waiter arrives for our orders. He speaks French slowly, with a strong accent; his nametag identifies him as Klaus from Dresden. Rach orders off the English menu. Sam orders in German. I do the same. Cast number two.

"*Sprechen Sie Deutsch?*" asks Sam.

"*Ja, Sie anscheinend auch.*" You too, apparently. Before he can ask, I describe the Kessler clan's Korean-American-Swiss connections. Sam chuckles as I joke about the mishmash of accents in our ears, turns his chair toward me just a tad when I comment on the German inflection in his English. The question about his ethnic heritage is implied. Casts number three and four.

He willingly reveals his own tri-cultural mix: Puerto Rican and Black on his father's side, German on his mother's. He's hooked. With a few gentle tugs, more of his story unfolds.

His father was a Bronx-born US Army Sergeant stationed in Bavaria, where he met and married a local woman and later took her back to the States. Born in the USA, Sam was little more than a toddler when his father was killed in action in Vietnam. His mother returned with him to Germany, eschewing her rural village in favor of Frankfurt am Main, in the hope that a large, cosmopolitan city would be a more welcoming setting in which to raise her multiethnic son.

Sam's family on both sides made it a priority for him to know his multiple cultures. His growing-up years were spent primarily in Frankfurt, with summers and every other Christmas in New York. After completing compulsory military duty in Germany, he attended university in Washington, DC.

Sam returns his chair to neutral position. He asks Rachel about her roots, what led her to become a therapist. She looks up, surprised. She's been intent on her stomach, probably didn't expect to be of any more interest to him. I tap her foot lightly with mine; Sam leans in toward her with a reassuring smile. She says her parents took their Scotch-Irish roots literally; that steered her toward mental health. After last night I realize the hidden cost behind the familiar wisecrack.

We're comfortable now, but not fully relaxed. The purpose for our new association has yet to be addressed. I'm about to ask about the mystery car when Sam's cell phone vibrates.

"I'm sorry; this is important." He diverts his attention to the newly received text message, types a quick reply. He apologizes again, this time for an abrupt departure. "Let's meet again for lunch." He flashes an exquisite smile. "I'll have information for you."

Rachel's eyes follow Sam as he exits the dining room. I expect a classic Rach comment, something along the lines of, He's gorgeous. Instead comes, "Well, that was a waste."

"A waste?" I pat my stomach.

"Of time." She pats her wristwatch. "I hate jibber jabber. He was supposed to find that car for us. He obviously didn't. Why couldn't he just say so?"

"Looks like that call was it."

"Then this could've waited till lunch."

"Rach," I say, "it wasn't a waste at all. Consider this your first lesson in the art of collectivist communication. Getting to know your allies. The man was vetting us as much as we were vetting him."

"Huh?"

"Okay, so I was vetting him. Puerto Rican, Black, and even though he grew up in Frankfurt, his mom's a small town gal. That combo makes him a probable collectivist. The fact that he read and responded correctly to my cues confirms the diagnosis. He also now knows that I'm one too and you are not." I wag a finger at her. "Clues on how we each operate, my dear Watson."

"I wondered what the deal was." She pushes back from the table. "So we've got the skinny on him, too. And knowledge truly is power."

"Exactly." I squeeze her hand, proud of her. "Reading between the lines, we can also surmise that he and his mother had some hard times in both countries, maybe even with both sides of the family."

Rachel's face clouds. I wait.

"Y'know those clients who never came back?"

"Yeah."

"They did the same thing, got up into my business that same way."

I hold my tongue, look away.

"You're not surprised."

"No. I get it all the time from prospective clients – collectivists and kids, anyway. Especially teenagers. It's a test. If I'm vulnerable with you, will you reciprocate? They want to see if we'll really go there with them, honor their effort. Trust-building goes both ways."

Rachel rubs her temples. "From day one they drilled it into us: boundaries, boundaries, boundaries. Self-revelation is a cardinal sin."

"And just who were *they*? We had White instructors training us to enter what is still a predominantly White middle class profession. As far as they were concerned, their rules applied. Wrong. In the wider world, boundaries are relative."

"How'd you know? I sure didn't."

"What they said turned me off. I knew if I were a client, I'd never work with any of 'em. I decided to be the kind of therapist I'd seek out for myself. Sam follows the same process. Did you see what he was doing?"

"No. What?" She fiddles with her bracelets.

"The security version of what we do, tapping into the vibe."

I see Rachel replay breakfast in her head. Reyes had been constantly scanning, aware of not only our interactions, but of the action surrounding us.

I continue: "It's the same radar we use, keying in on things that don't fit. We feel for ripples in emotion, behavior, the energy flow between people."

Her body springs to life. "It's how we smell an affair. Abuser and victim, addict and enabler." She taps her spoon on her coffee cup. "The security version, eh? He'd sniff out hunter and prey."

After foolhardily wandering the Latin Quarter without a map, Rachel's relying on me, the one with decades of European experience, to navigate our way back to the hotel. Lost cause. Somehow, no matter which route we take, we end up back at the church of Saint-Etienne-du-Mont. We peer upward into the contorted faces of long-necked gargoyles, eroded by age and the elements. They glare back at us, *bloody tourists* in their expressions.

This time, instead of turning right, I turn left down what looks like a back alley. Halfway down, we both recoil at the stink of stale urine.

"Oh, gag!" she says. "How can anyone in a modern western society do that to their own neighborhood? And in Paris, of all places."

I point to a spent champagne cork in the gutter. "At least there's a higher pedigree of piss here than in Pioneer Square."

At the end of the alley we turn right. Another block down is the Hotel Monique.

Sam is waiting, cell phone in hand, workbag slung over his shoulder. He leads us to a neighboring *boulangerie*.

"A lot of people say a lot of bad things about British cuisine," he says as we inspect the dizzying selection of sandwiches. "It's getting better but whenever I'm in Paris, I have to agree."

We take a table in a far corner. Sam pulls a large manila envelope from his bag and places it on the table. "We tracked down the Mercedes."

I decide not to pursue the plural. Sam snaps an index card face down on top of the envelope and slides both toward me. Rachel looks on; I can practically feel the itch in her fingers.

"The owner," says Sam. "She must be the person Amy wanted to meet."

Rach crosses her arms; her voice oozes skepticism. "How can you know?" Her turn to vet the poor guy.

Reyes lifts an eyebrow a fraction of an inch. That's probably as much irritation as the man allows himself to reveal. "It was Amy's behavior that caught my attention in the first place, even before I realized it was her."

In an exhale, Rachel whispers, "Radar."

"She was incognito," continues Sam, "dark glasses, baseball cap with the bill pulled low, the whole bit. She scanned the traffic, waved the vehicle over. When it pulled to the curb, she stooped to say something through the passenger side window. It was too far away for me to hear, but *she* opened the passenger door. She got in voluntarily."

I flip the card over. *MIREILLE GASTONEAU* is printed neatly in bold capitals, an address in Nice and a telephone number in smaller print below. Finally, something concrete. A real lead, no matter how slim.

I pull a black and white photograph from the envelope. A young woman with attitude. Light hair cut in a severe chin-length bob, meticulously parted down the middle. A dark leather jacket over a white V-neck t-shirt. An indifferent expression. Something in her features catches my eye.

"Looks like a driver's license or passport photo." I pass it to Rachel.

"Or mug shot," she says.

"I'm headed back to London," says Sam. "My contact in the Paris Police Prefecture is expecting your call." I add the officer's card to the envelope. "Good luck with this." Sam stands and shakes hands, first with Rachel, then with me, enclosing my hand in both of his. "I hope you find the bastard."

Back in our room I fire up my laptop. According to the internet, Mireille Gastoneau is an expert on antique jewelry at a well-respected auction house in Nice. A link leads to the color photo of a stylish professional in a royal blue silk blouse, a pear-shaped sapphire and diamond pendant resting in the hollow of her throat, an inviting half-smile on her lips. Yes, the photo in the manila envelope is of a much younger Mireille. Here her hair is swept back into a loose chignon; she looks to be in her early forties. Although her facial expression, like her hair, looks softer than in the black and white, the eyes contain the same canniness.

The telephone number on the index card is the one listed on the auction house website. I punch the number into my cell phone. Of course, the message is in French. I put it on speaker phone. Rachel shakes her head; her two years of high school French were too little, too long ago. Willem's hometown is near the French-speaking part of Switzerland. He and the kids speak French, so I never bothered to learn.

Frustration turns to relief as the message is repeated in English. Madame Gastoneau is currently unavailable and will return messages as soon as is convenient. This is repeated in Italian, followed by a chime heralding the chance to leave a message. I move to hang up, but Rachel impulsively grabs the phone. She says something stilted about family jewelry for sale and requests a return call.

"Okay," she says, "I hope that didn't sound too phony."

I hug her. "Thanks. It was fine. Good idea." I admire her initiative, some of that boldness I need to absorb.

"Now what?" she asks.

"We wait for her to call back." I check the clock. "In the meantime, we have an appointment with Allan and the gang."

No one, not even Mohamed, has heard of Mireille Gastoneau. And neither he nor I know of Amy ever expressing an interest in jewelry, antique or otherwise. Allan wants us to head down to Nice tomorrow. He's expecting detailed info on Ms. Gastoneau's background, hopefully in time for whatever meeting we can finagle. Expecting it from where and from whom?

Before I can ask Natasha says, "Renting a car's cheaper, but the train's faster." My tech-savvy daughter, the coordinator of this group video chat, is quick on the draw. Before we're finished discussing the photos, the transportation research is already done. I make an executive decision to drive.

"What do we do once we're there?" I ask.

Allan says, "Go to the auction house and pry."

"And who'll bail us out when we're arrested for stalking this woman?"

Mohamed grins mischievously. "I'll send Sam to your rescue."

Liz speaks up from her house. "On your way down, think on this. Ang and I figure — "

"Fuck," I say for the nth time. The screen is frozen. Again. A notice reappears on my laptop screen informing us of a weak internet connection. No kidding.

Liz's image jerks back into motion. The audio descrambles enough for us to decipher "— weird cartoon of a she—" before there's another freeze.

"What? What do you figure?" yells Rachel. "Weird cartoon of a she—what? Fuck!"

Our video chat is no more.

"So much for modern technology," I say.

"Let's call," Rach says, breathing heavily. "A regular *phone* call."

Irritation laces my response. I scratch my scalp in aggravation. "Not worth it. We got enough. Let's try again from Nice." I email the group with that suggestion.

She upends the last bottle of mineral water into her mouth. "I'll get more," she says, rummaging through her purse. "And some snacks for the road. You want anything special?"

"No, whatever is fine."

I'm still researching the best route when she returns. "This oughta hold us." Rach unloads half a dozen assorted packages of cookies and what looks like enough water for a week. She rips open a bag, tosses me a madeleine. "What's with you?"

"It's a fucking nine-hour drive, and that's without stops."

"I've always wanted to see Nice."

"Tasha's right. The train's a few hours quicker. Nope, we need the flexibility." What Rach said finally penetrates. I scrutinize her over the rims of my reading glasses. "We're not going to sightsee."

She sends a challenging glare right back. "That's what you said about Paris."

"We won't have any spare time." I calculate out loud. "It's a day down, another back. A day there, if we're lucky."

"Then a day back to Seattle leaves ten days till the deadline. Not that anyone's counting."

I appreciate the fact that she is. I bite into the madeleine. It's stale. Rach either doesn't know or notice; she's on her third. "Let's hope what's her name is there."

Meet her where she's at. I finish the disappointing cookie; Rach smiles as I reach for another. "Mee-RAY. At least that's close enough. The bigger question is how to get her to talk about Amy."

Rach's expression is sly, her inflection ironic. "We'll have to figure out how Mee-RAY operates, and use it to our advantage." She waggles her eyebrows.

Stay with her. I say, "She's French."

"According to what I've learned, it'll help to know if she's city- or country-raised. I read once where most of the French live within spitting distance of Paris."

"She's a city dweller now. Your hypothesis, my dear Watson?"

"Most likely an individualist, my dear Holmes."

"I agree. Let's keep in mind that the whole collectivist-individualist thing is a spectrum. A dyed-in-the-wool collectivist can have very individualistic tendencies depending on the circumstances. And vice versa."

"Hell's bells!" says Rach. "We're therapists, for god's sake. Our whole schtick is getting people to talk."

DAY SIX

•••••••••••••••••••••••••••

Amy was twenty-three, a college grad whose band was drawing increasing attention in local clubs. She sat, rubbing at the faded scar on her left forearm. I ran through a mental list of anxiety-inducing possibilities.

I finally took the bunny from the bookshelf and threw it at her. "Do something else with your hands, please. I can't watch that anymore. It's making me nervous. What's going on?"

Amy started stroking the bunny's ears, a familiar, automatic action. She looked up with an evil grin. "You're in charge of your own emotions, IJ. My bad habits aren't making you nervous, your reaction to them is."

"Nice try, smart ass. Answer the question." Unfortunately, she was right. Warning sign number one.

The young woman sat forward, excitement in her eyes. "I'm going for broke. We've got our first tour booked."

I wanted to clap my hands and laugh. Instead, I bit my lip to stop myself and said, "Hey, congrats. That's great news." She deflated as she wrapped the bunny's right ear around her left forefinger. I was thankful for her silent clue. "Have you told your family? How do they fit into this whole ORB thing?"

"That's always the final Jeopardy question, isn't it. How do they fit into anything?"

"They're not trying to stop you, are they?"

She frowned. "No. But they're not terribly encouraging either. My parents are waiting for me to fail."

I chose a turtle puppet and slowly rotated it in my hands. "What about your siblings? Your sister has been supportive in the past. Is Martha still on your side?"

"Yeah, I think so. She's always believed in me; she'll want me to go for it. But it could be different when I actually leave. And Bill? Bill's oblivious."

"Understatement could be your middle name." Amy looked up again as I continued. "Reality is usually different from what we expect. Your sibs will miss you."

"Maybe Martha. Yeah, she'll be the only one."

"Don't underestimate your brother. I think you mean more to him than you realize."

Amy was standing now, pacing. "Billy Blue? He thinks I'm a pain in the ass, always on him about his studies and steering clear of the neighborhood trash." She dropped the bunny into the swivel chair and knocked against the window, startling a sparrow out of the maple. "Maybe my parents will be relieved when I'm gone. Maybe it'll be ..." She ran her hands through her hair, today brightened with orange and indigo flames. "They don't get me, never did. It'll be a lot easier with just the other two in the house."

Amy had taught me long ago that once redirected, she could focus on the positive with new energy. Before she could retreat further into a useless funk, I switched gears. "You told me once how you got your name. How about Martha and Bill – where do their names come from?"

Amy caught what I was doing and went along. "You know how Asians think you are what you eat? They'll eat cow brains to be smarter, stuff like that?" I nodded. "My mom thought the same might apply to names. You know where mine comes from."

"*Little Women.*"

She nodded. "Martha's named after Martha Washington. My mom learned somewhere that Martha was a rich widow before she married George. I think she also liked the fact that Martha's husband was a war hero. In any case, Amy married money, while Martha was the one who came with it. What does that tell you?"

I didn't dare answer. She snorted approvingly.

"And you know how much boys are worth compared to us useless girls. When Bill was finally born, my parents thought their lives were complete. He'd be the brilliant one, the one to make it big and take care of them for the rest of their lives. They named him after the richest, smartest person they could think of – Bill Gates."

I laughed and nodded. "That makes sense. Your name and Bill's are pretty straight forward. Martha Washington seems a bit of a stretch. Your sister isn't married, is she?"

Amy shook her head. "And she has no money and there's no way she's ever gonna marry a future president, let alone a surveyor. At this point, my parents would be happy with any-thing with balls. But no, Martha will never marry."

"What makes you say that?"

"In our community, arranged marriages are still a thing. My parents have been approached about guys interested in Martha, but she always refuses, doesn't even want to meet 'em. She's big on family duty. Bill's destiny is to become a high-priced lawyer. I have no idea what they expect for me. Find me dead in a gutter, maybe. Anyway, Martha's job is to remain single and at home; she's the one left holding the pa-rental bag."

"That's rough but not uncommon. Years ago I led a sup-port group for college-educated immigrant women having trouble in the working world. A few of them had the same role in their families. They felt that their parents had given up everything to come to the States; that meant giving up having their own lives in return."

This time Amy nodded. "Fuck. That's Martha, all right." She raised her eyebrows at me; a challenge was coming my way. "There's a Bible story that always reminds me of Martha. Now these ladies too. Can you guess which one?"

I thought for half a second. "Abraham and Isaac." This had come up in the group.

"You're good, Doc." She opened the cabinet that held the art supplies. "Are you Catholic?"

"No. But guilt isn't denomination-specific."

"I guess not." She smiled. I wasn't sure if it was because of my comment or the ample selection of brand new, extra fine Sharpies at her disposal. "Yeah, in my head, Martha's always been our sacrificial lamb. It's good to know she's not the only one out there. It's also quite disturbing."

"I totally get that." Memories of my brother Matt threatened to flood my consciousness. I pushed them away.

Amy looked at me keenly. Shit, she'd picked up on it. Warning sign number two.

"Y'know," she said, "Martha's the person on this planet who knows me the best, but in a lot of ways, she's still a mystery to me."

"That sounds a little sad, a little lonely."

"It is. Lots of both."

"How much of a mystery do you think you are to her?"

"Ah, mysteries. Mysteries and secrets and lies, lies, lies. My family's full of 'em. I'm so sick of 'em."

I wasn't sure if she meant the secrets or the family. Smarter not to ask. "So what do you want to do about it?"

"What can I do? They're out of my control. Hell, they're out of control, period. I have to look out for myself, find myself, do for myself, like I've done all my life. Only now, I'm doing it because I want to and *get* to, not because I need to. It's time to finally hit the road Jack." She hummed the tune.

"Well, take good care of yourself, Amy. I'll be thinking of you and ORB." I stopped myself with a jerk, feeling much too motherly for comfort. Warning sign number three.

She quit humming, looked alarmed. "I didn't mean this road, not you and me, Doc. I still get to come here if I need to, right?"

"Of course, if you want to." Whew. A deep breath and snark are always good for a little distance. "Only now that the band's making money, you'll have to pay me. I want an autographed copy of every CD."

"Fair enough." Amy watched the wind whip through the last of the candy-colored maple leaves. When she turned to me, a playful twitch pulled at her lips. She cackled as she produced a flat square of plastic from her pocket, spun it Frisbee-like onto the sofa next to me, and sauntered out the door.

It was a homemade CD. I recognized the black and white cover design, the globe within the tear that was ORB's logo. It had been cheaply reproduced via copy machine, the paper carefully trimmed to fit the CD cover. And it was autographed.

Another sleep-deprived night. Restless enough that around 2:00 a.m. Rachel ended up throwing her pillow at me in indignation. Can't blame her.

She scowls as she slathers orange marmalade onto a warm croissant. "What the hell were you doing?" She takes a vicious bite.

"It occurred to me that Paris is probably the last place where Amy was actually happy." I'm not ready to share the details of that session and the sketch of a sacrificial lamb, the weird cartoon of a she-ep, that resulted.

Her next bite is slightly less ferocious. "Were you on your laptop all night?" In addition to disturbing her sleep, I got her up at an ungodly hour to pack before breakfast so we could be on the road ASAP.

"Sorry I kept you up." No use getting us both down. Time to switch gears. "I'll have you know I spent some of that time researching a way to make it up to you."

She plunks a warm croissant onto my heretofore empty plate. "Wait, wait, wait. You were looking for a way to make me feel better while making me miserable?" I give her my best I'm-dangling-the-juiciest-carrot-you-can-imagine look. "Just tell me, why don't you."

I sip nonchalantly at my coffee, offer her my phone. "Here's where we're staying."

She grabs the phone and takes a gander. "Oh, honey, now we're talkin'." It's a monster-sized suite with a marble bathroom and a magnificent view of a sandy beach that goes on seemingly forever. Rachel crams the last of her croissant into her mouth. "Jax," she says, swallowing hard, "this'll cost a fortune. You don't have to —"

"It's one of those cut-rate last-minute deals. We're worth it, don'tcha think?"

She closes her mouth and high-fives me in response.

At that moment a waiter approaches bearing a small, ivory envelope. My name's on it.

"Who is this from?" I ask.

He answers in perfect English. "It was delivered by courier, with instructions that you receive it straight away."

"Maybe from Sam," Rach says, cheerfully chugging her café au lait.

I read the note, sit back. Rach snatches it from my hand. She sits back too, dejection puckering her face.

It's an invitation. The hand-drawn calligraphy is elegant and precise. Mme. Mireille Gastoneau requests our company.

A taxi cab will collect us at our hotel at 15:00. There's no request for an RSVP. A command appearance.

I shudder.

"Well, that's creepy," she says. "How does she know about us and where we are? Maybe we should call Sam."

"No, his part's done." I check my watch. "Ten o'clock back home. Maybe Allan's still up."

No answer. I leave a message. So much for his promise of round-the-clock back-up.

Rachel says, "I don't like the sound of it."

"I don't like the feel of it, but we don't have much choice, do we? I mean, this is why we're here."

"You better cancel the car and that awesome, amazing, bury-me-in-that-bathtub hotel room."

I nod. "Sorry."

She shrugs, pinches her pale, pouty cheeks, and raises a hand to get our waiter's attention. "Garçon," she says, "we're staying after all. May we please have more of everything?" She picks up the invitation again. "Fifteen hundred hours," she says. "Military time."

I tap my watch. "It's also European. And a taxi cab will *collect* us. At least we know she's not American."

"Her name tells us that."

"No, nowadays you can't tell by names or faces."

Rach glowers. "I can't help but think that two days after meeting with this woman, whoever and whatever she is, Amy Nguyen was dead."

"There's a happy thought." From Rach's expression, she's thinking what I'm thinking: the same thing could happen to us. "No use freaking ourselves out. Amy felt safe enough to meet with her alone. That's a good enough endorsement for me."

"So why do you think she did it then?"

"What? Kill herself?"

"No, dummy." She thwacks my forearm with the back of her spoon. "Why'd you say that? I meant go back home."

I wish we'd ordered room service. I don't want to fall apart in public. The arrival of more croissants and coffee is well-timed.

"Rach, I have to apologize again. The way I acted at Angie's. I was so mad, so scared that … maybe you were right."

"About what?" She sounds tentative, tender.

"What I've been telling myself all along. That if Amy Nguyen did commit suicide, I was a contributing factor."

"Anyone who calls you a Svengali doesn't know you."

"The other day Mona Chen and I talked about counter-transference."

"Eat like a normal person, will you?" She points with her knife at the shredded croissant littering my plate.

I smile wanly at her, knowing we share the same opinion of the word *normal*, and obediently eat the buttery flakes with my spoon. Nice try, Rach; I refuse to be distracted. "What you both said got me thinking."

She sighs. "That's always dangerous."

I think about Rachel's recent revelation. If I'd known the truth about her mother earlier, I might've dared this conversation earlier too. Nope. Can't and won't blame that on her. C'mon, Jackie, here's another opportunity to make good on your vow to do something different.

"I always thought it was my father who pushed Matt too far."

"What does your brother have to do with anything?"

"I've been thinking about why he died. His relationship with our father was no-win. Now I'm wondering about him and my mom. And I'm wondering what kind of pressure I put on him without even knowing. I mean, he was the son, the Golden Child, the one to bring glory to the name Chol. I thought so too, and he knew it."

"You caused your brother's death as much as I caused my mother's." She seizes my hand. "Namely, not at all."

"I know. I know, up here." I point to my head. "But in here?" I point to my heart. "He was my smarter-than-the-average-bear big brother. It never occurred to me he could be having an even tougher time than I was."

"It's not a contest. You both had it tough. But getting back to our mission – and we did choose to accept it, damn it – you didn't force Amy into anything. You had some influence, but she made her own choices."

"But that's the point. *How* did I use my influence? She said more than once I nagged her into it, whatever it was. Sure, she was joking, but if I hadn't put those expectations on her, like I did with Matt…"

"You're talking crazy. Is that a Korean thing or a Jackie thing?"

Before I can say, What the fuck, she reaches across the table and pushes my forehead with the flat of her hand hard enough that I fear whiplash. "Be healed!"

Luckily, I see the twinkle. Instead of jumping down her throat as originally planned, I say, "I love you, you nasty woman, you." And I mean it.

The main living area of Mireille Gastoneau's third-floor corner apartment has high ceilings supported by ancient-looking oak beams. Heavy drapes lining the street-facing sides of the room are tied back, exposing wide windows set into the deep stone walls. Carpeted stairs lead up to what must be bedrooms. The only jarring note is the austere, almost industrial-looking kitchen, its gleaming stainless steel appliances contrasting with the general feel of antiquity.

"This is wonderful," Rachel remarks.

"Our family seat is in Nice; however, this has been our pied-à-terre since shortly after the First World War. Upon my mother's passing, it became mine." Ms. Gastoneau motions us into an antique settee. The delicately worn upholstery looks hand-embroidered.

Our hostess is an intriguing subject. Seated in a matching chair across from us, she tucks an errant lock of hair behind her ear with a well-manicured hand. Her movements are tidy, deliberate. The elegance belies a certain tension. The photo on the auction house website is obviously old too. Or well-doctored. Seeing her up close, I guess her to be around my age, in other words, a decade or so older than she first appeared. And she takes pains to disguise it. Her hair color is a shade too light. Her cosmetics are artfully, but a touch too heavily, applied. I feel for her. Another woman not completely comfortable in her own skin.

Mireille tells us that during her childhood, she and her mother came to Paris often. They spent their days exploring the city, inventing stories about the intriguing scents that wafted from seemingly every door, the colors and textures within every shop window. "They hinted at all the mystery and adventure the planet holds," she says. "Best yet, each excursion was celebrated with a pain au chocolat."

I smile, picturing the young Mireille's delight. "What a wonderful way to spend time together."

"So much has changed in the intervening years. Many of our old haunts are gone." She seems to falter, regroups with a breath. "In any case, it was only natural that I continued in this vein as a professional."

While Mireille's furnishings are European, several of the decorative pieces, the lamp bases and vases, have an Asian flair. At first impression the combination works. But on closer inspection, like the woman, the overall effect comes across as studied.

We converse about mundane topics, carefully choosing our words and judging the results. Mireille is amused by our inability to escape the gravitational pull of Saint-Etienne-du-Mont, our orbit returning us to those soaring spires and tortured gargoyles again and again. Rachel's knee bumps mine. She mouths *vetting* at me, disguising it with a smile so wide, it looks like it hurts.

Enough of this polite bullshit; I'm ready to bite someone. I say, "What a happy coincidence to be in Paris at the same time, Ms. Gastoneau. Perhaps we're ready to address this meeting's true purpose."

"As you wish, Mrs. Kessler." Mireille gives me an appraising look. "There's no need for *any* further pretense. Do not ask me to believe that you traveled all the way to France to sell family jewelry which I do not for one moment believe you possess."

I'm relieved at not having to continue the charade; however, I'm also a little offended. There's a gold and silver bumblebee locket tucked beneath my blouse. My mother-in-law gave this Kessler family heirloom to me when Willem and I celebrated our tenth anniversary. Willem half-joked it was her way of welcoming me into the family. If need be, that was the piece I would have presented for sale, with no intention of actually going through with it.

Rachel takes a breath to speak; I butt in.

"Traveled all the way?" I ask. "How do you know how far we've come?"

"I was told by – what is your quaint American phrase – a little bird that a woman from Seattle, Washington had come to Paris to locate the owner of a particular motor vehicle. My motor vehicle. Then I surprisingly receive a telephone call from that same woman. However, I believe it was you, Mrs. Darby, who left the message?"

Rachel and I exchange a look. Rach says, "We didn't expect such a quick and personal invitation."

"I was curious. And you were very easy to find."

I'm curious too. "This little bird wouldn't happen to work for the Paris Police Prefecture, would it?"

"Assume what you wish, Mrs. Kessler. Please tell me what you want."

More than a hint of a dare. Given the circumstances, I don't find it inappropriate. Neither of us knows what to expect. In any case, I respect her ballsy approach. Might as well take the plunge.

"Ms. Gastoneau –"

"Madame, if you please."

"Pardon me. Madame Gastoneau, we mean you no harm. We did indeed come a very long way looking for help in solving a mystery. Circumstances led us to you."

She examines us as if we're objects on display before repeating her question. "What do you want from me?"

My guess is she wants confirmation of what she's already learned. "We're looking into the death of the American singer, Amy Nguyen. There's no need for you to look surprised or deny that you knew her. She was seen entering your motor vehicle on July 19 of last year. Two days later she was found dead. We want to speak with you about that meeting."

"Yes, we met." Her voice is flat. "No, I didn't kill her."

"Why would you say that, Madame? I never implied that I thought anyone, let alone you, killed her. It's commonly known that Amy Nguyen died by suicide."

Rach adds, "And it happened in Seattle, thousands of miles away from Paris."

Mireille's gaze intensifies. "Why would two mental health therapists investigate a confirmed suicide? It may be you're writing a book, but I'm sorry, neither of you looks the literary type."

Rachel coughs; I can't help but smile. I cross my legs, one of the signs we devised to signify the passing of the interrogative baton. All yours, honey.

Rachel swallows, clears her throat. "Mme. Gastoneau, do you think Amy Nguyen was murdered?"

"Yes," she says. "Do you?"

Rachel crosses her arms. My turn. "We do, as do others. We're here on their behalf as well as our own."

There's the slightest hesitation. "So I am a suspect?"

"No. But you are, to use another American phrase, a person of interest." I echo Mireille's words. "Why did you come all the way from Nice to meet with an American rock singer? And now us?"

She gives us a measured stare. "As therapists, you must know that family secrets will come out. But for you to fully understand, we must begin at the beginning. Let me introduce you to my family."

She moves to a richly carved credenza and lifts a picture frame containing a faded black and white studio portrait. A slim, dark-haired man in US Army dress uniform stands behind an unsmiling girl. She looks to be around nine or ten. The girl's face is tilted downward toward the light-haired woman seated in a wingchair beside her. The woman's iron-clad visage is downright stony compared to her husband's. The photo leaves no doubt of the source of Ms. Gastoneau's severity.

"As you can see, my father was an American soldier, an officer. My parents divorced a year after this photograph was taken. Happier times."

Rachel raises her eyebrows, a subtle that-ain't-what-I-call-happy move.

Maybe Mireille meant the happier times came after the divorce. She hands me the photo. The father's eyes, his body type. The image makes me catch my breath, the same reaction I had to the photo of Mireille that Sam gave us. And there's that dare again. Or maybe it's a different type of invitation. Might as well see.

I say, "Like you, I'm fascinated by stories, especially when it comes to families. How did your parents meet?"

She explains that after finishing university, her mother celebrated by visiting family friends in America. These friends introduced her to Anthony McMillan, then a young lieutenant.

She shows us an image of her father, older, with silver oak leaves on his shoulders. He stands beside a simple steel desk, his posture mirroring the flagpole bearing the Stars and Stripes behind him.

Mireille speaks slowly, deliberately. "After my father's death, his lawyer informed me of an unexpected inheritance, a depository of the colonel's, shall we say, secret history." She uncrosses her ankles only to cross them the other way. "The collection included a personal journal and photographs of my father which I had not before seen, with people whom I did not recognize. It also held a most precious and disturbing letter, written in my father's hand and addressed to me. It was both confession and apology. And it pointed me to Amy Nguyen. To my sister." She looks as though the words feel foreign in her mouth.

"Your sister?" I try to hide my surprise. Rachel stiffens.

"My half-sister, to be precise." She looks pleased at her disclosure's effect. "She was becoming quite well-known. She was even easier to find than the two of you." We share a reluctant smile.

Mireille learned all she could about Amy, her music, her family. She yearned to meet her, and the opportunity finally arose during the ORBit tour.

"I left a letter at her hotel, not knowing if she would respond."

"And she did."

"She did indeed."

"Did Amy know who her biological father really was?" asks Rachel.

"No, she did not." Mireille recounts Amy's adamant denial of the possibility that they could be related. Amy very much resembled her mother in features, so she never doubted her father's identity. But Mireille then presented her with proof.

Again, there's more than a hint of satisfaction as she says, "She was really quite upset."

"Imagine that." Oops. Didn't mean to let the sarcasm slip. Time to switch things up. "Pardon my bluntness, Mme. Gastoneau, but you also more closely resemble your mother than your father. I guess your father to be multiethnic. Is your heritage part Vietnamese?"

Yeah, lady, you're not the only one with surprises up your sleeve. Waves of excitement start to pour off of Rachel.

Turns out Mireille's paternal grandfather was one hundred percent American, Kentucky-born and raised. He rose to the rank of sergeant in the US Marine Corps during the Second World War, served in the Pacific, and was captured by the Japanese.

"He was held in a prisoner of war camp near Saigon."

"I didn't know there were POW camps there," says Rachel. Neither did I.

"Not many do," says Mireille. "I only know because it is such an integral part of my family's history. When the war ended my grandfather was too weak to return home right away. While recuperating in Saigon, he fell in love. He took his bride home to Kentucky and their son, my father, was born shortly thereafter. So soon after the war, my father and grandmother were regarded by many with suspicion. My grandmother was, by all accounts, exceptionally unhappy, and my father fared not much better. He was often bullied."

I say, "I can only imagine."

"That is how he became a ferocious fighter. He defended himself and his mother well." The woman's face is still, but her ankles cross and uncross again. That's her tell. Rachel uncrosses her legs, brushes the side of her foot against mine; she caught it too.

"What about his father, the sergeant?" Rachel demands. "Where was he?"

"Ah, Mrs. Darby, after the war, he became a traveling sales representative. He spent more time on the road than at home. His wife and son had to fend for themselves. This was especially difficult because my grandmother never spoke English fluently. In fact, my father's first language was Vietnamese."

There go the ankles. I now appreciate Mireille's previous satisfaction at messing with someone else's identity, given the complicated history of her own.

"What brought your father to France, Mme. Gastoneau?" asks Rachel. Good. I would have asked the same thing.

"His family roots." Like her apartment, Mireille's smile is more formal than warm. "My American grandfather's father was a doughboy in World War I."

"Who married a Frenchwoman."

"Yes, Mrs. Kessler. My great-grandfather also returned with a war bride. The men of my family gained a reputation for being more than slightly eccentric in that regard.

"After graduating from West Point, my father wanted to retrace his grandfather's war experiences and meet the relatives he'd heard about yet never known. It was on that journey that he met my mother."

Rachel's eyeballs roll up into her head as she works out the connections.

I say, "History was repeated through the generations."

"It was indeed," Mireille answers. "However, it did not serve the family well. My parents married young and impulsively and came to regret it. There were too many differences they could not overcome."

Rach says, "That's quite a complicated lineage."

I enjoy having someone else supply the multicultural history lessons. How come Rach can take them from an outsider better than from me? But then, many a kid client can't hear sense when it comes from a parent, whereas they're able to accept the same thing quite easily from their therapist.

"My roots are perhaps more widespread, but here in Europe you will find a multitude of similar stories. War and its aftermath have a way of dislodging people and sprinkling them about." Mireille sweeps her arm in an arc to illustrate her point.

"Which brings us back to Amy Nguyen," I say. "You said your father's papers prove him to be her biological father."

"Yes." She retrieves a leather-bound notebook and tells us that her father's bilingualism and familiarity with Vietnamese culture were particularly prized during the war. As a liaison officer between US and South Vietnamese commands, he knew several South Vietnamese officers well, befriending one particular officer and his family. When this man was killed in action, Mireille's father took it upon himself to ensure the family's survival. He arranged a job for the widow, working for the Americans. Before Saigon fell he arranged to get them out, but in the chaos of the evacuation, the widow and her daughter never made it onto a helicopter.

"My father later located them in a refugee camp in Thailand," Mireille concludes. "I am ashamed at how long they remained there."

She hands the volume to me. The cover is worn and smooth, the corners bent and dull. I open it at random; the lined pages are filled with dated entries written in a spidery, masculine hand.

Several photos had been carefully placed within. Rachel shifts closer. We study a black and white image of two men in uniform standing collegially beside each other. The taller of the two is obviously Mireille's father; the other man wears the uniform of what must be the South Vietnamese army. A young Vietnamese woman stands nearby holding the hand of a girl whose other hand reaches toward the Vietnamese officer. The woman looks uncertainly at the camera. The resemblance between her and Amy Nguyen is striking.

Mireille recounts how Amy had gasped in recognition. She had held that same photo flat in her palm, as if encouraging it to fly away. It did indeed depict her mother holding the hand of the young Martha. The men were strangers to her; however, Amy had recognized the Vietnamese officer's face in Martha's.

He was as Martha had described during nights cuddled together in bed, the soft Seattle rain thrumming against their bedroom window. Amy had come to regard her sister's stories as the most wonderful of fables, and she had longed to have this heroic man as her father too. Rather him than the distant, mercurial man with whom their mother fought so bitterly in the next room.

"The widow remarried in the camp. My father arranged entry to the United States for the entire family."

She takes the notebook and briskly thumbs through it, stopping at a two-line entry dated 24 Feb 1991: 'Birth of daughter. Mother and child well. Nguyen to assume parental responsibility.'

"Doesn't get clearer," says Rach.

"Amy admitted the same. It seemed that many things she had pondered in the past now made sense, especially her father's attitude toward her. She had no choice but to believe me."

Now knowing that Martha's stories were true, Amy was at once comforted and devastated. Anger came with the next document shown to her, a letter written by Amy's mother while still in the camp. She recognized her mother's script but could not decipher the French. Mireille translated the words which reminded McMillan, now a colonel, of his obligation to further their petition for refugee status in France. "This you owe us."

Amy was shocked and confused. She had never known of her mother's facility with the French language. She had, in fact, often despaired at the woman's long resistance to English. Knowing that her mother had wanted and expected to emigrate to France changed things. She was not in America by choice.

I sit back, breathless from this unexpected gut punch. Not in America by choice. She'd never actually admitted to it out loud, but my mother had, in many ways, indicated that she was not there by choice either. I'd always assumed it was because she was unhappy living with Dad. And vice-versa. But what did I actually know about how and why my parents came to the United States? The story they'd told had always stressed how pleased and proud others were for them, never how excited and happy they were for themselves. I'd assumed they felt something more than relief. Honor and a great hopefulness, perhaps. Here was the prize for their years of grindingly hard work and early academic successes. But my brother and I never heard mention of this.

Throughout my childhood, my parents regularly sent money to their parents in South Korea. Matt and I accepted the resultant lack of extras in our household as the price of our parents' monumental opportunity. It was also the one regret our mother actually spoke about. Supporting her parents meant she'd never be able to see them again. It was only after our grandparents had died that we could afford a trip to Korea. I'd always thought sharing this regret was how she instructed Matt and me on our future filial responsibilities. How wrong could I be.

For her part, Mireille was disenchanted and disillusioned. Her father had been an enigmatic figure, floating in and out of her life. According to her mother, he returned from Vietnam a changed man. Now Mireille had another hint as to why. She mourned anew, grieving the father she had thought she'd known. This newly discovered man was a stranger, someone who acted shamefully in her eyes. Even though he had ultimately assisted the family and watched Amy develop from afar, an honorable man would have claimed his child, not waiting until after his death. But then, even with his legitimate daughter, he had a poor track record as a parent.

"You're aware that Amy left for Seattle the day after your meeting?" I ask.

"Yes. She wanted urgently to confront her mother and hear the truth from her lips. I advised her against this, to allow herself time to think carefully before taking action, but she would not be dissuaded."

"Did you hear from her after that?"

Mireille turns to face the window, shades of Amy in that maneuver. "No. I heard nothing until I read of her death."

Ankles.

"Thank you, Mme. Gastoneau. We appreciate you sharing such sensitive information with strangers."

"You're welcome, Mrs. Kessler, but I expect something in return. You must understand that I also want to know who killed Amy. It cannot have been suicide. As we parted company, we agreed to meet again in Munich. We were both very much looking forward to knowing one another better. Such plans are not so abruptly abandoned. I do not believe for one moment that she deceived me."

I'm struck by her certainty, her unwavering resolution. Perhaps this is a result of being raised in a military family, where one needs clarity and a very thick skin. I feel a kinship. Military families are another unseen minority.

"Perhaps it is fitting," says Mireille, "that you found yourself again and again at the final resting place of Saint Genevieve. She is a patron saint of Paris, you know, having saved the city and its people from Attila the Hun and his attacking hordes. She is still very popular, with special significance for us women. Perhaps it was she who called you. Perhaps this was the saint's message to you that she is on your side."

I swallow, feel Amy's tug on my heart. Perhaps it was the saint's way of telling me not to fuck up.

Back at the hotel we call the team to share the latest. Mireille had allowed me to take pictures of her family portraits, which I'd emailed to Allan. He, Mohamed, and Willem are grouped around our dining table, prints of the three photographs spread before them. Rach and I take turns reciting Mireille's family history. When we're done, Allan fills some holes.

"Lt. Colonel Anthony McMillan had a fatal heart attack two years ago. The mother, Georgine, died of breast cancer in 2009. Mireille's a single child, born in Kentucky in 1971. She and her mother returned to Paris when the dad shipped out to Vietnam. They never moved back to the States."

Rachel says, "That pretty much confirms what she told us. Except that they actually lived in Paris. She told us Nice."

I think back. "No, she was actually vague on that. She said the family seat was in Nice."

"You're right," says Rach. "She was sketchy on the details. Collectivist communication?"

"Maybe so. In contrast, the colonel left evidence as concrete as anyone would want or need. We saw journal entries he'd made about Amy and a binder full of articles about ORB." These had been carefully clipped and collected in a separate binder.

"It makes sense," says Mohamed. "That night in Paris, before the last show, Amy was distracted. It was not her usual nerves, even though she insisted that's what it was. Now I understand."

"Yes," I add. "Amy bemoaned the secrecy in her family, especially about the war and refugee camp. Whenever she asked about how they survived, how they made it to America, her mother would be evasive. Once, though, her mother let slip that they had help from a friend. More information than that, such as their benefactor's name, Amy never got. I remember she was totally frustrated by this. She resented being denied her own history."

Rach says, "Mee-RAY tried to talk her out of confronting her mother, thought it might be too much too soon."

"I can imagine how that went," says Mohamed. "Amy would insist on knowing the truth."

I smile, having been on the receiving end of Amy's response to well-meaning advice more than a few times.

"Okay, now we know why the man Amy thought was her father treated her so poorly. Of course he paid attention to his bio son, Bill, and he was civil to stepdaughter Martha. She was older and her father was on record. He barely paid Amy any notice. But then, why would he? Especially if he knew who the real father was."

Allan checks something on his phone. He says, "The family entered the US in late 1990. Based on her birthdate, Amy was conceived in the refugee camp. If her mother married Nguyen there, it must've been a practical arrangement."

"Yes," agrees Mohamed. "She would have needed a man to protect and provide for the family and give legitimacy to Amy."

I say, "Maybe not to provide. Amy never did tell me what the man she thought was her father did for a living. She hinted that he was on permanent disability."

"Yeah," says Rach, "from a war wound."

Willem scratches his chin; that's one of his tells. "Maybe this was how the colonel fulfilled his obligation. What a tidy way for a family of Catholics to hide a big, fat sin."

"It would be a fair trade. Nguyen probably saw this family, with its connections, as his ticket to the west. I saw that often enough," says Mohamed. "No one is happy, but in a sense, everyone benefits."

I sigh. "Allan, what's next?"

"You two did a great job. Come on back; we'll pick up the threads here in Seattle."

Mohamed nods his approval.

"Before you return," Willem interjects, "I have just one question. This woman, Mme. Gastoneau, has been surprisingly forthcoming. In a situation like this where family secrets are exposed, one might say she has been overly eager. I know," he says, anticipating Allan's response, "she said she also wants to find Amy's killer. But doesn't anyone else find this rather convenient? We know very little about this woman. How do we know she's sincere?"

It's a strange comfort to know that my husband is as keen a cynic as I. I hadn't wanted to raise my own doubts for fear of the group criticizing my negativity.

"It's not as if she's pointing a finger at anyone in particular," says Rachel.

Willem scratches his chin again. "No, but she adds to the abundancy of lies and secrets in this family. I must issue a caution about believing anyone too quickly."

DAY SEVEN

● ●

Rach and I are booked on a late-afternoon flight back to Seattle. This whole enterprise has me feeling surprisingly energetic. Using my skills in this new way has sparked the same feelings of curiosity and engagement that originally got me hooked on therapy. I'm still feeling unsure of myself, though, a toddler taking those first tentative, wobbling steps, grasping at anything within reach in search of security and support.

I lean over the balcony railing and send a message of thanks to the powers that be for my inimitable team. Without them, I probably would have caved to Wayne's pressure to settle days ago. Look what we've accomplished. True, every day brings more unanswered questions, more threads to pick up, but for the first time since this started, I'm truly hopeful. Those three generations of female Asian war refugees are still at my side, whispering in my ear. But now they're saying I can do this. In search of a way to honor them, I step back into the room and thumb through Rachel's Paris guidebook.

Rachel double-checks the armoire. "Jacqueline Kessler, you're a travel snob."

"Well, we *don't* need souvenirs and there *is* enough time for the catacombs."

"We said no museums. And since when are you into the macabre? The last thing in the world I want to end a trip to Paris with is looking at human bones. That's downright icky."

"It's not as if we'll recognize any of the bodies. And if we're lucky we can get both birds – they probably sell t-shirts. This is a piece of Paris history, after all."

"Seattle's got history too, without the skeletal remains."

"Oh yeah? Where would you go for that?"

"I don't know." She shoves her bangle bracelets as far up her forearm as they'll go, anchoring them in place. "My history – history you and I have shared, by the way – has always been at places like Twin Teepees and the Bon."

Of course. Eat, drink, shop. "Both are long gone, Rach. Next it'll be Zesto's and Chubby and Tubby."

"Oh, break my heart, why don'tcha. I still miss them."

"Thank you for proving my point. Even though the places are gone, the memories remain. That's history. The people may be gone, but their memories live on through their bones. Their lives deserve to be acknowledged, even honored."

"If that's all you need, let's get some mimosas and toast their memories." She stops packing to give me an intense stare. "And Amy's."

I return the look. "And Stan's." Neither of us mentions her mother or my brother, but I know that she knows that we're both thinking of them. That's shared history.

"All right," she says, her manner brighter, "but we do have to shop. Seriously, if Liz and Ang went somewhere great without us – Iceland or Tahiti or someplace – wouldn't you want a souvenir?"

"Rach, our big RAJE trip is next year; that'll be a real vacation. Germany, Switzerland. Your roots and Kessler whatever you want to call 'em."

She wags a threatening forefinger at me. "We're not going back empty-handed."

"We have those jawbreaker cookies you got for the road."

"Oh, you're hopeless." She moves onto the balcony and plucks two brilliant geraniums. "It's our last day of a very short yet very successful trip. Lighten up, will you?"

Stubborn broad. I check the time. Might as well get that drink and go shopping. I won't admit it to her, but it does sound more fun. I sigh my apologies and thanks to the spirits of those women. "Just no tacky tchotchkes, okay?"

"Okay." She carefully presses the blooms between the pages of her guidebook, trying hard not to look too triumphant. "At least we'll always have Dick's and Bartell's."

At the street market, we bicker over berets and I muscle her away from a dismayingly large display of sterling silver bangle bracelets. Other items are too big, expensive, or fragile. That leaves food. We reject the cans of foie gras and hover over handmade pralines. Then we remember the glorious patisserie we saw near Mireille's apartment yesterday. We grab a cab, direct the driver to le Marais, and ask him to wait.

The place is imbued with the sweet, buttery scent of pastry heaven. There's a delectable assortment of *viennoiseries*, but the delicate wonders would never survive the jostling of the trip. We thankfully agree on an assortment of distinctly colored macarons in flavors neither of us has ever seen in Seattle. After they're packed in tins embossed with old-fashioned scenes of Paris, we're set.

Back at the cab, the driver is gesticulating and cursing. A delivery truck is double-parked, effectively blocking our exit. The driver of the truck returns with another man who helps him unload boxes from the back. Our cabbie yells something out the open window. The truck driver screams something rude in return and continues his work.

As this unfolds, I look up the street to Mireille Gastoneau's building. It's dignified and graceful, a true grande dame. Then there, on the sidewalk, another drama unfolds.

"Rach." I nudge her shoulder and point.

Mireille Gastoneau shares a lingering kiss with a man in a well-tailored suit. He hands her into the passenger seat of a metallic silver Mercedes Benz sedan. The man seats himself behind the wheel and smoothly eases the car into the flow of traffic. The man is Sam Reyes.

"Holy shit," says Rach.

My first impulse is to have our driver follow that car, but we're still penned in. I pound the seat in frustration. "Little bird, my ass. A little bird named Sam. He must've been vetting us for her, not himself."

Willem's warning flashes across my consciousness. Rach must be thinking the same thing. "Do you think the stuff she showed us was fake?"

It takes a while to regain control of my mind. "No. Who in the world would go to all that trouble? The detail in the journal was too precise, too personal, too thorough. The articles alone. Shit, I've got some of those. The *Rolling Stone* piece, the *Seattle Times* profile."

"You have an Amy scrapbook?" She looks at me like I'm a stranger, one she'd like to keep that way.

"What can I say, I'm a fan. But I never saw her onstage. The closest was when she ran poetry past me in session."

Rachel shivers, grabs my arm. "That must've been the car Sam *allegedly* saw Amy get into of her *own free will*."

"Yeah, and if so, he took down the license plate number of a car he conveniently drives."

"Fuck," she says. "We've been had."

With the truck finally unloaded and Sam and Mireille long gone, we direct our driver back to the hotel. My head fills with scenes from the past days. The link to Mireille is Sam. The link to Sam is Mohamed. It was Mohamed who insisted on Sam's initial involvement. He arranged for Sam to get us into the investigative swing; he is paying Sam's fee. What do I really know about Mohamed except what Amy and he himself told me?

Rachel slugs my arm. "Hey, have you heard a word I've said?"

"Uh, no. I'm kinda freakin' out here." I share my doubts about Mohamed.

She runs a hand through her hair to the familiar, now somehow reassuring tinkling of those bangles. She takes a deep breath. "Okay, try this. Mohamed, Sam, and Mireille are a client family. They're stonewalling you, and you need to get them to talk. What would you ask?"

"What the fuck is going on?"

She laughs. "Good one, but probably not the most therapeutic."

"Depends on your definition. Besides, in this case it would be interrogation, not therapy."

"Hey, we get at the truth too, without a lamp in the face."

"Point taken. How about you?"

Rachel peers out the window, uses her sleeve to wipe a smudge from the glass. "I'd probably let them think I know more than I do and see what they cop to."

"Remember, we're not going to see them all together. When we're back, it'll just be Mohamed. How can we tag team him like we did Mireille?"

"Lotta good that did. She lied. So did Sam." She scratches at the window with a fingernail. The smudge is on the outside.

"So did Mohamed; he didn't tell us everything he knows. But a lie of omission is different from a lie-lie."

"Not in my world."

"In mine, omission is quite useful. Especially if it's someone close to you, you can feel in your bones when that person's holding back. Chasing down the missing pieces is another matter. From earliest childhood I was expert at knowing just how much to tell my parents when something happened. However, I always left space for them to ask for more. They knew full disclosure would only cause them grief, so they never pushed it. Their choice; both sides were spared. Point being, if you leave things out and no one asks, there's no lie."

While she thinks that through I consider the things I've not yet asked Mohamed. The things I never asked Amy. When Rach has it, she says, "We already figure Sam's more collectivist than not." She shakes a finger at me. "If Mireille is too, which is not a given, what do you think they're trying to spare us from? Or you, since this is your problem."

"I actually think Mireille alternates depending on the situation. Remember how she switched her approach?"

"Yeah, very clever, downright slippery. Just like Angie."

I look at Rachel sharply. That's the first time I've ever heard her say something critical about Ang. I've always considered them to have a stronger bond, like Liz and me. It's a clear mathematical equation: RAJE = (Rachel + Angela) + (Jacqueline + Elizabeth).

I choose my words carefully. "Yeah, Ang can be hard to pin down. That's part of what makes her so good."

"Good or infuriating, take your pick." She combs her hair with her fingers again. "Back to the business at hand."

"They could be taking a page from your book, pretending to know more than they do."

"Trying to get info out of us? There's a thought." She shakes her head. "No. Only out of you. I know diddly-squat about Amy. What would they think you know that they don't?"

"Maybe what we're all trying to figure out: who killed Amy."

"Playin' devil's advocate here." We grin at each other. "The flip side of that could be they're trying to figure out how far we've gotten. That could be what they want to spare themselves. Maybe they had something to do with it after all."

"They may have. We don't know."

"Okay, so we're back to Mohamed. What does he know about Amy that we don't? And, collectivist that he is, what could he be not saying?"

"A hell of a lot," I admit. "He was Amy's best friend, the person closest to her, by her own admission."

I haul out my cell phone and use the remainder of the drive to compose a text to Allan. My thumbs feel even clumsier than usual, mirroring my scrambled thoughts. I revert to pecking out letters with my forefinger, shushing Rachel, who's emphatically dictating her own additions.

When the message is released into cyberspace Rachel asks, "What do we do now?"

I check the time. "Grab our luggage and head for the Métro. We have a flight to catch."

DAY EIGHT

●●●●●●●●●●●●●●●●●●●●●●●●●

So much for yesterday's energy and confidence. Last night I took a sleep aid. I'm not keen on chemically-induced rest or the lingering muzziness it produces, but there's something to be said for being able to function.

The entire team is in my living room; there are two additional faces.

"Okay," says Allan, "we've got eleven days before the legal shit hits the fan. No time for niceties. I'd like to introduce our new recruits." He draws a woman forward. "Everyone, this is Eve Connelly, my former SPD partner." She exudes a warmth that matches her hearty handshake. "Her husband Walt here is another friend in a strategic place. He's with the local FBI. I asked him to look into a few things for us."

No wonder Allan was able to get the skinny on the McMillans so quickly. And if the Connellys are good enough friends to get roped into this crazy endeavor, maybe he hasn't been as isolated as Liz imagined. Walt doesn't fit my image of a G-man. The wide smile and accompanying crinkles in the corners of his eyes make him look much too jovial. I won't complain. Mohamed, however, looks like being near an FBI agent is on par with snakebite. Natasha sees it too; she beckons to him and he takes a quick seat next to her.

Walt gives my husband a respectful nod. "Willem, you raised some interesting questions about our Mireille. She married Emil Gastoneau, an artist, in 1993. They divorced in '96. She never remarried." He then turns to Rach and me. "What you ladies saw gave us more to dig into." He confirms what Mireille told us about her father's service in Vietnam. "We haven't yet uncovered anything about the personal relationships he may have formed; however, one interesting tidbit did turn up. The colonel was Sam Reyes's father's CO."

Rachel practically jumps out of her seat. "Ha! We knew it had to go back." She and I had spent much of our return flight pondering possible connections, but nothing we came up with had felt right.

"Wait," says Allan, "there's more." He gestures for Walt to continue. There's an eagerness about him that's new. Was that a gleam in his eye or the morning sun reflecting off his cornea?

"Mme. Gastoneau crosses the Atlantic a couple times a year. Officially she's on business, sticks to the northeast. Flies in and out of either New York or DC, makes routine side trips to Boston and Philly. March of 2017 she broke with tradition and flew directly to Seattle before heading to New York."

I say, "That's interesting."

"Here's something even more interesting. Sam Reyes was on that flight."

Rachel raises a triumphant fist. "There it is! She *did* meet Amy earlier."

Angie reaches to shake Rachel's wrist in celebration, but her hand meets empty air as Rachel offers me a high-five. I pretend not to see the move. Instead, I puzzle over Liz's little frown and the slight tilt of her head. Could be concentration, could be something else. Knowing her, it's the latter.

Another action pulls at the edge of my sight line. Mohamed's still squirming. Natasha leans toward him, says something sotto voce. Liz's curiosity broadens to include my daughter. I wonder what else has been developing these past few days.

I ask, "Now that we have this info, what do we do with it?"

Allan says, "Mohamed?"

Mohamed clenches the sides of his seat. "Allan asked me to contact Sam. To tell him I have need of him personally, which is true."

"What reason did you give?" asks Willem.

"We need his help with the investigation." Mohamed quickly adds, "Which is true. He said he must rearrange his schedule. There are some conflicts he cannot avoid; he will be here on Monday."

"That gives us time to dig a little more," says Allan.

I stare at Mohamed, trying to drill through that indecipherable expression and read his mind. I say, "Sam struck me as a very shrewd individual. Our advantage is that he doesn't know what we know about him."

He looks back at me, unblinking. "You speak as if he's against us."

"I didn't mean to." Even though it's possible I did. "But at this point, I don't know who to believe." Which is very, very true.

"Okay," says Allan. "Eve, Walt, you've got your assignments. Rachel, Liz and Angie will fill you in. Jackie and Mohamed, please wait for me."

RAJE filters off to my study. Willem and Tasha head next door. Allan and the Connellys walk and talk their way out to an old Jeep parked halfway down the block.

Mohamed and I fidget in the kitchen. I shove an entire purple macaron into my mouth. It's too sweet, so I practically swallow it whole. I don't know what the various assignments are, and I don't like not knowing what other people are undertaking on my behalf. What I like even less is being uncertain about whether I can trust someone. There's still my therapeutic instinct, shaky though it may be. I can only go by what a person shows me.

All right, Mr. Ahmad, it's just you and me now. Show me who you are.

"I didn't mean to cast suspicion on Sam," I say. "I know he's a good friend to ORB."

"Yes. He is."

"How are you doing with all this, Mohamed?"

"I must admit, it's strange. There are many new people."

After ORB's experience of the FBI, I know he means the law enforcement officials, not the rest of us. I skip over this detail, tell him I'm the same, and remind him that civil war tends to warp one's sense of trust. Both of us have that in our family legacies, not to mention our individual experiences. And the more people there are in the room, new or not, the more relationships there are to juggle and the harder your radar has to work.

Mohamed turns a bright green macaron this way and that, looking at it as what it is, a foreign object. "Yes, well, I feel I can trust you with this. I have few memories of Somalia. I don't remember the war. In Kenya it was just my parents, my sister, and me. The rest of the family…" He puts the cookie down. "My parents did not allow talk about what we left behind. Their attitude was, 'Why dwell on that? We left in order to have a better life, so make a better life, insha'Allah.' Perhaps they did not trust their own children with the past."

I don't know how to take this intimacy. Right now I'd rather hand it back. The feeling in my gut that says he's sincere is kickboxing with the caution flare in my head. There's only one way to respond. He laughs ruefully when I say, "Our parents could have been related."

"Then we are family."

Buddy, you don't know how loaded family status is for me.

Allan steps into the kitchen, rubbing his hands.

"What are the Connellys doing next?" I ask.

"They're revisiting those threats made against ORB." He mentions the letters and Amy's drawing of the shark-toothed yellow car. "They've contacted your manager, Mohamed, but they need more help. Are you two up for it?"

With Allan and Mohamed gone, it's just RAJE, following Wayne's orders by filtering through my history with Amy.

"I'm confused." Angie massages the bridge of her nose. "I still don't know which direction to head."

Rachel says, "We need to exonerate Jackie."

Angie puts down the poem she's been reading. "That's the prob. It may be a waste of time and energy."

"Oh? What do you suggest?" I'm surprised and upset by her sudden negativity.

"The way the lawsuit's presented, the suicide is a given so the pressure's on you." She waves her hands at the papers strewn about the room. "This is a diversion, designed to keep us off track. Think about it, Jax. You're a solid clinician, as good as they come, yet we're here trying to prove your competence. Meanwhile, a murderer's going free."

"Once I prove myself, the authorities will have to listen. We need to keep that avenue open, too. That's why we're here and the crime fighting pros are out there looking for Amy's killer."

"Hold on. I get what Angie's saying." Liz's head is down, cocked to the side. "We might be in a better position to do that. Maybe we should flip assignments."

This stinks of pre-planning. I sigh and sag, misery-bound. "They don't know how to interpret my case notes, and we're not FBI profilers."

"Oh, oh, oh," says Rach, "but we *are* profilers. I never thought of it in those terms before, but we spend our entire professional lives using what we know about human nature to figure clients out." Her voice picks up speed and volume. "Come on, Jackie. There are more than a hundred years of clinical experience in this room." She nudges me. "This isn't about you and Amy; it's about Amy and someone else."

"Right," says Angie. "Patterns develop in every relationship. If we focused our search on the pattern that led to Amy's death, what would we be looking for?"

Liz rapidly and repeatedly clenches and unclenches her fists. "What are the three things that point to a murderer?"

Rachel jumps in. "Means, motive, and opportunity."

RAJE energy is contagious. I look fondly at my friends. This is us at our best, playing off each other's strengths.

Angie taps her chin. "The means are clear. Figuring out the why should lead us to the doer. We need to go beyond someone with a grudge."

I say, "We already listed motives on the whiteboard."

"Oh, how to explain." Angie bangs her palm against her forehead. "Wayne the Wonderful has us mired in bullshit. He doesn't understand what we do. I don't think Allan and the Connellys do either. Not fully, anyway." Liz's raised hand quickly lowers. "They're going after this case *their* way. We need to go at it *our* way. We've been tracking Amy's therapeutic progress. What would happen if we tracked other people's dysfunction instead?"

Liz is thoughtful. "It'd definitely give us a different angle."

"There you go," says Ang.

Rachel snorts. "I still don't see how going through all this stuff'll help us find someone crazy and/or hateful enough to waste Amy."

"Don't be dense. It's called reading between the lines."

Rachel mouths *dense* at me while pointing to herself.

Angie sees it, raises her eyebrows questioningly. "If you think it's such a dumb idea, we'll just forget it."

She takes several poems from the top of the pile. Rachel, looking repentant, stretches her hand out. Ang gives her a long look, hands over a few sheets. Rachel waves them in the air, says, "Amy had a sense of humor. Look for something that could be an in-joke or riddle, something no one else would get but her."

"When did you become an expert on Amy Nguyen?" says Liz.

"Well, it's obvious, isn't it?" Rach shoots back. "Anyone who'd work with Jax for so long would have to appreciate the absurd." No one laughs. At least she tried.

I say, "Nothing else is working, and Angie makes a strong point. We should do what we do best. Why not follow the dysfunction?"

"We've only got evidence of Amy's," says Liz.

I'm annoyed by their refusal to see Amy the way I saw her. "She wrote and drew to externalize things so she could approach them objectively. It helped her work through the toxicity in her family system and beyond. To me, that's the opposite of dysfunctional."

"However," says Liz, "before she started the healing process, she was part of that system and shared the responsibility."

Angie sits up, readjusts herself. "Jackie, you said she communicated through the garden gate. Would she have used that method hoping other people would get the drift?"

I mull that over. "Yeah. After a tough session, she'd often start the next one by handing me something to read or look at, something that showed how she'd processed it. It saved time and, I think, embarrassment. We'd go from there. Why?"

"She played with names and initials, like in 'Enigma.' A-N equals Amy Nguyen, right? What if her work was even more externally focused than we thought? What if we look for connections between songs and other people? We can look for nicknames. We already know she had one for someone who harmed her."

Rachel coughs. "You think the evil math teacher did it, Ang?"

"Of course not. But may I remind you of this RAJE motto: Everyone's entitled to their own brand of crazy. Look for connections, where Amy's crazy crossed with someone else's. Forget the obvious; focus on the obtuse."

What's gotten into her? She's not usually so directive.

They attack the stacks of paper. I sit back, eyes closed, the plush bunny in my lap. I stroke the long ears then squeeze them tightly in my fist.

"Every color has its meaning." I leap to the bookcase, seize an LP, and play ORB's cover of 'True Colors.'

"Why're we listening to this?" asks Liz.

"Amy loved Cyndi Lauper, called her a genius."

"That doesn't answer my question."

"Be patient," says Rach, "she'll get to it."

"Since when are you an expert on Jackie?" demands Liz, her attitude surprisingly sharp.

Now I'm thoroughly annoyed. "Hello! I'm right here. Rachel, I appreciate you wanting to defend me, but I can do it myself. Elizabeth, back off. And frankly, I'm not supposed to need defending, not against you guys."

So much for our best. Rachel huffs and continues reading. Liz turns her back to me, fuming. Angie has visibly wilted. My heart's pumping and my skin feels electric. It feels like I'm about to burst from my own body.

Too much is out of my control right now, but there's one thing I can actually do something about and get instant results. The bunny goes back on the bookshelf and I head outside.

It's me against the boxwood hedge. I work with a pickax to better expose the root system. Suddenly Liz is next to me holding a hatchet. I move aside and she hacks away the lower branches. While our attention is on keeping limbs and digits intact, Rach and Angie appear with more garden tools.

We work steadily, saying only what's necessary to get the job done. It takes all four of us to wrench the last obnoxious bush from the ground. Using our combined weight and strength, we rock the stump back and forth until there's enough space for me to attack with a saw. The final stubborn roots give up their hold with a powerful spray; clods of earth and pebbles pelt our hair, trickle down the backs of our shirts. We blink dirt out of our eyes, cheer and high-five each other. We start to laugh. Then to cry. There's no difference between the two; we cling to each other as if life depends on it.

Willem and Natasha set out a burrito bar, bless 'em. I dip a tortilla chip into salsa, scoop Tasha's renowned homemade guacamole with it, and cram the heaping thing into my mouth. I've emptied almost the entire bowl of green stuff by myself.

Rach returns with a reloaded plate and lands next to me with a thump. She says, "Jax, the harsh thing about your reaction earlier is that I really have been defending your honor."

"Oh?"

"Uh huh. No need to thank me, but this morning I went to the networking breakfast." She bites into her burrito.

Early in our careers we'd jointly attended these monthly gatherings for local mental health professionals. We stopped when it became clear that RAJE was enough.

Rach swallows. "As you can imagine, you were the hot topic. Some of them said you'd really messed up and were giving us all a bad name. They didn't want to be tainted by association." She sits up straighter. "I'll have you know I gave them all a piece of my mind."

"Since when do you go to those again?" I put a loaded chip down. The lightness I'd basked in just moments ago is gone. What the hell was she thinking?

Rachel looks flustered. "It was the first time in a while. Y'know, a lot of rumors were flying around. It was the least I could do, y'know, as your friend, to make sure people knew the truth." Her shoulders rise in response to my deepening glare. "In other words, I stood up for you in the most stalwart of ways."

"Rach, I don't feel the need to answer to any of those condescending yahoos. I ask you to cease and desist."

"That's the thanks I get for upholding your good name?"

My throat is raspy. "You just said no thanks are necessary, and I must agree. If you're truly my friend, quit gossiping about me."

"I wasn't gossiping; I was defending. God, Jackie, this thing is doing a real number on you. Get a grip."

I choke. Liz and Angie stop moving.

"I'm sorry," Rachel says rapidly, reaching for a hand which I pointedly withdraw. "Look," she says, "we *are* in it together, whether you want to admit it or not." Liz and Angie make sounds of confirmation. "We've all had shit fly at us at hurricane velocity. When Stan died, the boys and I never would've made it without RAJE. Now it's your turn to be on the receiving end. Don't shut us out because you think we don't get it. Give me another chance. If you don't, you're being a hypocrite. I'm trying, you know I am."

She looks unnaturally contrite. And I do know it. I felt it in Paris. Oh well, she asked. Let's see if she can take it.

"You have no idea what it's been like. For most of my life, people have wedged me into their image of me. If I object, I'm judged. You confessed to it yourself. Even when I tell you something hurts, it gets turned around so it's my problem. You don't know what it costs to be your friend."

"Wha--y don't you tell me?"

"Honesty, respect, and good intentions, right? Rachel, sometimes you are – there are so many times I bite my tongue. I know you mean well. I really do, but you made it very clear very early on that you aren't interested in things that don't concern you. Specifically, the things that make me different from you. For someone with my face, that's really, really hard. I know I don't always understand you either, but bottom line, you three have each other. No matter how much I work at it, a lot of the time I'm an automatic outsider, not only because of the color of my skin."

Rachel turns away. "Accidents of birth. We can't help being White."

"What do you mean you work at it?" asks Angie. "Do you feel discriminated against by us?"

"Not discriminated against. More like not fully understood. Or maybe you take the differences for granted because they don't really affect how you have to operate. It's been like that between me and my friends for as long as I can remember. I learned not to push it to keep people I care about from fading away. When the four of us met, I didn't do anything different. That was my choice. I own it. But sometimes it's lonely."

"I'm sorry," Rachel says quietly. "Help us, help *me* understand. I want to understand."

I look at the forgotten chip without recognition. On the one hand, I don't want to do their work for them. On the other hand, this is about us, RAJE. If I don't let them know me, that's it, my call. We each still have work to do. This is my chance to do more of mine, and Rachel's giving it to me.

"How did you first realize that not everyone's like you?" I ask. "And when that happened, did you think, Oh, that person's not like all of us, or was it, Oh shit, I'm not like all of them? For most every member of a minority population it's the latter, and they have distinct memories of it. I do.

"First day of kindergarten. Each of us has to stand in front of the class and tell about ourselves. In my family that's something you actively avoid because it's selfish and prideful. When my turn comes I'm stymied, so Mrs. McLaughlin tries to be helpful. Did I mention I'm the only ethnic minority?

" 'Jacqueline,' she says, 'We'd all love to hear you say something in your language.' Say what? My language? My language is English. I have no idea what she means. I stand there paralyzed, so she says, 'I can help. I speak a little Japanese.' I'm thinking, Japanese? I'm Korean. But I can't correct her because she's the teacher, and the teacher is always right. To correct her would be disrespectful."

I grip the tops of my knees. "Now she's annoyed and says, kind of snippy, 'Your parents must sing you lullabies in your language. I'm sure we'd all enjoy it if you sing us one of those.' Here's the rub: I can't. My parents never sang to me. Ever. There was no room for frivolities such as music in my parents' house. Second, I was five years old and had never heard the word before. I didn't know what a frickin' lullaby was. Now everyone's laughing at me, including the teacher, and I feel like an idiot. That was my first oh shit moment."

I tell them I didn't speak for the remainder of the school day. That evening I overheard my mother on the phone. After the call, she informed me that the school principal recommended I be placed in a special program. She was proud, thinking only one day in kindergarten had exposed her daughter's genius. The next morning we were in the school office to arrange the transfer. That's when things got cleared up. The principal had called to ask if I was mute. My mother, whose English was actually pretty good, hadn't recognized the word. She'd been too embarrassed to ask, so she said yes."

"God, Jackie," murmurs Angie.

"My parents were so ashamed. That taught me to fit in, no matter what." I turn to Natasha, who's trying to remain unobtrusive while replenishing the guacamole. "Tash, do you remember the first time you knew you were different?"

"Oh, easy." She licks a green fingertip. "I was little, not in school yet. Remember Casey, Mom?" Oh yes, I remember the nasty little twerp. Tash says, "He was a few years older than me, lived a couple houses down. I was out in our front yard. He was on his bike, kept riding past, making faces and calling me *Nacho.* "

Rachel's "I love nachos" is undercut by Angie's "That's terrible. Did you tell anyone?"

"No," Tasha responds. "I didn't know what a nacho was, but I could *feel* it was mean, that he was being intentionally mean. In any case, I didn't know what to do. I was really glad when they moved."

"See, that's what we deal with," I say. "Did strangers ever ask if you were your child's nanny? Happened regularly to me. At the playground people would comment on how good I was with the kids and ask how much I charge. And racist crap still flies my way. Tasha?"

"Way too often. My all-time favorite question is 'Where are you from.' "

I turn back to the others. "That's a classic, right up there with 'How'd you learn to speak such good English.' And there's the difference. We all get discriminated against because we're women. And we," I indicate RAJE, "get a double dose because we're of a certain age. But *we*," I point to myself and my daughter's retreating back, "get even more shit handed to us, and a filthier grade, because we're women of color. How much can you relate?"

The silence is answer enough.

"That still doesn't tell us why you've never said anything to us," says Liz.

"I've been bleaching my persona so long it's automatic. Why would I mention it to you?"

Angie whispers, "Because that's what friends do."

Liz says, "Rach, I need more from you too. That night at Angie's, what did you mean when you said you're done?"

"I meant I was done with blaming culture for whatever ails us. People do what they do for their own reasons. They need to take responsibility and move on. All of us do."

"You, me, Liz – we're White," says Angie. "We have no idea what it's like for Jackie. Have you ever tried looking at things from her point of view?"

"Ah, yes, that's what you're good at, isn't it." Her mouth has that hard, Rachel look to it. "The clever devil's advocate, constantly shifting position, putting others on the spot. That way you can't be held accountable. Very slippery. Very sly."

"Conflict avoidance runs in my family."

"Don't you start with family culture."

"It's real, though. I've always liked Jackie's definition: culture is what we live. That covers pretty much everything. There are lessons to learn and choices to make in terms of the whats and hows. You're right; being a moving target has its benefits. That was an integral part of my family's whats and hows."

Liz rushes in. "Come on. We're all tired and stressed out. Ang and I worked really hard while you were gone, and we're really glad you're back. We need you. Both of you."

She offers Rachel a bunch of red grapes. Rach accepts it begrudgingly. I give Liz a thankful smile.

I say, "I hope and pray we never have to go through something like this ever again, never ever, not for any of us. This is one of the worst things that's ever happened to me, and I want you to know what having you here means to me. I need you too. All of you."

Liz says, "Here's to friendship."

"Here's to RAJE." Rachel is quick to raise her glass. "Jackie, we really *are* in it with you."

Rachel's revelation in Paris still makes me cringe. She showed me how thick my own ethnocentric lens is, how quickly I come to false conclusions and hold them as truths. It's so easy to judge even my best and oldest friends. What other prejudices do I hold without even realizing? The thought is both horrifying and liberating.

"C'mon," says Liz, "we have work to do." She leads the way to my office.

Amy had just completed her last final exam of freshman year. She was in a subdued, pensive mood. This meant I might be able to con her into revealing more than she ordinarily would.

"Tell me about your family."

"Think fast!" The stuffed bunny came at me like a bullet. She laughed when I ducked too late. "What do you want to know?"

"What are they like? I hardly know anything about them."

"Count yourself lucky."

"No, I really want to know." I lobbed the rabbit back to her.

"Oh, all right." She stood, tossed the toy into the air and tried to catch it behind her back. "Mother – frigid bitch. Father – total asshole. My sister – basket case. My brother – total asshole in the making. Good enough?"

"They can't be all bad. You must love them for a reason."

"Habit?" She snorted when I crossed my arms. "Save that for your next victim, Doc. You know, it's hard to take you seriously when you try to look severe."

A smile escaped. I uncrossed my arms, relaxed the muscles in my forehead, and waited.

"While we're at it," she said, hands on her hips, "it wouldn't hurt if you dropped that my-wardrobe's-like-a-rainy-day thing. Tell you what, I'll make you a shirt, a shibori." She tugged on her own, a stunning raspberry red number. "You could also do something with your hair. You'd look way younger." She riffled her own glorious locks, the black punctuated by bright pink and blue.

"Thanks in advance for the shirt. As for the hair, I like seeing what Mother Nature does with me, and the money I save goes elsewhere."

"Like where?" She tried the behind-the-back catch again.

"Some friends and I have this thing. We each pick a non-essential expense like designer coffee, professional manicures, or *hair dye* and refrain from the indulgence. Twice a year we add up the bucks and donate to a worthy cause."

"Not shabby." She looked impressed for once. I didn't know if it was from what I said or the fact that she'd made the tricky catch twice in a row. "How'd you decide to do that?"

"My parents came here after the Korean War with a suitcase full o' nothing. What they went through helped me become who I am today. Now I'm in a position to pass it on, even if it's a little at a time."

"What worthy causes do you give to?"

"Nope. Nice try. That's my business."

"I bet I can guess. Something ultraliberal," she said, the slightest question mark at the end.

"Would my politics matter to you?"

She sidestepped. "My parents came after a war too. Did yours go through a refugee camp?"

"No, they were spared that experience."

"Yup, they were lucky. I like to tell people I was conceived in a refugee camp. Nobody normal knows how to respond to that. It's an automatic conversation killer. I call the place of my creation a waystation to freedom – my family's own WTF."

I sputtered and laughed. Amy's expression went blank, her invitation to pry. "Have you ever asked Martha what it was like for her in the WTF?"

"Yeah, right."

"Okay, it'd be a wasted effort. Too bad. The juicy stuff is always hidden deepest, right?"

"Yeah. Sucks, doesn't it."

"Yeah. They don't get that knowing could help us understand. In cases like this, knowledge really is power. If we understood, the world might make more sense and we could do something differently. It might make it easier, better for everyone. But that's trauma for you. Who wants to go back to WTF territory, even in memory, if you don't have to."

"Yeah. I suppose you're right. Whatever happened, well, it really fucked up my family. I don't know how my parents can stand it. I think they remind each other of the What-The-Fuckness. They really are not good together. They used to fight constantly but now they just ignore each other. They're like igneous rock – they heated each other up until they melted, then they cooled into hard, sharp bits of obsidian."

This was a simile I could go with. The two things I remembered from eighth grade science were Mr. Vogel introducing us to the glory of rocks and the day he dissected a black tom cat the size of a small Doberman. "What kind of rock is Martha?"

Amy stopped again to consider. "Petrified wood with an even grain? No. A bug eternally suspended in amber. Fossils are forever." She continued her game. "And Billy Blue's sedimentary, like the Painted Desert, streaked with colors bold and true, stunning to behold, yet subject to erosion."

"Those hills look more red and purply than blue."

"Way to kill both metaphor and simile. He's *blue* because he's *depressed*. You of all people should get that."

"Oh, sorry. Of course. And you? What kind of rock are you?"

She showed her forgiveness by twirling with a light, fairy step, arms swaying above her head. "Once I was that and now

I'm this. What will I be tomorrow? Metamorphic, that's my name. Speckled and veined, I'm not what I seem, shot through with indigo, scarlet, and green." She stopped suddenly and waggled her eyebrows conspiratorially. "Every color has its meaning."

I finish channeling Amy and plunk into a chair, dizzy from the twirling. Fuck. I definitely need more sleep.

"Are those direct quotes?"

"Pretty much. Some moments with her are permanently engraved." I point to the center of my forehead.

Angie purses her lips, taps her forehead. "I dunno, Jax."

I know she's commenting on my mental health, not my memory; I choose not to follow the detour. "Hey, it's a short step from Billy Blue streaked with colors bold and true to 'True Colors.' You said to look for the obtuse. This fits the bill."

They all groan. Liz says, "Such a bad pun must be punished. No more fancy French cookies for you." She eats the macaron in her hand. That's a good sign.

"She said he was subject to erosion," Rachel muses.

I add, "Sedimentary rock is easy to shape."

"Yeah, that's just the kind of thing that would've gotten Amy going," says Rach. Liz gives her an exaggeratedly keen look; Rach sticks her tongue out at her, finishes with a wink.

Angie taps the table with her knuckles. "Children, children." When we settle she says, "Are we agreed – 'True Colors' is a message for Bill?"

"A way Amy could tell him things without causing trouble for either of them," says Rachel.

Liz climbs on board. "Exactly. Don't let yourself be worn down or reshaped. Show your true colors."

"What if his true colors only show with erosion? You know, like the Painted Desert."

"Angela, were you born this way?" Liz huffs.

"Family lore suggests the affirmative. But it does result in the occasional headache." Angie rubs her temple. "I appreciate Amy's subversion," she says, returning to the original subject. "If this song was for Bill, maybe there are others for the rest of the family."

"Yes, there are," I say before correcting myself. "Rather, knowing her, there would have to be."

"Which ones?" Liz calls, thumbing through the papers.

"I don't know off the top of my head. There are more than a hundred poems and pictures to choose from."

"Don't worry," Rachel says. "We'll find 'em, but you'll have to figure out which songs go with which people. Jackie, anything else you can tell us about the Nguyens' culture around relationships would be good."

She and I exchange a long look while Liz and Angie stare at her in disbelief. Then I draw a quick Nguyen family tree illustrating the power structure, emotional ties, and divisions as I knew them. The clinical notes are forgotten as we filter through the remainder of Amy's art.

It isn't long before Angie waves a sheet of paper in the air. "Here's one about family secrets," she says. " 'Second.' It's gotta be about her mom and the colonel."

Even from a distance, I know it. About her mom and the colonel? Maybe. And so much more.

After weeks of painstaking debate, Amy had signed up for her high school's poetry slam. The penalty for my nagging was to serve as her test audience. She was only slightly miffed when I settled back and claimed it as a reward rather than a penance.

Standing stiffly resolute, she tossed her bunny friend onto the sofa next to me, rolled her shoulders, massaged the back of her neck, and declared, "I'm ready. Remember, don't pay attention to the grammar or anything stupid. Just tell me if it's a go."

"Okay." I reached over and picked up the abandoned bunny, squeezed it tightly.

Amy showed me the poem, handwritten in fine point green Sharpie, and indicated a word near the top, thickly circled in purple. "See here – it's called 'Second.' It's how I feel about being second generation." She took a deep breath, exhaled slowly, a relaxation exercise we'd practiced many times. She gave me a sharp look; I smiled encouragingly. She cleared her throat, rolled her shoulders again and recited, ignoring the sheet of lined paper crumpling in her fist.

"I have a tale, my tale to tell
I'm a Second and it's plain hell
I've got no way to be or try
Not knowing is no alibi

I've watched her now through all these years
She thinks I'm blind, don't see her tears

Seconds have to do or die
to get our piece of the American pie
Of sacrifice I hear so much
when all I want's a healing touch

'Do more, be more, have all that's sweet'
Must lie and cheat, or it's the street

What came before's a secret tale
I don't know what she has to veil
Some piece of her that's also me
I want to know my history!

I've held my secrets, too, from her
A Janus life, you can infer
Survival's cost means lose yourself
If you get wounded, heal yourself

She claims our burden: 'Know the score'
She says it's better than it was before
'Keep your head down, make no fuss'
Deeper feelings aren't discussed

Would she think that she had failed
if she knew you knew my tale
my hopes and dreams and hates and screams?
I know that nothing's as it seems

I learned quite young to block a fist
Other weapons just don't miss
'Fucking gook, you fucking dyke
You freak – I'll call you what I like!'

Why'd we come? What brought us here?
What'd you trade for hate and fear?
Don't know who I am, can be
Living here's a mystery

Hopes eroding, tempers flowing,
counting pennies, job with bennies
Have to make it – it's a job so take it!
Home defeated, soul depleted,
it all ends in silence."

I blinked once, hard. When my eyes refocused, they
latched onto hers. It hit us simultaneously, that flash of mutual

recognition, of understanding. Amy sighed and her shoulders came down; I started breathing again.

She held a tissue box out for me. "I guess that means you liked it," she said, a smug smile on her face.

I wiped tears away. "Yeah, it's a go."

"Here." She handed me the sheet of paper.

"You don't need it?"

"Nah." She tapped her forehead, tapped her heart.

"Thank you." I couldn't think of anything else to say that would fully express what I felt. Instead I proffered the paper. "Where's the autograph?"

"Brat," she said as she signed and dated it.

Rach and Ang are gone, done in by the demands of the day. At least we ended on a high note. Liz sets a tray of dirty dishes on the kitchen counter. She asks, "Where's Willem?"

"Next door." I load the dishwasher while she washes her hands.

"Good. Mohamed's next door too. He and Tasha went walking earlier?"

"Yeah, they took the cat out." I recognize the tone, abandon the dishes to say, "What are you insinuating?"

"I'm not insinuating anything. Just wondering. I mean, Mohamed already looks like a member of the family. He and Natasha got cozy awfully fast." I keep my mouth shut, hand Liz a dish towel. "It's common knowledge that he and Amy Nguyen had a thing, but I guess knowledge that's common isn't necessarily true. Tasha should be careful." She dries a glass and spins the topic dial. "Do you think he's gay?"

"First you hint that he and Tasha have a thing. Now you wonder if he's gay. What's up with that, and does it matter either way?"

"I suppose not," Liz answers only the latter question, and spins again. "What about Amy?"

I plant my palms on the edge of the sink to stay steady. "What about her? Spit it out, Elizabeth."

"Don't judge me. Just thinking out loud here, from a purely clinical perspective." She continues carefully. "The Black community is still pretty homophobic. If Mohamed's gay, what would he do to stop his cover from being blown? Maybe Amy covered for him. To protect him."

"You're imagination's running away with you."

"C'mon, Jackie. Couples are my thing. The dots don't connect. There's something between Mohamed and Sam, not necessarily sexual, but there's a vibe." I turn my back to her, but she keeps pressing. "Watch Mohamed when Sam is mentioned. You'll see."

"What's your point?"

"Sam's team protects ORB. What if Sam had to choose which ORBer to protect, Amy or Mohamed? I'm telling you, Natasha should be careful."

My hands slowly lower to my sides. I hate to admit it, but Liz isn't the only one to notice Mohamed's reaction to all things Sam. I have more pieces to the puzzle than she does, but that doesn't make me feel any better. She just arranged them in a new, unsettling way.

I'm on the sofa with Bonkers buzzing sleepily in my lap. Tasha hands me a mug of black tea spiked with a splash of rum before sitting on the floor at my feet. Next to me, Willem kicks off his shoes and lifts his feet onto an ottoman.

"How're you doing, Mama?" Tasha asks.

"Hangin' in there, thanks. It helps to actually be doing something instead of just fretting."

"You've got a dream team."

"They're good people," Willem agrees. "I'm very grateful that Allan brought Eve and Walt. That speaks for him. At first I had my doubts, but he's all right."

"I remember him from Liz and Theo's barbecues," says Tasha. "I thought he was weird, kind of stand-offish."

"He was a hurt kid for a long time after his mother died."

"Then he went off to college and stopped coming," Tasha muses. "Next thing I heard he was a cop. Then he was married. Then his wife was killed. Horrible what he's had to go through."

"Love and pain are partners." Willem rubs his feet together with a concentrated effort and takes a deep swallow from his own mug.

"Speaking of love," I say, "is there something going on between you and Mohamed?"

Tasha tilts forward. Her eyes fly open and she twists to face me, her expression guarded.

"Jackie," Willem warns.

I picture Mohamed listening intently as my daughter whispered into his ear. "You two spend a lot of time together."

She presses a forefinger to her bottom lip. "He knows Amy told you he's gay. So let's see – if it's not romantic, what kind of relationship could he and I possibly have? Here's an idea. We're becoming friends. And here's another thought. Turns out he and his extended family want to live close to each other but no longer under the same roof. They're looking for ideas. I'm an architect. Hmmm."

"You're working for him?"

"I will be."

Having made her point, she leans back again. The restored warmth feels good against my shins. I comb her hair with my fingers, the way I did when she was a child. Her head tilts back and her eyes close. The artful way she handled my idiocy instills a warped degree of satisfaction and pride. My daughter is part of a new generation, one more step removed from the family trauma. She has the feistiness I often wished for myself.

I turn to Willem. "You knew about this?"

"Sure," he says. "I'm the boss."

"God, what else have I been missing?" I lament. "The world's passing me by and I'm not even aware."

"That's okay, Mama. You're doing what you need to do."

I bend forward, upsetting the cat. "Liz thinks there's something between Mohamed and Sam Reyes."

Tasha sighs patiently. "I love RAJE, Mama, but you do tend to stick your noses in where they don't belong."

I am included. "We're therapists. We can't help it. I have to agree with her that there's a vibe."

"Haven't you ever had a thing for someone who didn't reciprocate?"

Willem sighs. "I'm done for the day. Gute Nacht, you two. Be kind."

I sit as if hypnotized by the pool of warm lamplight. I let my mind wander, attempting to pry apart the events of the past week and rearrange them into some sense of order. Somehow reality has twisted into an Escheresque illusion that dips and swirls.

"Here." Natasha moves to stand behind the sofa and massages my shoulders.

"Oh, that's nice," I purr, flinching as she attacks a particularly stiff knot of muscle. "I'm really sorry about all this."

"It's not nearly as bad for us as it is for you. You're one tough cookie, Mama. I'm proud of you."

There's heat behind my eyes. "I'm proud of you, too."

I reach back, and Natasha clasps my hand. "You don't know what that means, especially now." Tears cloud her voice. I keep myself from turning and ruining the moment. "I know we had some crappy years. I'm sorry about those."

"We both made mistakes. We're both making up for them. Now you're back from California, and what do you get? None of the quality time we promised each other."

"Yeah, well, there was no way to predict this." Tasha's free hand rests lightly, yet possessively, on my shoulder. It feels good to be claimed. "I never realized how much of a toll the job takes on you."

"Ordinarily it doesn't, but some clients make a bigger impact. Protecting myself, and you, from that is part of the job. Sometimes I didn't do that great. I'm really sorry." It's an apology worth repeating.

"You spent so much time in the office."

"I worked as much as I could back when Papa was getting his business off the ground."

"I used to think it was your excuse for staying away. I thought there was something wrong with me that made you love your clients more than me."

There's that word. "Oh baby, I'm so sorry I ever gave you cause to think that. That was never true. There was never anything wrong with you. Not with either of us. We had some really tough times, but we came out okay, didn't we?"

"Yeah, like you always say, the goal of adolescence is to survive it."

"And we did. It wasn't easy and we carry the scars, but those reminders keep us on track. To be honest, there may have been times I *liked* my clients more." Natasha gives my shoulder a playful swat. "But I didn't have to live with them, and that's a vital difference."

Tasha comes around and sits close. I savor the pressure of that young arm against my own.

"Mama, Amy Nguyen. What was she to you?"

I bite my lip. "Ordinarily, I wouldn't work with anyone so close in age to you and Stef, but Amy needed someone fast and I figured there were enough differences. She came into my life right about the time you and your brother were deep into hating each other. You were so eager to leave childhood behind and had no patience for Stef – for any of us, for that matter. He was devastated that his big sister was treating him like a worm."

Natasha shakes her hair back. "I liked worms; Stef was a lesser life form."

"Yes, you made that eminently clear. And there was nothing your father or I could do about it. Do you know how rotten it is for a therapist to feel so helpless in her own family? It's crap on a stick."

"I was a butt for a while, wasn't I?"

Bonkers launches herself back onto us. Balancing her back legs on my lap, she kneads Tasha's thigh with her front paws.

"Yes, you were. All developmentally appropriate, but that didn't make it okay. Anyway, your dad and I felt like we couldn't help you at all because we didn't know what life was like for you. I have the Asian experience; he has the White. He's an immigrant; I'm second generation; you're second and third. I could feel you holding a lot of stuff in. That's the Chol blood in you."

"The Kesslers are pretty expert too."

"Mmm, too true."

"The life of a mutt."

"You put it so charmingly." I take Tasha's chin in my hand and shake gently before letting go. "Even with our differences, it felt like Amy and I had more in common than you and I. We connected and understood each other in a way you and I couldn't because she and I had shades of the same life. Her I could actually help. I clung to that.

"By the time she was doing better, so were you. Only the way I saw it, you'd pretty much done it on your own. Yeah. She meant a lot to me." I reach over and envelop Natasha with as much love as I can muster. "But she was always a client, never my daughter."

DAY NINE

• •

It's been a long while since I was last in this house. Rays of morning light expose a light layer of dust coating the hardwood floor, the same floor RAJE had had beautifully refinished as our wedding gift to the newlyweds. A conspicuously clear path runs down the hallway, connecting kitchen to sofa. I run my fingertips across the paint samples that arc across the living room wall, each broad curve another shade of soft, mossy green. Using this location had been my suggestion, a way to track the qualities of the different hues as the light changed throughout the day. The rainbow shape had been Zoe's lighthearted response to Allan's observation that green is the color of rot. Maybe leaving the rainbow is one way Allan keeps her with him.

Eve and Walt watch quietly from the sofa as I squish into an easy chair. In his haste to assemble us, Allan had forgotten food and drink. Not that refreshments are necessary, but he'd been embarrassed. He'd taken drink orders and hustled out the door with Mohamed, who was more than eager to help. He still doesn't want to be anywhere near the Connellys.

I'm overwhelmed by a flush of energetic need. This may be my only chance to ask the questions that have been boring through my conscience since we first met.

"Eve, Walt … what are you doing here? I mean, you must have more important things to do."

It's Eve's turn to contemplate the green rainbow. "Allan's doing this for Zoe. We're here for both of them."

"Is what you're doing legit?"

Walt says, "We're not involved in an official capacity."

Eve winks. "In other words, we're doing this on the sly."

"What happens if you get caught?" The palms of my hands start to itch.

"We know what's at stake." I know she means their livelihoods. "But trust us," she says, "we're good at what we do."

"I don't want anyone to commit a crime on my behalf." I don't know how much I really mean that. One thing about this adventure, I'm finding out how seductive the dark side can be.

"The only crime would be getting caught," says Walt.

There's obviously more to this operation than I know about. That's both comforting and alarming. Is this why Allan refused to go to Paris, one of the things he had to handle?

I'm untangling this in my head when Allan and Mohamed return. Mohamed's long legs cover the space from door to living room in just a few steps. Whatever he and Allan talked about seems to have calmed him; he looks reassured, almost relaxed.

Walt accepts his matcha latte. "Mohamed, I know the FBI let you down before, but you have an ally there now. It'll be different."

Eve adds, "We'll find whoever killed your friend."

Allan makes a fist. Mohamed looks from me to Allan to the Connellys. "You want to know more about Amy and ORB. How can I help?"

My mother nearly elbows me in the face as she reaches unsuccessfully for the maple syrup. I pass the bottle to her. "It's easier if you just ask."

She ignores me. As well she should. In our family's language, she asked quite clearly, and I responded quite correctly, except for the disrespect.

She crams another less-than-ladylike wedge of French toast into her mouth. Mom's always been a sucker for anything sweet and high carb, probably a result of having gone so hungry for so long in her youth.

Speaking of asking… "Mom, what was it like for you when you left Korea?"

"What?"

"I was just wondering how it felt for you to come here." She's stopped chewing, is staring at the fork in her hand. Give it up, Jackie – this is a no-go. She's shutting down. Nope! Time to do something different, even with Mom.

"You told me once how happy your parents were that you and Dad got to come. How about you? Were you happy, excited? Did you want to come?"

She cautiously swishes more eggy bread through the pool of syrup on her plate. "Of course."

"Of course you were happy and excited, or of course you wanted to come?"

She looks me square in the eye, something she hasn't ever done when I've asked about her past. My nerves are jangling. This new territory is uncomfortable for us both.

"Of course, I had to come. Why are you asking? Your kids left home too. They always far."

"Tasha's back."

"Because her father is sick. What about the boy? Are you missing him? Why he have to go so far? Maybe he didn't want?"

"He wanted. It was his idea. And he's a grown up. It's not as if we could stop him, even if we wanted to." Yikes! Please don't take that as a criticism. I know exactly what and whom she's thinking about.

"He go so far." That's what she'd said when Matt packed for New York. Only he hadn't had a choice.

Whoa. That's right, turn it around, lady. I learned from the best. Time to reciprocate. I put another half slice of French toast on her plate. "Mom, did you want to come to the US?"

"Want to come, had to come. No difference. That doesn't mean I wanted leave Korea."

This is the closest she's ever come to talking about either her or Matt leaving home. The deterioration of her English shows her level of upset.

I jump at the low buzz signaling a freshly received text message. That shows my upset. God, what rotten timing.

"You better read." My mother's conversation shut down.

"I'd rather talk with you."

She pauses for a fraction of a second, considering her options. Her expression goes blank. Yup, we're done.

She says, "Could be him." She means Willem; she's right. I check the text and sigh.

"Is he dead?" The deepening of the lines around her mouth hint at her true emotion. She loves Willem. When I told her of his stroke, she'd said, "Better if it was me."

"It's not him," I say, relieved. "It's a client emergency. Sorry, Mom, you'll have to finish without me."

"Who has weekend emergency? I don't understand why you want to work with crazy people." Back to Mom-basics.

I could comment on the craziness of the person I'm sharing brunch with, but there's no need to end on that note. She's entitled to her brand too. "It's my job to care about other people. You taught me that."

She blinks sourly at me. "Too much food," she says. "Take some. I'll wrap it." She reaches for a pink paper napkin, delivering another elbow.

I disrupt the French toast operation with one hand, lower her flying joint with the other. "Thanks, but I've had plenty.

Besides, I can't eat in the car. I'd drip syrup all over myself." I kiss the back of each of her hands. "I love you, Mom."

Her surprise is glorious. Ours is not a kissy relationship. I take advantage of her momentary stupefaction to plant another buss on her forehead and, as I retreat, am treated to the sound of her grousing in Korean.

The waiting area of the hospital's pediatric psychiatry unit holds the usual assortment of kids and grown-ups, all in varying degrees of distress. I've been here with clients before, but that doesn't make it any easier.

The word *suicide* provoked an instant response. It took the entire drive to calm down. Thankfully, I was never here with Amy so I'm spared that association. And the fact that she never had to be readmitted is an important, hopeful thing.

It's been over a year since Devon's last attempt. He had jumped from the roof of his former foster parents' house and broken his leg. Lucky they lived in a rambler. He was still in the hospital when his caseworker had come calling.

After a few rough months he and his new foster parents, Candace and Ray, hit their stride. Devon's been doing really well, and we'd recently discussed cutting back on sessions. Now I'm second-guessing that move. With twelve tumultuous years of life under his belt, Devon does not like change. In addition, he's a huge ORB fan. I never told him about my connection with one of its founders, but who knows what he's heard or how he's reacted.

To be honest, since the lawsuit, I'm second-guessing every move. Note to self: Make a doctor's appointment. These heart palpitations can't be good.

The large waiting room smells as institutional as it feels. My client sits in a molded plastic chair at a molded plastic table. I acknowledge Ray with a nod, readjust my game face, and slide into the seat across from the boy.

"Hey, Devon. I'm so proud of you for doing the right thing."

His eyes bulge with we're-in-the-psych-ward perturbation. I tilt my head at Ray, offering him the baton. Thankfully, months of hard work bear fruit; he proudly pats Devon's shoulder.

"Yeah, he did exactly what we agreed." Okay, we need more work on getting him to speak directly to Devon. "When he told us how bad he was feeling, we asked if he felt safe, and he told us he needed to come here," he says loudly, as though trying to drown out the oppressive hospital atmosphere with an overly jolly voice.

Ray's proclamation has caught a flash of attention from an Asian girl in her early teens. She and what looks to be her parents sit nearby. Just as quickly, the girl casts her eyes downward to match her parents' postures. They say not a word, share no physical contact. I send out feelers. Nope, no emotional connection either; rather, quite a bit of chilly distance. They're so still, they remind me of Waiting for the Interurban without the occasional adornments that make the statue so fun throughout the year. I itch to festoon these people with bright feather boas and ridiculous oversized hats, drape them with outrageous color and texture.

Boa Girl dares another move. Her head turns ever so slightly, her ears and eyes swiveling for better reception.

Devon's head is now face-down on the table. I lean in toward him until our heads almost touch, speak quietly but emphatically. "Way to stick with your plan, dude. I know it must've been hard. You're taking good care of yourself." I lift my head; he lifts his. I offer him a high five. He reluctantly responds. His palm is clammy and his cheeks are downright chalk-like.

Oh, fuck. Adrienne's on duty. I duck, but she beckons me over to the front desk. Of all the social workers in this unit, she's been here the longest. She's also a dependable, if irritating, referral source. I don't mind being the lady's ethnic minority go-to; however, it would be real progress if she sent me the occasional Euro-American kid. But then, I owe her. She sent Amy.

"Jacqueline Kessler," she says, also not bothering to turn the volume down, "fancy meeting you here." I wonder what the hospital's confidentiality protocols are. Not that she would care; I'm not a patient, so my privacy obviously doesn't count.

I answer at a much lower decibel level. "Good to see you too, Adrienne."

She aims an opossum smile at a passing co-worker, adds a head twitch in my direction. His consequent stare makes me feel like something in a petri dish.

"Hey, I was so sorry to hear about your … current situation. I really regret sending you-know-who to you way back when. Who'da thunk it'd turn out the way it did." Her eyes are gleaming so brightly, I'd like to smack the polish off. When I refuse to respond, she looks at me more warily. "Well, I'll be more careful about who I send from now on. Wouldn't want to cause you any more trouble."

Amy was pure joy. "You aren't responsible."

"Well, still."

At this point, I'm summoned to participate in my client's intake assessment. I wave a cheery goodbye to Adrienne. As I turn to exit stage left, Boa Girl and I make what almost amounts to eye contact.

During Devon's solo interview with the intake coordinator, I take advantage of alone time with Ray. "What do you think set him off?" I expect a report on a recurrence of the vicious bullying Devon had been subjected to for years or an unexpected failing grade despite his best efforts. Or that Devon felt betrayed by me.

Ray chews the inside of his mouth, says, "Jackie, there's something you should know." I've come to dread that phrase. "We got word yesterday. His mother signed away her parental rights."

"Oh, shit," I say. That would more than do it. Through all the years of heartbreak, that's what kept Devon going, the hope that his mother would turn herself around, as promised, and that someday they'd be reunited.

Thank the stars, his current suicidal ideation has nothing to do with me. Note to self: Enough with the self-pity and self-importance.

Ray tells me how much he and Candace rely on my input and support. As we talk, I set aside the jitteriness and uncertainty that had filled me. A couple hours and one extremely detailed safety plan later, I'm equally nervous and relieved that Devon's going home. I imagine the two of them pulling into the driveway, Candace and Todd, Devon's younger foster brother, listening for their arrival. Ray's already booked weekly appointments for the next month. "We'll all come," he'd said. "We'll get through this as a family."

The walls of that house are thin, and Todd's old enough to understand. He's also a sensitive, intuitive boy with a record of closely scrutinizing, if not following, Devon's footsteps. Thankfully, Ray and Candace are great foster parents. They took the lesson about minimizing the possibility of future regrets very seriously. It's a lesson I wish my parents had learned. I fend off my own decades-old what-ifs and if-onlys. And I wonder which coulda-shouldas have haunted Amy's family since she died.

DAY TEN

●●●●●●●●●●●●●●●●●●●●●●●●●●

Having imbibed bucketsful of coffee at my house, Mohamed has invited me to a place of special significance. He hasn't been in Beancounters since he and Amy last shared this table. The young man shifts uncomfortably in the creaky wooden chair, taking occasional sips from the thick mug clenched tightly between his hands. I'm across from him, one hand circling my teacup, the other under my thigh to keep myself from squirming. Our chitchat is forced, our smiles even more so. Mohamed's bodyguard sits apart with a clear sightline to us. So much for acting naturally.

The rich smell of freshly roasted coffee beans permeates the large room. There's a low buzz of conversation from two tables away, a trio of college students intent on a laptop screen. Other customers are sprinkled throughout the place, further away. Mohamed's gaze darts from one person to the next. We both involuntarily turn our heads toward the counter; a man and a woman just walked in, are chatting and laughing with the barista. They pay for their drinks and, it being a cloudy yet dry late May day, exit the shop to sit outdoors.

Mohamed finally makes eye contact. "I spoke with Isha," he says, keeping his head down, his voice low. "She asked me to give you her greetings."

His halting delivery is alarming and I put my teacup down to look at him. "Is she all right?"

"Yes, she's fine," he says reassuringly. "She wants to be known only as Kick now. Kick Dorji. This does not yet come naturally to me."

"Good for her," I say. To me she's always been Kick.

"She asked me to convey another message. She and her mother have been talking. She said you would know what this means."

Ah. It means satisfaction. Mothers and daughters, that cosmic relationship. I hoped and trusted she would follow through.

The bells attached to the front door chime again. Mohamed checks out the new arrival, does a double take. Sam Reyes exchanges a casual glance with the bodyguard before ordering.

Mohamed and I neither move nor speak as Sam approaches, beverage in hand.

"Mind if I join you?" he asks, taking a seat.

"Sam," says Mohamed, "it is, it's good to see you. What are you doing here?"

"I thought it would be better if I caught an earlier flight."

I make a disbelieving sound in the base of my throat. Another sneaky move, initiative thief. Monday, my foot.

I speak without preamble. "What's your relationship with Mireille Gastoneau?"

Wait. Where was the eyebrow move? He wasn't surprised. Seems our cab driver's screaming fit didn't go unnoticed after all. Sam gives me an appraising look and we spend what seems like years inside each other's heads.

Might as well put it out there. "Since you don't like that question, Mr. Reyes, try this one. Better in what way? That you face us before we ferret out whatever it is you and Madame Gastoneau have been going to great lengths to hide?"

Busted. He sips from what looks to be a double espresso then sighs deeply. "Colonel McMillan was my father's CO in Vietnam. When Dad was killed, the colonel wrote a letter of condolence to my mother and me. It meant a lot. The colonel was stationed at the Pentagon before he retired. I contacted him when I was at school in DC. He invited me for dinner. Mireille was visiting. We were just kids then, having fun. She and I stayed in contact for a couple years, but life happened and we lost touch. Mireille let me know, though, when her father died. I was in the States at the time and attended the funeral. We reconnected."

"Why the duplicity?"

He succumbs to a fraction of an inch eyebrow lift. "It wasn't meant that way. After Mireille discovered the truth, she asked me to keep an eye on Amy. When ORB was looking to hire security, going for the job was a given. Mireille came with me when I flew out. She hoped to meet Amy, but an opportunity didn't open up so she waited. The ORBit tour made it easy to get a letter from one to the other."

"What would she have done if Amy hadn't responded?"

"She would've tried again later. She didn't want to force Amy into anything. Afterward, when she heard about your investigation –"

"When you told her."

Another fraction of an inch. "– she wanted to help however she could. It would've looked suspicious if all of a sudden I had material on Amy that no one had ever suspected. The plan wasn't elegant, but it served its purpose." He downs the rest of his coffee.

Mohamed watches silently, his face impassive. It's clear he wants no part of this.

I keep pushing. "Why should we believe you? Mme. Gastoneau hasn't been crossed off the suspect list yet." Neither have you, buddy.

"Mireille is the first to hold herself partially responsible. She's convinced their meeting set off the chain of events that led to Amy's death."

"What do *you* think?" I lean forward. The move reminds me of Wayne. I straighten up.

"I know she regrets not being able to talk her out of going back."

This time my eyebrows rise. I glance at Mohamed; he still says nothing. Sam stands. "You have my number. I'm at the Four Seasons."

I think quickly, blurt, "One more question. What was Amy doing with a gun?"

"Damn," says Sam. "I need more coffee."

As we wait, Mohamed's body collapses in on itself. His eyes are red-rimmed as he says more about the consequences of ORB's political activism. In addition to the threats, police had to be called to more than one standoff between fans waiting for a concert and detractors carrying xenophobic signs.

Sam rejoins us. He explains that his approach with any new client is to get to know them, their personalities and habits, in order to keep their protection as minimally invasive as possible. ORB originally rejected the idea of bodyguards, saying they wanted to stay approachable.

Mohamed interrupts: "We didn't want people with dark glasses and darker expressions between us and our fans. Sam presented reasonable alternatives."

This included pressing them to buy small caliber handguns and learning how to use them. At first Amy had been vehemently opposed to the idea; however, she was outvoted. Sam took the ORBers to a local firing range and trained them himself. Amy surprised herself by enjoying it. Shooting, she discovered, was good stress relief. She joined a gun club and periodically went to blow off steam.

"She was a good shot," says Sam. "A natural."

The conversation with Rachel about lies of omission comes back to haunt me. I turn to Mohamed. "What else haven't you told me?"

"Nothing. Truly, this is the last."

"Why, Mohamed?"

He turns aside. "If I said it out loud, perhaps that would make it true."

I know he means the suicide. Suddenly the anger fades and I feel my insides shrivel, just as Mohamed's did moments ago. Sam takes this opportunity to depart.

Gobsmacked. Mohamed and I discussed ORB's security measures not that long ago. Why had he not told me about the firearms? He says there's nothing left to divulge, but it's hard to believe him.

The team has assembled to discuss the latest and reorganize our strategy. I wonder what Mohamed is thinking now that the whole story's out. I keep him in my peripheral vision; his head turns from side to side, keeping an eye on the others' reactions. It occurs to me that every time Mohamed has offered new information, it's been to me alone. With the team, his main contributions are answers to direct questions or add-ons to others' thoughts. This could be cultural. Maybe it's a response to the group itself, a bunch of mostly White people, some of whom are cops. Then again, I could be totally off the mark.

Then there's taking Sam's info at face value. The Amy I knew blamed violence in its many shapes and forms for all the damage done to her family. She would never have touched a weapon. But then, she was the first to admit she came from a long line of accomplished liars. She was bound to excel at any of the family traits she chose to maintain.

A current of renewed doubt agitates my insides. My ears start to ring. "How could I have been so gullible?" I ask, more to myself than the group. "Could she have killed herself? Maybe I did get it all wrong." I have a sudden impulse to check up on Devon.

"You're being self-pitying," Willem warns, low and stern.

I round on him, temper flaring. A lecture is the last thing I need. Then there it is, a mischievous spark of satisfaction. I shake my fist at him in mock rage. He catches it in his own and playfully gnaws on my knuckles.

Allan's phone buzzes in his pocket. "And?" is all he says. "Thanks. We'll be here." He stows the phone. "Eve and Walt are on their way."

In the meantime we fortify our guests with a simple meal of seaweed soup, rice, and kimchi, the pungent pickled cabbage that is as vital to a Korean's diet as comfortable shoes are to a therapist's wardrobe. Setting the food out, I'm reminded of a former client, a South Korean immigrant. She and her Euro-American husband divorced due to irreconcilable differences, namely culture clash. The breaking point had been his refusal to allow her to eat, let alone store, kimchi in their home. During their courtship they'd been vaguely aware of their cultural differences; however, they had assured themselves that their abiding love was enough. Turned out it wasn't.

I purposefully place the bowl of kimchi within sniffing distance of Rachel. Her nose stops, mid-wrinkle. Have to hand it to her. She doesn't take any kimchi, but she doesn't say anything either. And she stays in her seat.

Walt hands Allan a manila folder. "Merry Christmas."

Allan peruses the contents with an evil grin. He hands it to me with a hearty, "Ho, ho, ho." It's a copy of the dossier on Amy's death, a piece of evidence my lawyer refused to share with me, saying there was no need as it only served to prove me wrong.

"How'd you get this?"

Eve smiles. "We have our ways. We also tracked Amy's movements the day she died."

"You did this awfully fast." Liz's voice is sharp, critical, questioning.

What a goody two-shoes. Fuck, ten days ago that would've been me.

"It's a high tech world," says Eve. "We tracked her by her rental car's GPS records."

I'm about to repeat my line about wanting no one to take any risks on my behalf when Walt adds, "We also did it with official backing. The evidence so far is circumstantial, but in front of the right people it was enough to generate some real interest and, I have to say, concern."

Eve butts in. "Long story short, the investigation of Amy Nguyen's death has been reinstated. Walt and I are now officially part of the team."

"Weren't you always?" says Angie.

The laughter punctures my anxiety. I've always envisioned anxiety as a seething red-gray mass festering within my system. This time, instead of succumbing to its sinister yet familiar presence, I force it from my body through the jagged hole. The further away it floats, the more diffuse it becomes until I can blow it away. What a relief! I'd been so afraid that the Connellys were going to end up in big trouble on my account. No matter that they're doing this out of loyalty for Allan and Zoe. I'm the one who will ultimately benefit from their efforts, and I feel responsible for any trouble it could cause them.

Eve puts us back on track. "That afternoon Amy went from Sea-Tac directly to her parents' house."

"She confronted her mother?" I ask.

"We don't know what she did or who she talked with," Walt answers. "We only know that the car was there. Either way, it's her activity right after, in the hours before she died, that's interesting."

I reach for Willem's hand as Eve pulls a sheet of paper from the folder with a flourish, suspends it in front of my face. It's a dated sign-in sheet from a gun club, complete with Amy's signature and in and out times.

"How in the world?" says Willem.

Eve smiles as she says, "I toured the place under the pretext of joining, told them I was drawn by their exclusivity. The guy who showed me around tried to impress me by dropping a name or two." I'm not surprised that the attractive detective would spark the man's interest. "I let slip I'd heard Amy Nguyen used to be a member. One thing led to another," she sneers, her expression now delightfully wolfish. "So much for respecting members' privacy."

Allan takes over, full of nervous energy. If I had as much coffee as he's downed since his arrival, Willem would be peeling me off the ceiling. "We now know why there was gunpowder residue on Amy's hands."

My thumb rubs against the spot near my left knee. "Too bad GPS doesn't track who's in a car as well as where it goes. If someone went with and knew about the residue, that someone could have kept her from washing it off."

"And could've killed her and made it look like suicide." There's my Liz, sharing my wavelength.

"That's it exactly," Eve says approvingly.

Angie steps to the whiteboard. It's still divided into two columns that list potential suspects and motives: *Fan, Family, Friend, Intruder. ?, Finances, Hate Crime, Suicide.*

"I'm more than slightly overwhelmed," she says. "We've got suspects coming out our ears."

"We can't let Sam and Mireille off the hook yet either," adds Rach. "I mean, if Sam's really on our side, why isn't he here?"

Angie adds Sam and Mireille to column one.

"There are eight and a half more days," says Willem. "How do we attack this?"

"We should start with the Nguyens," I say. "If Amy did have that showdown with her mother, the entire family would have been aware. They would also have known that Amy would eventually expose their dirty laundry through songs. There's no saving face from that."

Eve indicates the dossier. "We have everyone's whereabouts at the time of Amy's death. The parents were at home; they alibi each other. Sister Martha was easy to track; her routine's pretty predictable. Outside of home and the church, she doesn't have much of a life."

"Brother Bill is the moving target," says Walt. "He claimed to be on a solo run at Seward Park. No one could vouch for him, but since the death was ruled a suicide there was no reason for further confirmation."

It's agreed that I will team with Allan, Eve, and Walt to investigate the Nguyen and Dorji families. I turn to my therapist colleagues. "Wayne wants something to work with, right quick. Are you still in?"

The response is immediate and unanimous. This is why I love them.

DAY ELEVEN

$$\bullet$$

After yesterday's intensity, the call of the garden is too powerful to ignore. However, the weeding I'd expected to do has been sidelined. I stand wide-legged on the grass, shovel over my shoulder, contemplating the dark shape lying near the shaggy pile of boxwood debris. In the background Willem tells Liz about our discovery.

"That is so bizarre," says Liz, approaching from behind. "It's been, what, a couple years since the first one, right?"

She and I approach the form, a dried out, leathery turtle carcass. "Yeah. It's buried beneath the cedar." I point at a neat rectangle of bricks in a back corner of the yard. "Only that one was fresh and juicy. This one's practically turtle jerky." We look skyward, searching for clues. "Maybe we're on some sort of bald eagle flight path," I say. "I mean, what else is big and strong enough to pick up a turtle? A hawk?"

"Maybe some sicko is chucking them into your yard from the road."

"Not aerodynamic enough to carry that far." I start digging a hole next to the old grave.

"You attract more than your share of weird shit. Have you called animal control? With this being the second time, maybe they'd investigate."

"Yeah, sure. Great way to put our tax dollars to work." I look down at the desiccated remains. "Another mystery. Just what I need."

Liz walks over to inspect the gaping space where the hedge once stood. The mid-morning sunshine releases the sweet fragrances of rock roses, lilacs, and lavender. The combination is a comfort as I scoop the mummy into the deep hole and shovel soil over it.

Liz rubs lavender leaves, sniffs the oil on her fingers. "Speaking of which, how're you feeling, my friend?"

"Burned out."

"You're not burned out."

"No? What am I then?" I say it in a way meant to warn.

I can feel her staring at my bent back. She says with cold finality, "You, my friend, are scared shitless."

I straighten up. "Fuck you."

"Well? Am I wrong?"

"Of course not." I stomp on the mound. "The *fuck you* was for noticing."

"It wasn't hard." Her reply is gentle. She waits a beat. "I can only guess at how much crap you're holding in. Uh uh, don't deny it. It's practically spilling out your ears."

"What the hell are you getting at?" She quails at the look I give her. It's quite gratifying.

We cover the grave with old bricks to discourage any marauding animals. I wedge the last one into place with my foot.

"I'm glad Rachel went to Paris with you," she says, "but she can be hard company. I just want to remind you that you can always talk to me."

She's avoiding eye contact. If Liz were a dog, her tail would be between her legs. Despondency doesn't suit her.

I say, "You're my best friend, not my therapist."

She twitches her shoulders back, cocks her head. There's my girl. "You can go on nodding sagely, spreading your Zen," she says. "But listen here, I'm pretty sick of you pretending you've got it all covered. You're coming apart at the seams. Come on, Jackie. Let it out. What's going on in your head?"

I can't remember her ever asking why I do what I do. It's what I've told myself I've always wanted, but now that it's happening, it feels so unnatural. I feel myself fading away and kick the brick. Hard. Time to do something different.

"You don't want to be in my head." I throw my work gloves onto the grass. "Since this started I've been going over every memory I have of Amy, and it's making me crazy. You know that ORB song, 'Chapter and Verse'? Amy wrote it after we talked about what it's like to be Asian, born with shame in our DNA." I regurgitate the lyrics.

"'I can recite chapter and verse every mistake
     I've ever made
And you know what's even worse is there's no way
     to make them fade
All attempts to move beyond are countered by
     my programming
Generations of regret hold fast and are
     my soul's damning.'"

"Fuck," says Liz. "It's more like 'Chapter and Worse.'"

"I should've become an accountant the way my mom wanted."

She elbows me. "You, a number cruncher?"

"Yeah, maybe not." I pull the golden head off a dandelion, wipe milk from the broken stalk onto my jeans. "Who the hell are we to mess with people's lives?" I crush the blossom in my fist; it releases a bitter scent. "What gives us the right? Look what happened. I mean, what if Amy and I had never met – would she be alive today?" I take the shovel and aim a vicious swipe at another dandelion. "I wouldn't wish this on anyone. On top of the personal hell, I'm causing misery for my nearest and dearest. Allan and Mohamed, too. And for what? Maybe Wayne's right, maybe I am nuts."

"Stop taking yourself so seriously. For one thing, maybe more people believe in you than you realize. Wayne took your case and is sticking with you, so that says something no matter how much you despise the guy. Which leads to your nearest and dearest; you're not causing us any misery that we don't choose to take on." She takes the shovel from me before I can annihilate more weeds. I want it back but she and her long arms keep it beyond my reach. "No, hear me out. Point number three: therapists don't mess with people's lives. Clients come to us for perspective, to learn they have what they need, and to figure out how to tap into it. Amy was incredibly gifted." Her speech slows as my breathing evens. "Frankly, her talent would've propelled her into the arts anyway. You nudged her along, but come on – in the vast scheme of things, we're minor blips on our clients' radar screens. As for second guessing yourself, join the club."

I'm surprised. Liz has always seemed so self-assured, even smug about her abilities, her knowledge of right and wrong.

"Therapists are human." She's reading my mind. "We all make mistakes; it's no good dwelling on past miseries. We have to forgive ourselves and keep in mind the good stuff. It's only fair."

My body sags. "Fair? What the hell is that? Amy Nguyen ended up with a bullet through her head. So did Zoe. Is that fair?"

"All we ask is that you be fair to yourself." Liz lifts my arms above my head to force a deep breath. I can't help smiling. She hugs me. "Don't be so pig-headed. Give this a chance. You can only do so much."

Be fair to myself? Forgive myself? What peculiar, foreign notions.

Amy couldn't sit still, constantly tapped her fingers on the swivel chair's armrests as she stared out the window, ignoring me. I took this as a sign of her abiding distrust and anxiety in my presence. The hospital's therapy requirements had been completed and, according to state law, she was old enough to direct her own treatment. She'd wanted to continue, but did *not* want her parents to know; they'd fought her therapy from the start. Amy couldn't pay so I'd offered her a pro bono slot. Not that there'd been much progress. My efforts to establish an easier relationship were obviously not working. Stubborn kid. One thing was for sure, I wasn't dragging her here every week. And I was tired of working so hard.

I sat silently, watching, mentally adding my name to the list of therapists that hadn't made the grade. Time to end this. Then movements that at first seemed nervously random took on a distinctly coordinated look.

"Do you play the piano?" I asked.

"Yeah." She sounded not only surprised, but suspicious. "How do you know?"

I gestured with my chin toward her ever-moving digits.

She gathered her fingers into fists, rubbed her thumbs back and forth against her knuckles.

"What're you working on?"

"Mozart. He's complicated."

"So I've heard." That was about all I knew about classical music. "How long have you been playing?"

"Since fifth grade." Five years.

"I didn't know you have a piano."

She turned red and muttered, "We don't. My parents don't know. You won't tell them, will you?"

What? How does a kid learn to play a musical instrument, especially one as big as a piano, without the parents knowing? Time to see if she was playing me.

"No, of course not. I only tell if someone's in danger or … How did you learn?"

She grabbed the stuffed snowy owl from the top of my bookcase, wrapped her hand around the beak, shook her head in rejection. Next she looped the four-foot-long python around her neck, quickly loosened it. She stroked the wolf, pulled her hand away from the coarse faux pelt, then settled on the ever faithful and dependable brown bunny.

"My fifth grade teacher kept an electronic keyboard in the classroom." Amy snuggled the bunny close, making her words hard to decipher. "I was messing around with it one day during rainy day lunch. She gave me lessons after school until I graduated."

"Wow, that's great. She must've seen some real promise in you."

Amy scowled. "It's not as if it was for free. I had to tidy up, put books away, clean the whiteboards, stuff like that."

"Sounds like a fair trade. And since then?"

Her eyes grew large at my apparent idiocy. "Middle schools and high schools have music programs."

I covered a smile by saying, "Yeah, but you can't take individual lessons there, or can you?"

"No." She flushed red again. "I go to my old teacher's house once a week. It's still not for free," she added quickly. "I mow her lawn and walk her dog."

"Another fair trade. Wait a sec. After all this time your parents still don't know?"

"Of course not. I'm not stupid."

No, Ms. Nguyen, you definitely are not. There's plenty I didn't tell my parents either, for what I could guess were exactly the same reasons. No need to drop the subject, though.

"They don't worry when you come home late?"

"They don't give a shit about me as long as I don't cause trouble. And I'm not about to get them to look my way."

I wiggled my fingers in the air. "Then if I were you, I'd watch out for unconscious keyboard fingers."

She dropped the rabbit into her lap, wiggled her fingers in response. "Yeah," she said before returning to silent mode.

Score one for me! That was the first time she'd positively acknowledged one of my offerings. That was one day made. It also meant I wasn't the first adult she'd corralled into helping her on the sly. I wondered how many more were out there. I hoped for dozens. And she was a compartmentalizer, a secret keeper. Hmmm, what else did she have to hide?

"Wait." Her body went rigid. "Does this mean I have to clean your office or something?"

"Of course not." She relaxed. "There is something I ask, though." She stiffened again. "Give this a chance." I gestured between us and received another *duh* expression for my pains.

"I'm here, aren't I?"

The Dorji residence is a typical 1970s split-level painted boring beige with a chocolate brown border. The camellias could use deadheading and the rhodies are rangy, but otherwise the yard's compact and tidy. Not bad for an immigrant widow on a housekeeper's salary. Amy must've paid well. Or maybe it was Kick's ORB money that bought it.

Allan and I are parked on the street, a few houses away. I have my doubts about anything happening.

"What if no one shows?" I ask.

"Stakeouts require patience. More coffee?" We've each already had a large latte, and the turkey sandwiches he supplied are gone.

"No, thanks." I don't want to have to pee. "So what did you used to do during long stakeouts to keep from going nuts?"

"Eve and I used to tell family stories. She has some doozies." He slides a sideways glance my way. "What you told me about your family." My guard is instantly up. "My granddad fought in Korea. He told a story or two." Lucky him. "After what you said about how your parents wouldn't talk, I couldn't stop thinking about it, how lucky I am that Granddad did."

"It's definitely a different approach to life. I hope you remember those stories, maybe even write them down. They're precious."

He stares out the windshield, but his eyes are unfocused. I can practically hear his grandfather's voice as Allan replays the stories in his head. I mark the time. One minute. Two.

He blinks, says, "You really don't remember any? Not a single one?"

"My mother is notorious for hinting at things she then vows to never talk about, and communication and sharing weren't Dad's strengths. My brother and I got bubkes."

"That's hard to imagine," he says. "But then I only know what I know." A polite pause. "Your parents didn't pass on any Korean heritage?"

Nosy bastard. He could be a therapist.

I strain to remember. It was hard enough to forget. "The entire point of our being here was to become American. I know Korean food names; that's about it. My dad told me a story once, though, a Korean fable." I lift a fresh cup of coffee from our dwindling supply. When, not if, I need a restroom, there's a Safeway within trotting distance.

"It wasn't long after my brother had died. I was still barely speaking to my parents. My dad had always been hard to predict, emotionally, psychologically. Since Matt's death, it was many times worse. I remember on this day Dad was in quite the singular mood, even for him. He was subdued, almost philosophical.

"I was watching TV when he came and sat next to me – again, something he did not ordinarily do. I don't remember where my mother was. Anyway, he sat down and announced he had a story for me, one that was important because it was from Korea and explained a lot."

"Sounds deep. Ominous, even."

"At the time it felt like both. There was nothing I wanted from him, least of all lame explanations or excuses."

"But something kept you listening. Now, looking back, what do you think he wanted you to know?"

"I'll tell you the story, then you tell me."

"Game on."

"All right." I put the coffee down, rub my hands together. "Back when tigers smoked – "

Allan's head comes up. "What?"

"That's the Korean *once-upon-a-time*."

He smiles in appreciation, and I begin again:

"Back when tigers smoked, Dog and Cat were the best of friends. They relied on each other and shared everything. Over time more animals arrived, forcing hard competition for food and living space. Dog and Cat's easy being evolved into a partnership for survival.

One day, Dog bounded back to their shelter. 'Cat, Cat,' he said, practically bursting with excitement, 'the birds are all atwitter. The king of all creatures knows of our plight and is setting a contest. In the unknown territories on the other side of the river, he has hidden an enormous cache of food. It is enough for a lifetime and will stay forever fresh. Whoever finds it first wins it all! The way will be long and perilous, but the birds who flew over the site discussed the location among themselves. Now *we* know! What do you think?'

Cat continued preening. 'You trust those pesky feathered things? They must've known you were listening and decided to do us a mischief. They hate me because I thin their numbers. If the story is true, they'll easily claim the prize.'

'No, no!' Dog insisted. 'The birds came upon this by chance. The contest will soon be announced, and birds are disqualified because flight is an unfair advantage. Besides, they already travel far and wide to feed themselves; they aren't starving like the rest of us.'

This was news indeed. But Cat, ever resistant to displays of over-excitement, took his time. He stretched and yawned. 'If we position ourselves for a head start, we'll have an excellent chance. But how will we cross the river, my friend? You know I don't swim.'

'You're the clever one. Come up with a plan.' Dog's mouth watered at the thought of stilling his stomach's constant rumbling.

Cat thought and thought, then finally said, 'You're right. Even if this is a trick, there's nothing left for us here. Here's what we'll do...'

They camped near the shortest river crossing and preserved their energy as they waited. When the king's contest was announced, the other animals were caught unawares. As they ran frantically about, lost in their desperation to prepare and depart, Dog calmly flexed his still-mighty muscles. He stretched, paws forward, head down, rear in the air. Cat climbed the ramp of Dog's back and carefully balanced. Dog stepped into the frigid water and began the arduous swim.

After struggling to the middle of the river, he grunted, 'Cat, you are heavier than you look, and the current is hard to fight. When we reach the other side, I will need rest. You must race ahead and claim the reward on both our behalves.'

'Don't worry, my friend,' said Cat. 'All will go according to plan. Now stop talking and concentrate. I'm getting wet.'

'I am an expert swimmer,' said Dog. 'You, though, could be a more considerate passenger. Sheathe your claws!'

'Your back is slippery and the water is cold. Stop thrashing!'

Suddenly, Cat fell into the river with a mighty splash.

'Cat! Cat!' Dog dove, desperate to save his friend; however, he saw nothing except the water's turbulence as it pulled him downstream. It took Dog's last strength to make it to the far shore. He howled in sorrow at the death of his dear friend, and cried himself to sleep.

Upon waking Dog heard the sounds of other animals making their ways across the river. 'I must complete our mission,' he said to himself, 'if only for brave Cat's sake.'

He took off running, following the course the birds had described. Yes, there were the landmarks. Ha ha, yes! He avoided this trap and that misdirection. Finally, there it was, a mountain of the most delectable grub! And yes! There was Cat, lying atop the lifelong feast, happily combing the fur of his distended belly.

'Cat!' cried Dog, 'I'm overjoyed to see you! As you promised, all has gone according to plan. You have claimed the prize for us both. I am hungry, so hungry. Move aside and let me eat.'

'I'm terribly sorry, friend Dog,' Cat purred. 'The rules were very clear. Only the first to arrive claims the prize. I'm afraid you must remain hungry.'

'But what am I to do? I will starve.' Dog ran in crazy circles, chasing his tail in despair.

'There are new creatures on this side of the river. Humans, they call themselves. They seem rather stupid, but they have plenty to eat. Make friends with them; perhaps they will feed you.'

Dog was devastated. 'I have no choice and will do as you say. But Cat, you must first tell me – I tried to save you, but you were gone. How did you survive?'

Cat cleaned his whiskers. 'I didn't appreciate the dunkings you gave me, so I slipped off your back and swam to shore.'

'But Cat, you can't swim!'

'No, I heartily dislike getting wet so, since meeting you, I *don't* swim.'

And this is why Dog chases Cat."

"Quite the story," says Allan.

I shrug. "You asked what I thought my father wanted me to know. Besides contemplating what would feed every type of animal, my ultimate teenaged takeaway was that you should never trust anyone. Now I wonder."

"Wonder what?"

"Given what had just happened with my brother, I wonder what Dad was saying about who he felt more akin to, Dog or Cat. What do you think?"

Allan has a faraway look. "Maybe both." He straightens, his voice is hollow. "Maybe he was talking about Matt."

I'm hit with a shiver. "Maybe. We live in an and world. There's yin and yang in each of us. When pushed to our utmost limits, we each have to choose." I take a deep breath. "Bah. Lately my dad's voice and his frickin' story have been stuck in my head."

"What do you think *that* means?"

"I'm not sure yet." I store the question away for the future. Time to pivot. "From what Liz has said, your mom loved stories too."

"Yes, she would read stories to me. Zoe, on the other hand, had lots of family stories and a great imagination. In fact, she kept a story journal. I haven't been able to read it yet." He turns his back to me, pretends to find something interesting out the window.

"What a special thing to have waiting for you."

Allan clears his throat. "I heard you had to deal with your brother's death by yourself. That must've been rough."

At first I'm appalled at Liz's freedom with my particulars. But then, what did I expect and what does it matter? It's all in the family. I say, "What made it even harder was that it was totally unexpected. Though maybe it shouldn't have been."

Silence. After a minute or twenty I say, "I had something special to remember Matt by, too. In college I used the backpack he carried all through high school. It was a constant reminder, a motivator to make the most out of my life."

"That sounds kind of miserable." Allan's still staring out the window.

"Part of my grieving process," I say. "Misery is definitely one of the ways I kept Matt close. However, it was also a comfort, depending on my mood and attitude. The danger was in letting it become a constant companion."

He holds his right hand in his left as if cradling a wound. "I get that. There's comfort waking up every morning with the same wrench in my gut that I fell asleep with."

He and I have something in common. The major men in my life, Willem being the exception, have all left me. The major women in Allan's life, Liz being the exception, have all left him. The difference is that Allan lived through what I only feared with Willem.

Another long silence, this time companionable, until a car pulls into the Dorji's driveway. Allan and I slide down in our seats to be less visible.

A dark-haired man emerges from the rear of the vehicle, opens the front passenger door. He helps an older woman, whom I assume to be Dawa Dorji, extract herself. The driver, Kick, circles around to join them. The man lays his arm across Kick's shoulders. She slips her hand into the back pocket of the man's chinos. They follow Mrs. Dorji into the house.

As the man closes the front door, we catch a fleeting glimpse of his face. It's enough.

A light, surprisingly warm breeze flits through the kitchen where Allan and I have been huddled. Plan in place, we head next door to talk with Natasha. I'm not pleased to have my daughter on the hot seat, especially without warning.

I begin. "Tash, when are you meeting with Mohamed again?"

"We're having dinner tonight. First he's taking some design ideas to his folks then meeting with the band. He said to call if you need him. Do you need him?"

"No, we're actually here to talk with you."

"Sure. What's up?" She leans back in anticipation.

I let Allan continue. He says, "Natasha, we need to clear something up. A theory's been floated that there's more than a working relationship between Mohamed and Sam Reyes. Your mother thought you'd be able to help us."

Natasha spins in my direction. "Why, Mom? We've already gone over this."

"Tasha, we're investigating a murder," I sputter. "We don't know who to believe. Help us believe Mohamed."

"Is he a suspect?"

"Not yet," says Allan, "but we're looking at a possible motive."

Tasha tightens. "What he told me was in confidence, friend to friend."

"I understand you're working for him and his family," Allan counters.

"Yes, and?"

"Do you see?" I say. "He hired you knowing you'd give him close, personal attention. This was the same reason ORB hired Sam. If it turns out their relationship is a little too personal…"

"This is ridiculous. Mom, you're no homophobe."

"This has nothing to do with his sexuality. It's about how he is in relationships. We all care about Mohamed, but with everything happening so fast it's easy to forget we've only known him a short while." I've had Natasha wait on the sidelines until now; pulling her in like this feels dirty, dishonest. "He's the link to a lot of our investigation, which means he can sway things depending on what he says and how believable it is. We need to know how much we can trust him."

"You just said he's not a suspect."

I want to introduce this as gently as possible but there's a risk in being too vague. "From what we know, Amy came back mid-tour intent on exhuming family skeletons. What if Mohamed was afraid of which skeletons were exposed? They presented themselves to the public as a couple. He told us himself Amy was planning on coming out in a public venue, maybe even during the ORBit tour. What if he thought that meant outing him at the same time? What if he felt the need to guard himself? Who would he turn to for help?"

It's a relief to see Tasha's shoulders gradually lower. "He'd turn to a friend." She looks toward Allan. "Do you think he's telling the truth?"

"Sam is connected to both Amy's best friend and her half-sister. They each had reasons to want Amy's secrets to stay that way. We only have Mohamed's word that Sam's people weren't watching Amy when she came back to Seattle. We also know that Mohamed's been misleading us in other ways."

I cut off Tasha's response. "Mohamed told me that Kick Dorji's mother didn't like Amy and wanted Kick to leave the band. Earlier today Allan and I saw both her and her mom with Bill Nguyen. Kick and Bill are a couple, and Dawa Dorji has no problem with it. How does that jive with what Mohamed said?" Natasha's face blanches. "Tash, until this is ironed out, you need to be careful."

"I'm your daughter," she says. "I'm always careful."

Eyes closed and feet up; shameless eavesdropping made effortless. Those two sound so easy with one another. Natasha's self-assurance continuously surprises and impresses me. The difference one generation can make.

Tasha's voice comes from the kitchen where she and Allan are loading the dishwasher. "World War II was different for my dad's family because, being Swiss, they were never in danger of invasion or losing their lives." Allan's reply is a muffled rumble with a question mark at the end.

"Yeah, my friends used to be jealous because we spent every summer in the Alps. They couldn't understand that we weren't gallivanting around Europe. It was family duty; Stef and I spent our vacations working on the farm. It was our equivalent of visiting relatives in Puyallup."

"Better scenery, I'll bet." His head must be out of the dishwasher.

"Who cares about the view when you're cutting hay by hand? That was a party, let me tell you. But it did teach us one practical life skill. We're all good with a scythe."

There's a deep chuckle. That's the first time I can remember ever hearing Allan laugh. "What about the Korean side?"

"Don't know much about it. I do know it tends to be on the woo-woo spectrum."

"The what?"

"Traditional Koreans, at least the ones I know, cling to their superstitions. Take my great-grandmother. Every year she hired the village shaman to chase evil spirits out of the house. And there's family lore of strange things happening, especially premonitions that came true. It happened to me once and taught me to trust my gut. Speaking of which, I'm quite the fan of Korean food. That's the part I know best."

Now I'm regretting my decision to listen in. Shit. The only Korean elements Tasha connects with are superstition and the cuisine. She's my daughter, all right. I head outside, suddenly in need of fresh air. Too bad we don't have another spare hedge.

Oh, this can't be good. Mrs. Dobbs only talks to me to complain.

"Mrs. Kessler," she says, waving at me from the middle of the street. "I have something to discuss."

"Good evening, Mrs. Dobbs. How can I be of assistance?"

"A lot of strangers have been coming and going lately."

"You don't say."

"Yes, I do say, and I don't like it. I'm taking down license plates."

"Why are you telling me?"

"Some of those people look suspicious, and they knock on your door. Have you started some sort of charity?"

Lady, if I started a charity it'd be a program to combat willful ignorance, and you'd be first on the list of prospective enrollees.

"Mrs. Dobbs, are you spying on me and my visitors?" Of course you are.

"I want you to know that if there's any criminal activity, even a *hint*, I'll turn those people in to the police. They don't belong here." The old biddy. She means Mohamed.

"Mrs. Dobbs, if it will reassure you, please show me your list and I'll vouch for the owners."

The hand-drawn chart records license numbers, colors, and makes, plus the dates and times they were parked on the street. Her penmanship is as crabby as she is. She hands me a freshly sharpened red pencil to make check marks validating each vehicle's presence. RAJE is there, as is Allan. Two entries are starred. The first of these, of course, is Mohamed's. It can't be his thoroughly respectable Tesla she objects to; it must be his black body. I bite my lip at number two. Eve and Walt will have to pay her a visit; it seems their beat up Jeep screams *criminal element*.

A couple entries aren't familiar. Sam's people? Now I'm getting paranoid. I need to run this past Allan.

"Mrs. Dobbs, may I please hang onto this for a day or two? I'll return it as soon as possible."

The sound of a car slowly rumbles toward us and Mrs. Dobbs's arthritic forefinger points down the street. "There's that one back again, too," she says. "That man drives like he's up to no good."

It's probably nothing but I watch anyway, curious to know what up-to-no-good driving looks like. Oh my. She's right. The car approaches slowly, suspiciously. Then the driver sees us watching, her pointing. He turns his head and uses the sun visor to keep his face out of view. The car speeds up and turns at the corner.

"That one isn't on your list."

"It didn't park," she says, slightly defensively. "But it drove past, just like that, only yesterday."

Oh, Mrs. Dobbs, I could kiss you.

"Well, we should definitely add that one. Let me." I quickly scribble the license plate number, add a star, and run to get Allan. We just found ourselves a scrubby yellow Honda with a shark-toothed grille.

DAY TWELVE

L ast night the Connellys made the Honda hunt their top priority. This morning Allan and I address our to-do list. We agree that Bill Nguyen is the most elusive and, based on recent revelations, most intriguing member of the Nguyen clan. Allan's idea is to call the law offices of Meldon, Moore & Flores to see what we can ferret out.

He says, "If a woman answers, I'm on. If it's a man, it's all yours."

"You expect me to charm some potentially young thing? I don't have that kind of charisma. Face it; I sound like the middle-aged lady I am."

"You have another suggestion?"

As a matter of fact, I do. Natasha was on both her high school and college improv teams.

The call's on speaker phone. "I'm sorry, but Mr. Nguyen is no longer with the firm." The male receptionist's voice is bright and energetic.

It's been a long time since I've seen Tash perform. She goes full throttle. I stifle a giggle.

"Really?" she says with Marilyn Monroe breathlessness. "That's too bad. Bill and I are … *friends* from school. When we reconnected last year he gave me this number and said when I got back to town he'd give me a tour. See, I'm considering the legal profession and he told me good things about your firm."

"Oh, well, any *friend* of Bill's is a *friend* of mine." We all roll our eyes. "You didn't miss him by much; he quit not long ago. He told me being here helped him in a big way, though. He figured out that lawyering isn't for him."

"Oh, that *would* be good to know."

She's laying it on a bit thick. I shake my head at her; she waves me off.

"Yeah, right?" he says. Tash flashes me a told-you-so grin. "I wasn't surprised, though. I mean, everyone here is driven. Bill just didn't seem to be that into the work, you know? No ambition. Unlike myself. You said you saw him last year? That must've been during his leave of absence."

Allan scribbles a quick note, shoves it at Natasha, who reads it quickly. "No," she says, "we reconnected on-line. He didn't mention taking time off."

"That's Bill all right, really private. Like I didn't know for the longest time Amy Nguyen was his sister. It sucked, what happened to her."

"Yeah, right? Is that why he took that leave, because she died?"

"No, it was before. He took time off again after, of course, but he didn't want to talk about it."

Allan writes another note. Tasha nods.

"No, who would. Remind me, when did his leave start?"

"Hold on a sec; I'll look it up. You know, since you're in town, I'd be happy to give you that tour."

Tasha artfully sidesteps the invitation and ends the call. We calculate back. Bill Nguyen's leave of absence started two days after ORB's European tour began, eight days before his sister's death.

"What makes this vegan?" Angie regards the plate of warm banana bread with suspicion.

"No butter. There's olive oil and macadamia milk instead." I force a slice onto my skeptical friend.

"I like butter."

"Too bad. Willem and I are eating healthier. There's ground flax seed in it too."

"Flax seed. That's supposed to make it okay?" Angie takes a reluctant nibble, chews thoughtfully, swallows. When it doesn't come up again, she takes a larger, more enthusiastic bite. "What's for lunch, beet burgers?"

"We'll never eat that healthy."

Walt brings us to order. "One thread we were following has been resolved. Thanks to Jackie, we nabbed the driver of a certain yellow Honda who was also the author of certain letters." Mohamed is clenching his hands in his lap. "Turned out to be a barista at Beancounters. For years he's been in a band that can't land a recording contract, let alone a decent gig. At one audition they were told they were no ORB. He took that very personally."

Mohamed lifts a hand. "We're most thankful."

It's difficult to look at him directly; I don't want him to see my concern. My gut tells me he's sincere, but with suspicion still whirling, I'm not sure how much to trust my instincts. New mantra: *Innocent until proven guilty. Innocent until proven guilty.* Hmm… Mohamed or me? I guess it can do double duty.

And even though he hadn't meant it to, Mohamed's idea to revisit Beancounters got things moving. No one trying to stymie our investigation would do that on purpose. Replacement mantra: *Innocent and on the same side.*

I lean toward Mohamed. He locks his long fingers with mine, gives a squeeze. I say, "That's a huge relief. We can thank Mrs. Dobbs. The other loaf of banana bread is for her."

"Offering her treats?" says Tasha. "She'll think you're trying to kill her."

Even that poor old bat ended up helping. One never knows. A fresh wave of energy floods me, head to toe.

"Another issue has also been resolved," says Eve. "All of Sam's people have been accounted for, and Mireille's also in the clear."

Allan had already told me. With this reassurance, I had given him the green light to recruit Sam for one last assignment.

Allan stands before the whiteboard, wipes *Sam* and *Mireille* from the list of suspects. "This is what we have so far." He erases *Fan*. "Given what we know, this doesn't fit." *Intruder* is the next to go. "There was no sign of a break-in or struggle." The only remaining suspect listings are *Family* and *Friend*.

I step to the board and use the side of my hand to wipe *Suicide* off the motive list, leaving only two, *Finances* and *Hate Crime*. I add *Lover* and say, "This is something we haven't even mentioned. Mohamed, what do you think?"

"Amy's energies went into her music."

After what happened with Kick's mother, I'm sure they did. But there was that unknown woman. I phrase my question in collectivist-speak. "Yes, romance would be difficult."

A noncommittal sound rumbles at the base of Mohamed's throat; the sphinx look reappears. Eve steps in. "We have no reason to suspect her guest," she says crisply.

Not so unknown after all. Looks like the Connellys already know about whoever-she-is and have cleared her. Yet another piece I didn't know about. That category could fill a whole new whiteboard. No, it's good enough that *Lover* disappears from this one.

Allan's cell phone vibrates on the table. He glances at the caller ID and answers immediately.

"Where are you? Be right there." He turns to us, smiling. "Sam helped us take a closer look at Colonel McMillan."

Allan nods to Walt. They leave the room; Allan returns with Sam Reyes in tow. Introductions are made. There's a strangeness floating through the room, a mix of wonder, suspicion, relief, exhaustion.

Mohamed sits up expectantly as Sam's voice fills the void. "My contact at the Pentagon found a report that mentioned the death of one of the colonel's Vietnamese liaisons, Captain Duong Thanh. The captain and his aide, Corporal Le Dai, were traveling between command posts when their jeep was shelled. Duong died at the scene. The corporal was severely injured, but survived. Duong had a family, a wife and daughter."

"Amy's mother and sister," I say, disappointed. "We already know that."

"Here's something you may not know," says Sam. "McMillan was supposed to be with them but bowed out at the last moment without explanation. In his debrief, Le claimed McMillan must have been forewarned of the danger. Why else would he change his plans so suddenly? By saying nothing he sent them on a suicide mission. A subsequent investigation found no evidence to support the accusation, and McMillan was cleared."

I ask, "What do you think, Sam?" He gives a noncommittal shrug. No surprise. The colonel was his father's CEO, after all. The fact that he says nothing, though, says enough.

"Do we know what became of the corporal?" asks Willem.

"He was not evacuated when Saigon fell," Sam replies. "I don't know if or how he survived."

"How is Madame Gastoneau doing with this news?" I ask.

A familiar female, French-accented voice replies from the hallway: "I've long known my father to be flawed." Mireille

and Walt step into view. "But this has been particularly difficult, as you can imagine. At least I now know the truth, and I
must make my peace with it."

"Madame Gastoneau," I say, rising. "Welcome."

"Please," she says, grasping my hands, "call me Mireille."

Sam moves to her side, slips his arm around her waist.
Mohamed's shoulders slump and his face turns to the wall.
My heart hurts for him.

"Next steps?" asks Willem.

Allan rubs his chin. "A plus B equals C," he says. "Time to
put it all together and find us a murderer."

That's right. We're after Amy's murderer. In the pause that
follows, I consider the remaining list of suspects and motives
and tap into my considerable store of rage.

I say, "Amy was killed in her home, her sanctuary. Only
her inner circle would be allowed there, and those closest to
her were collectivists." I give a quick and dirty review of collectivism and individualism for the newest members of the
team, and conclude with: "So far linear logic – A plus B
equals C – has worked, but it may not apply any further."

"Explain," says Walt.

"In situations like this you can't add A and B without considering elements L through Q. Which to include depends on
other variables you may not even know about. So it's best to
make educated guesses, keep your expectations low, your
eyes open, and your mouth shut."

"Okay," says Rachel, "that made no sense at all. To go
with Willem, what's next?"

"I get what you're saying, Jackie." Liz's head is down,
cocked to the side. "We're still minus a motive. To find
Amy's murderer we have to think differently, not like indi-
vidualists. We're looking at relationship but need to look both
deeper and broader, at all the ripple effects of relationship."

"At relationship to relationship," offers Angie.

My friends are brilliant. A shiver literally goes up my spine as another message in Dad's fable becomes clear. The story was both apology and sympathetic warning: *We can't control how loved ones leave us. What we can and must control is our reaction.*

Another piece of ancient bitterness dissolves.

I take a cleansing breath and say, "Now that's collectivist thinking."

Angie is back at the whiteboard. "What else goes here?" she asks, pointing to the short list of motives.

Liz calls out, "Jealousy." Angie adds it in her clear, flowing hand, a holdover from her days as a fourth grade teacher.

"Greed," suggests Rachel. Angie taps *Finances*. Rachel blushes and recedes into the sofa cushions.

"Shame," I say. "It's the main way collectivists keep each other in line."

Liz chimes in again. "What was it you said Amy used to say? 'Mysteries and secrets and lies, lies, lies?'"

"Yeah, add that too, please."

Tasha, who has been observing quietly, adds her bit. "Desperation."

"Please expound," says Eve.

Natasha smiles semi-apologetically at Willem and me. "Sometimes it's camouflaged, but in literally all her music is the piece about not fitting in. I've felt that way too. There are times when you don't know who you are or where you belong."

Rachel rocks forward in her seat. "Nothing makes sense. That makes you desperate for some way to feel like you have some control, some say over your own destiny."

"Yes, that's it," says Tasha. "Like you said, Mom, Amy's desperation fueled her art."

"And if Amy felt that way," says Allan, "who else close to her did, and what did they do about it?"

The image of Amy with a gun in her hands still doesn't fit. I take a page from her former playbook and produce two stick-figure sketches. The first portrays a humanoid shape, a pistol in its hands, standing over another humanoid lying on the ground in a small pool of blood. The second has the gun-toting figure aiming at a distant bullseye. Though the drawings bear little resemblance to their subjects, they're enough to remind me that Amy's favored mode of communication was symbolism embedded in her art.

Words and objects mean different things to different people depending on context. What could a pistol have meant to her? In one context it's a source of death and destruction, something she abhorred and would never touch. I can believe she'd never turn one against a living being, not even in self-defense. In another context, a gun was something she readily reached for, a source of stress relief, perhaps even recreation. I can see her appreciating, even savoring, the irony.

My original purpose this afternoon had been to scold her. I'm relieved to let that go. She hadn't lied to me.

"Hey, Amy," I say. "I brought a friend." I clear a place for the old stuffed bunny at the foot of her grave.

An echo swirls in on the breeze: *Whoa, Doc, that's not right. C'mon. Think again.*

Footsteps. Shit. I quickly return the toy to my bag. That woman is back. She nods at me. She looks to have aged since we last met. Was it really less than two weeks ago?

"Good morning," I say. "We meet again."

"Hello," she answers. She makes a move toward the grave of the wife, mother, and grandmother, thinks better of it, looks up at me with a shrug. It's a very familiar move. I make space for her, and she arranges her daisies at Amy's grave.

Birdsong fills the lengthy pause. "Do you know who I am?" Her voice is just above a whisper.

I look deeply into Amy's eyes. "You're Martha."

Her mouth sets in a tight line. "Why do you come?" Her plaintiveness echoes Amy at her most doubtful.

I look beyond her ear, catch sight of downtown. The tops of the skyscrapers are still swathed in fog. "You may find it hard to believe, but I was truly fond of your sister. I miss her."

Martha's face softens; however, her eyes remain suspicious. "I wondered, the first time I saw you. When I saw you again, I knew. And now you're here once more."

I shake my head, turn to leave. "We shouldn't be talking." Wayne would pitch a fit.

Martha speaks rapidly, urgently. "I know you didn't want anything bad to happen, but I know what is true. I am the one who found her. It was horrible, horrible. But no one could know what she would do. Not even I. I want you to know I forgive you."

"I appreciate you saying that," I say, suppressing harsher words, "but I don't feel the need to be forgiven." I turn to go again and feel a surprisingly firm grip on my arm.

"Wait. That was wrong. I know we shouldn't be together, but I wanted to meet you. You know, she wanted me to find someone like you. There was a time I wanted it to be you, but she wouldn't share." When I remain silent, Martha continues, her voice urgent. "I can help you accept the truth. When I found her, she was dead, on the floor. There was a letter."

I startle. "This is the first I've heard of a suicide note."

"This was not news to share," she says. "We – her family – we know. It's no one else's business. My mother wanted to burn it, but I keep it. I found it; it's mine."

My mind can't comprehend. I think of the time and effort so many people have poured into the investigation. "If this is true then I did miss something. It's all been a waste."

"Not a waste," Martha says, misinterpreting. "If Amy hadn't met you, she would have killed herself much earlier."

"Would you say that in court?"

"No. You see, it's also possible that if she hadn't met you, she would have learned to be content with what she was. You made her think wrong things."

I stand dazed and uncertain with my mouth hanging open. I think of other clients who've been on the edge. Taneesha. Devon. My goals for them have always included thinking for themselves. Amy did that from the start. All I did was help her challenge and stretch her thinking.

I square my shoulders, root myself into the ground. "No. I asked questions. The answers she came up with were hers."

Martha unzips an inner compartment of her handbag to retrieve a plain, letter-sized envelope. From this she extracts a sheet of paper and carefully unfolds it. The lines on it are written in Amy's precise hand with her favorite utensil, an ultrafine Sharpie, this time brown. Two words, a third of the way down, are thickly circled in purple.

"My sister's last decision. For me to find." The bitterness in Martha's voice is surprising. She grips her hair in her fist and tugs, another gesture reminiscent of Amy. "You see. All about her. Her pain. She was selfish like that because she didn't understand. What did she know of suffering? She was born in this country. She didn't know the war, the camp. She didn't know how good her life was. Complaining, feeling sorry for herself. She was good at that. This was the reason she left us behind." She shakes the page before handing it to me.

I gulp cool morning air along with the poem's closing words: "I lay myself down, I've done what I can / fate calls me to be a sacrificial lamb"

"I'm so sorry for what you've had to go through," I say quietly, "but you're wrong. I have this too, 'Sacrificial Lamb.' She wrote it when she was in college. It wasn't about herself. It was her tribute to you."

I return the page to Martha. Her face flushes red, defiant.

"What do you say?"

I no longer care. Holding so many secrets is exhausting, and I'm sure Amy would want me to reveal this one now. "She felt bad. She knew you were keeping things back to protect her."

"What things?"

"Early on she was convinced you were her mother."

"I? Her mother? That's crazy! It's not true!"

I reach out to reassure her. "She came to accept that, but as a teenager she looked for anything she could hold onto. This explained why her parents were so ashamed of her. And why you always took care of her, defending her from both of them. She felt you were more a mother to her than a sister."

Martha hugs herself. I continue cautiously. "When she gave up that dream, what you did meant even more to her, caring for your parents so she and your brother could have a chance at their own lives. She said you carried the burden with grace, but she was worried about how long you'd be able to survive before it crushed you. That's one of the reasons she was determined to succeed. She wanted to be able to help you, so you would be spared."

Martha's face freezes. "She felt bad for me." She holds the poem as if it might burst into flames. "I didn't want her pity. She should have pitied herself. She is the one who is dead."

A slow, loud breath. "I don't think it was pity. I think it was guilt."

"Guilt? Even worse. She was always good at making things up, twisting things. What was she guilty of? She tried to take responsibility for everything. She was not so important. Stupid girl!" She rounds on me. "You lie. Why would you say these things?"

"It's the truth. Maybe this is how I can help you." I fight the impulse to touch her hand. "This poem was important to Amy, important enough that she shared it with me. She planned on showing it to you someday, but not until the story was complete."

"Story?"

"She felt there were a lot of mysteries and empty spaces dividing the three of you – you, her, and your mother. First she wanted to know and understand."

"She showed you!"

"Yes, because I was her therapist. She knew I'd keep it private. You were her hero. This poem is about your life, your survival, not her death. I do have a poem she wrote about herself. It's a partner to this one. It's about determination and hope, things she said she learned from you."

"I must see it."

"It's at my office. Can you come?"

"I will come tonight." Martha's face is strained. "I know now how much she meant to you. I will do what I can."

"Thank you, Martha. Everything Amy told me about you is true."

"What are you doing meeting with that woman?" Willem takes my forearm, stopping me at the door. "Maybe she's trying to trick you. You don't know whose side she's really on."

He has to stabilize himself against the doorjamb, and I want to cry. I hate to put him through this, but it's something I must do. "No, I don't. But I'm willing to trust her until she proves the opposite."

"You are sometimes too trusting of the wrong people. The world is full of assholes."

"Not everyone's an asshole. I choose to cling to the belief that mankind is basically good."

"Yes," says Willem, "you keep hoping that. People can be basically good and still act like shits when it suits them. Call her and cancel."

"I don't have her number."

He reaches heavenward. "*Ogottogott*! I will be there. When is she coming?"

"No. You haven't had a chance to rest in days. Remember," I poke him in the chest, "we need to get you better and back to work ASAP. We might really need the money. Don't give me that look, and don't worry. I'll be fine. Besides, I won't be alone; it's Erica's long day. And Martha's tiny. If anything happens," I say in a playful manner I don't feel, "I can take her."

"Just be careful."

"I'm my mother's daughter and my daughter's mother. I'm always careful."

Willem gathers me into his arms and kisses the top of my head. "*Dummes Weib. Schade, dass ich dich so lieb habe.*"

"Yeah, too bad for you. You're stuck with me."

I compulsively reposition the two sheets of paper lying face down on my desk. There's a light knock at my open door.

Erica peeks in. "Hey. My seven o'clock cancelled, so I'm outta here. You're the last."

"Okay. I only have one more."

"Yeah, she's here. I'll lock up on my way out."

"Thanks. Have a good night."

"You too."

The front door opens and closes. I check my reflection in the mirror and smile to reenergize. I roll my shoulders back, breathe deeply in and out, and head down the hallway.

Martha stands motionless in the center of the room, head bowed, hands hanging at her sides. Once in my office she refuses a seat, remains standing rigidly near the door.

I lift my copy of 'Sacrificial Lamb' from the desk. "Here. You can see when she gave it to me." I point to the signature and date at the bottom.

"For me, because of my suffering," she says, disgusted.

"Believe me, it was her way of honoring you. She cherished you. And here." I offer her the second sheet of paper from my hand. "This is the partner poem. It shows that she was dedicated to life. She wouldn't have killed herself."

Martha reads, shivers with realization. "You have told the truth."

Relief bursts through my system, as welcome and cleansing as a thunderstorm after days of oppressive heat. She just gave me an in. How best to get her to cooperate? I don't want to scare her off. And Willem's caution remains in my ear. Best not to tell her how far we've already come.

"I'm so glad you see it. Please, talk with your family. We can work together instead of fighting in court. We can go to the police and have them reopen the investigation. We need to know who killed her."

I step toward her, my arm outstretched. She backs away.

"No. There is no need. It is best this way."

"Don't you understand? Your sister was murdered. Don't you want justice?"

"No one has to know our secrets," she replies, her voice flat. "There is no purpose in that. Only shame."

"There's no shame in finding a killer. Aren't you tired of secrecy and shame ruling your life? That's why she had to leave. She hoped to live a different way."

Martha's breath comes fast and shallow. "Her hopes were empty, like her words. She was a stupid little girl. Stupid and selfish, thinking only of herself. Like her father." She tears the papers apart; the shreds float to the ground.

I feel curiously detached, aware of myself watching her. "Her father did a dishonorable thing."

"He was a dishonorable man. Selfish. A liar." She paces, head down, her hands in tight fists. "It was because of him that *my* father was killed. My father, who trusted foolishly. Without protection, my mother could not fight him. Like David, he looked upon her and lusted. Like David, he killed another to take what he wished."

King David's treachery haunts us, plotting the death of Uriah the Hittite in order to take Bathsheba as his own.

I keep my voice calm and level. "I learned that he was repentant for what he'd done."

"If this is true, why did he leave us to suffer for so long? He broke his promises."

Their mother had written: *This you owe us.*

"Because of him," she says in a voice like steel, "my life, my mother's. We were ruined."

"Ruined. You explained this to Amy?"

"Yes, we explained all. It was time. I hoped it would bring her back to us."

She startles at the sound of the wind catching the old maple's branches, scraping them against the window pane.

I say, "She was bitter, not knowing."

"She was bitter, yet she was the one who was spared. She didn't know what it took to come to this country. She didn't care."

"She knew you made many sacrifices."

"All her life I told her that to survive, one must sacrifice. But it wasn't enough. That day, she demanded to know what we had given. She couldn't see that we gave nothing. All had been taken." She rocks back and forth. "The Americans ran for their lives. We were pushed out of the way and they left us behind. The communists were coming. They would have killed us. My father's man found us. His family hid us until he healed. It was he who arranged our escape."

"You all possessed great courage."

"On the water were bad men." Her voice takes on the sing-song quality of a child's, as if reciting a long-remembered nursery rhyme. "He fought them, but there were too many. His face was red and they threw him into the water and he floated away until he sank. I was frightened and began to cry. One of them pushed me down and tore my clothes. I heard my mother's voice. She cried and begged. They hit her and pushed her down. They hurt her then they did the same to me. I was only a little girl."

She opens her hands and holds them out to me, bewildered and pathetic, oblivious to the blood seeping from the wounds her fingernails cut into her palms. Tears trace the curve of her cheekbones.

"Sacrifice. What did she know of sacrifice and suffering? She told me to marry, to live my own life. She did not know how I was ruined. What man could I go to, I who cannot bear a man's touch? What life could I have? And I can never leave my mother, she who sacrificed everything for me."

She hugs herself again, smearing blood on her sleeves. The tears have dried.

"I hope she understood."

"She refused to listen, refused to return to us. She said she would leave forever and take him with her."

"She wanted to save him as she wanted to save you."

"He worked hard and became a lawyer, but he was unhappy. She told him to stop because the only important thing was to be happy. This she learned from you, and you were wrong. The only important thing is to care for your family."

Her stare is cobra-like, hypnotic, locking me in place.

I say, "Happiness can't be trusted. Safety and security in one's family is the most important thing. I learned this from my parents. They also survived war and nearly starved before coming here."

I sway with her.

"If you know the truth, why did you take her away?"

"I didn't take her away. When we met, she had just tried to kill herself. You found her. You saved her. I was trying to help you keep her alive."

"You told her we were bad."

"No. Never. That would be the same as saying my parents were bad, and that would be a lie. My parents sacrificed as yours did. They did everything out of love."

"Was it enough? Did you stay or did you go?"

There's no need to answer; she already knows. We slowly circle in tandem, my head filled with the scratch of branches on glass.

"She listened to me, she followed me until she met you. Then she began looking other places and doing other things. She taught him to follow her." She draws no breath; her words are a constant stream. "As my father died, his man gave his promise to protect us. He was killed because he did this. Once again we were alone. When the American came, again my mother could not refuse. Again, he lied and left us. To hide her shame my mother made a bargain with a man she did not love. For what? To give a name to the daughter of my father's murderer? But in this, my sister was the innocent one so I loved her. Then she grew and her blood showed, and she turned against us."

"You had to stop her."

"Yes. I went to her and begged her to make our brother fulfill his duty. She refused. I had to stop her before it was too late, before he became like her and her father, with no honor."

"You won. Your brother accused me."

"No. He tried to change their minds and they turned their backs on him. He then had to prove himself."

"He knew you killed her?"

"I didn't kill her. You did. She listened to you. Without you, she would have returned to us and done what was right."

I nearly collapse. Could this be true? Our dance is dizzying, disorienting, dividing me from reality. I will myself to find the answer. To claim it, I say it out loud. "No. She would have been dead at fifteen."

"The same ending, only we would have found peace and he would have learned. But it didn't happen that way; that is why she had to die. Now there can be no peace."

She extends her hands to me once more, as if asking me to fill them. At this moment she beholds her bloodied palms, and I break toward the door. She moves just as quickly and grabs my arm, twists me to face her, slaps me hard. I pull her hair, yanking her head down and away. I'm reaching for the doorknob when she hauls me back, grabbing hold from behind. She clasps me around the chest, pinning my arms to my body. Her mouth is beside my ear as she breathes, "I'm sorry to do this. I don't want to, but you make me."

I twist to wrench myself free, but she holds me too tightly.

Instinct and outrage take over. I flex my elbows, jerking my arms upward, breaking her grip. Grabbing her thumbs, I yank them in opposing directions. They snap into unnatural angles. She gasps. I spin and aim a mighty kick at her knee, but she anticipates the move.

My foot meets empty air, and I teeter off balance. There's a shove and a shattering crash as my head smacks soundly against the wooden floor. She quickly straddles my body and pins me to the ground. Determined savagery shines in her eyes as she squeezes her forearms against my neck.

I claw at her face, squirm and writhe, but can't dislodge her. Somehow my keys are bristling from between my clenched fingers. I'm bashing, smashing. There's a jarring sensation as metal points strike bone. She howls and thrashes. I pull my fist in an arc toward the back of her skull.

The raging woman screams again and presses on my throat with even more vehemence. I try to stab at her eyes as I'm being cut off from life. Is this what my brother felt in his last moments? I'm desperate to hold onto him, but the connection is severed by something wet and warm dripping onto my face.

Despite my eyes being tightly shut, I see a field of bright red. Random blobs of yellow flicker on and off. There's a voice, a male voice I don't recognize. I come fully to with a start and move to sit up. Strong hands hold me down and force something over my face. I try to yell but produce no sound. My breathing is jagged and raspy; my throat feels like it's on fire. I hit out with fists and legs, punching and kicking at whoever is trying to kill me.

"Mrs. Kessler, be still. We're here to help you."

I frantically continue to fight until I hear another voice.

"Jackie, it's Allan. You're safe." I force my eyes open. Allan is kneeling beside me, his warm, reassuring hand on my arm, a stricken look on his face. "You're safe," he repeats. "Let them give you oxygen."

With Allan here, I succumb to the paramedic's ministrations. "Other than your throat, where else are you hurt?" he asks. "Is this your blood?" I gingerly shake my head no. The back of my head throbs.

Allan looks up as another person enters the room. He makes space.

"Jackie, it's Eve Connelly. Do you know me?"

I blink twice in response. Allan and Eve share what I take to be a look of relief.

She says, "We have her, Jackie. You're safe." Thick tears leak from the corners of my eyes, unbidden and unstoppable. "Here. You can let go of these now." Eve's gloved hands gently force my fist open. I didn't even feel them in my grip, but I'm not so far gone that I don't notice her slipping my keys into a plastic bag. Evidence.

I push the oxygen mask from my face. "Dead?"

"No, in custody."

"And on her way to the hospital," says Allan. "You're not far behind."

"Willem." I try to sit up, but can't. "Call Willem."

"Already done. He and Natasha will meet you there."

The paramedics gently ready me for transport. Their heavy boots crunch strangely as they maneuver the gurney across the front room. I manage to look down; a mosaic of glass shards covers the floor. The large ceramic planter from the porch lies on its side, spilling its guts in the midst of the glittering mess.

This time I simply point.

Allan smiles down at me. "Sorry about that. The deadbolt was locked. It was the quickest way in." He sounds inappropriately jaunty, the little shit. Hmmm. That's a thought I'd reserve for a friend.

The crash I heard as I hit the floor must have been the window bursting. I shake my head weakly and push the oxygen mask aside again. "No sorry. Thanks." I pluck at his shirt sleeve. "Please with." As the paramedics lift me into the back of the ambulance, Allan gets a nod and climbs in. Now I notice that his shirt is stained with blood. "Hurt?"

"Don't worry. It's hers, not mine. That was some action on your part, by the way. We thought we were too late."

"How know?"

"Hey, when you hired me, you hired the best." Allan grins, evading the question. He turns suddenly serious. "The woman who attacked you. Have you ever seen her before?"

"Martha." I twirl a finger beside my temple to show my opinion of her state of mind.

Allan takes my hand, gives it a gentle squeeze. "You need to calm down," he says. "Don't worry. She'll get a chance to defend herself."

"No." I pull him close to whisper into his ear.

DAY FOURTEEN

••••••••••••••••••••••••••

Rachel and Angie are in the easy chairs while Liz and Theo have claimed a sofa. Willem and I are on the sofa facing them, holding hands, saying nothing. Stefan, who grabbed the first possible flight out of Zürich, helps Tasha and Mohamed bring chairs in from the dining room for themselves, Allan, the Connellys, Sam, and Mireille.

These people have walked alongside Willem and me throughout this entire ordeal. The emotional wounds are scabbing over and now they need answers. So do I.

"What the fuck were you doing with Amy's sister?" Liz demands. "I mean, damn it, Jackie, what the fuck?"

"Yeah, well, not one of my greatest decisions." The headache's gone, but my throat's still bruised, my voice still hoarse.

The implication jolts Rachel like lightning. "None of us saw it. I thought Martha was the one person in the family who actually loved Amy. I don't understand how this all happened."

"Have to back up." I haltingly tell the story of meeting Martha at the cemetery. Looking at Allan, I say, "It hit me then, our conversation about Dog and Cat. It's the only thing that made sense."

He massages his forehead. "Oh, my."

"Say, what?" Rachel wears her look of annoyance.

"It boiled down to the yin and yang within Martha, and what, or whom, she would ultimately choose." I look to Allan, passing the narrative baton while finishing a mug of licorice root tea.

"You had to have been there," he says, grinning. "Long story short, Martha pretended to help Jackie, but she was actually protecting the one person she was truly loyal to, the person who actually pulled the trigger. She thought a bogus suicide note would convince Jackie to settle the lawsuit and end this whole chapter. What she didn't know was that Amy regularly shared her poetry with Jackie."

Liz thinks it through. "'Sacrificial Lamb?'"

I tap my nose with a forefinger and point at her with the other. "Ding, ding, ding!"

"What's that?" asks Stefan.

It's Rachel's turn to supply information. "One of Amy's poems. It's about misery, sacrificing yourself for the greater good, and how doing that can eventually destroy you, become a personal Armageddon."

I say, "She wrote the companion piece a few months later. 'End Times' is about redemption, Armageddon averted."

"She wrote about things after she worked them out in her head," says Rach, as if confirming the thought for herself.

"Yes. 'End Times' signified the end of her suicidal thoughts and feelings and the beginning of her new relationship with life. She said she wanted a witness, someone to hold her accountable. This was the only time Amy gave me the original; she didn't even keep a copy. It's the second thing I showed Martha."

"I don't remember it," says Liz.

"Because you never saw it. I kept it separate, locked in my office. Every time Amy came she reread it, re-attested to it." I display it now, handwritten with an orange ultrafine Sharpie, the words 'end times' circled in chisel-point blue. Dated signatures in a variety of hues range across the bottom of the page.

The last few words were sandpapery. Willem hands me a throat lozenge. I look at Allan beseechingly.

He says, "Unbeknownst to Amy, Martha had been going through her papers for years. She was well-acquainted with the poems. When Amy died, Martha showed 'Sacrificial Lamb' to the sheriff and claimed she'd found it next to the body. With that in hand it was easy to rule the death a suicide. The supposed discovery was kept under wraps at the family's request to protect their privacy. Jackie's copy, signed and dated, would expose the lie. To top it off, 'End Times' proved that Amy was no longer a threat to herself."

Angie has her best skeptical look. "I thought Martha ripped them both up."

"I'm not a complete idiot." I bump Willem with the side of my head. "Color copies. You never know when you're dealing with an undercover asshole."

Liz allows me to bask in my own cleverness for a fraction of a second before shaking her head at me. "Jax, why didn't you show 'End Times' to us? That would've done the trick for Wayne."

"Wayne saw it. He said it proved nothing, might even be used to show how easily I was manipulated. After that I got paranoid and had real doubts about both Amy's honesty and my abilities. I needed corroboration first, for my own peace of mind, before showing it to you."

"Good gracious," says Ang. The best I can do is shrug.

Allan says, "Martha knew it was just a matter of time before you figured it out. You were already close, trying to convince her to go to the authorities with you. She panicked. She had to stop you."

Willem pulls me into his chest and wraps his arms around me protectively as I begin to sob. I weep for those three generations of women whose whispers urged me along. I weep for my brother, my family's sacrificial lamb, and I weep for Amy, who died trying to heal.

Allan waits until I unbury my face, hiccup, blow my nose, and wipe my streaming eyes. "After meeting you in the cemetery, Martha told her mother what you'd said. Right then Bill walked into the house. He was going to try one last time to convince his parents to drop the lawsuit. He overheard and immediately understood. Amy really hadn't shot herself, so who else could have done it? Only one of two people. He forced the truth out of them."

Eve turns to Mohamed and me. "When Amy got home from the gun club, her mother and sister were waiting. Martha told you the truth, Jackie. They tried to force Amy to give up Bill. When she refused, their mother got hysterical. Martha told Amy that she couldn't do that to her or the family. Amy said she didn't owe them any loyalty as none had ever been shown to her. While they argued, their mother picked up Amy's gun. Mrs. Nguyen said she didn't realize what she was doing; she just wanted them to stop. Martha staged the suicide scene. They've both confessed."

I sigh. "Martha said she would do anything for her mother. And I was stupid and gullible enough to meet her alone."

Allan says, "Thankfully, you told Willem, and even though he promised to let things play out, he called me." I look up into my husband's face. He grimaces at me; I squeeze his arm.

Allan continues. "Bill Nguyen called me right afterward, too. He was frantic, trying to track you down. He didn't know what his sister and mother were planning but knew it was nothing good."

"And people say there are no such things as guardian angels," sighs Angie.

Rachel reaches over to place her hand on my wrist. "You told Allan. How did you figure it out?"

"Her poem, 'Second.' When Martha told me what happened during their escape from Vietnam, I realized that even without knowing the details, Amy must have picked up on the fact that something even more horrible than she imagined had happened, and it preyed on her. It had to be the secret alluded to in the poem." I look at my colleagues. "Amy once called Martha 'a moth in the skein of truth.' We assumed correctly that 'Second' was about her mother and Colonel McMillan; however, our focus was too narrow. It also applied to her sister.

"It came together when Martha claimed to have found Amy's body. She first said that at the cemetery. Something niggled at me, but I was too caught up in my own crap and forgot about it." I knock the side of my head with my palm. "When she repeated it, I remembered. The news said that Amy's housekeeper found the body. The police report confirmed it. That's not something anyone would likely confuse. When I pushed her on it, Martha claimed to be in such shock after discovering the body and suicide note that she rushed home to her parents, didn't even think of calling the police. She said Mrs. Dorji must have arrived right after."

"How convenient," says Rachel.

"That's actually a plausible explanation. I know, I know. But it made sense – Martha could have reacted that way. But she sidestepped when I asked if she killed Amy. The way she did it was slick, through that garden gate. She was about to kill me. She had nothing to lose; why not admit it? Maybe because she didn't do it."

Eve chuckles. "That's quite the detective show cliché."

"Exactly. That's what made it easier for me to stay semi-objective, see it for what it really was – an act. She regressed, got erratic. It looked like she was having a psychotic break.

Luckily, I knew better. Her words were crazy but her behavior was not; it was very deliberate. Amy consistently described her mother as emotionally abusive, controlling, a master manipulator. When Martha attacked me, I wondered which of those traits she inherited. As she's strangling me, I'm thinkin', *Oh, insanity plea. If she gets off, who else could benefit?"*

"Jackie, your mind works in weird, not just mysterious ways," says Rachel.

Liz interrupts. "I have a question. How'd you figure Dawa Dorji was off the hook?"

Allan says, "Turns out Bill Nguyen and Kick Dorji are a couple." All eyes turn to Mohamed, who nods in confirmation.

I say, "A few days ago Allan and I happened to swing by the Dorjis' and saw the three of them together. We rang the doorbell. Turns out Mrs. Dorji really was afraid about Kick loving Amy. She was quite delighted to learn she loved Amy but was *in love* with Bill. After that she decided that all she wants is her daughter's happiness after all."

"Fame and fortune probably don't hurt either," adds Rach. She casts a surreptitious glance at Mohamed, who politely pretends not to have heard.

"What about Bill?" asks Tasha. "And where does that leave his father?"

"Bill will do what he can for his mother and sister. I think he understands how they became what they are and why they did what they did. He called his father a stoic man, someone who can take care of himself."

"You said he called you, Allan," says Willem. "How did he find you?"

"Through Mohamed. Thanks for providing that link, my friend." It warms me to see the musician and the former detective's ease with each other.

Mohamed beams. He addresses me. "It was difficult not to tell you about their relationship, but they made me promise. Kick told Bill about your talk at Green Lake. After that, Bill realized he had to steer his parents away from their path. He decided if they didn't listen, he would leave the family."

"What a hard choice," says Rach.

"Yes," I say, "choosing between loyalties. Holding onto the past and all its injuries, or moving forward. Amy said her family allowed no in-betweens."

Mohamed adds, "Amy showed him this was not true, that there are ways to bridge them both."

I lean against Willem, exhausted. "All my questions are answered," I say, "except for one."

"What's that?" he asks.

"IJ. Amy said I'd have to figure it out, but for the life of me, I can't."

Mohamed speaks up again, obviously enjoying another opportunity to contribute. "This is a mystery I can solve." He moves to the bookshelf and extracts an ORB album, Amy's parting gift to me. He points to the song list. "Here. 'Indigo.' She wrote this for you."

"'Indigo?'" asks Liz.

"We shared a favorite color," I explain.

Mohamed says, "It is also, as I heard many times, the color of intuition, honor, and wisdom. It was in those moments when you made her uneasy, when she learned something or wanted to emulate you in some way, that you, Jackie, were her Indigo, her IJ. That is why, after she learned to trust you, no matter what colors she had in her hair, one was always indigo blue. In this way, she carried you with her."

Amy and her wearable reminders. I pick up the old stuffed bunny and give it a tearful nuzzle. I whisper into its faded yet still silken ears, "Every color has its meaning."

DAY NINETEEN

I shoo Taneesha out of my office, slide one of her attention-grabbing campaign fliers into my desk drawer. The session ran long, but I wasn't about to interrupt her excited monologue. Most of the incoming senior class plus the entire girls' and boys' volleyball teams have already pledged their support, so there's little doubt her campaign will succeed. Taneesha will make a fabulous student body president, already has a long list of issues she plans to address. I pity the school administration.

The clock reads 4:02. I need a sec to reboot. I stand, stretch, glance out the office window. A robin skips along a branch of the old vine maple, stops to cock its head at me.

There's an assertive knock. The door opens, a young face looks in. There's a hint of a sneer. "It's late," the teenaged girl says. "I didn't know if you were here."

"Good enough," I say, doing a double take. "Sorry to keep you waiting. You must be Amy." I offer my hand. She ignores the invitation.

She immediately commandeers my fawn-colored leather swivel chair, the one with the therapist-sits-here look stamped all over it. I shut the door, take a seat on the sofa across from her, and wait.

She scans the room, avoiding eye contact.

"What'm I supposed to call you? Dr. Kessler?" she says warily.

I give what I hope is an encouraging smile. "Thanks for the promotion," I say. "I have a master's degree, no doctorate. You can call me Jackie. Okay if I call you Amy?"

"That's my name, isn't it?" She sits stiffly, rubs her right thumb and forefinger against each other.

I take a slow breath in and relax on the exhale as I clench and release my toes. I look down at what is without doubt the most important element of my professional wardrobe, comfortable shoes.

"I try to avoid making assumptions," I say. "For all I know, you have a nickname you like better. Or I could call you Ms. Nguyen. Up to you."

She focuses on the wall above my head. "Amy's all right."

Score one for the old broad. I love working with teenagers. They're my favorite clients, so honest, creative, stubborn. And endlessly entertaining.

Adrienne, the hospital social worker who made the referral, suggested I would be "a good fit for this patient." Based on our history, I figure I got the call because of my Asian face. Good fit indeed.

Amy shows no interest in proceeding. If this isn't going to work, might as well figure it out now. "If we decide to work together, Amy, what are you hoping will happen? What do you want to accomplish?"

Her expression remains blank. The info I got says she's burned through three therapists already. Maybe this is how she does it, with a brick wall demeanor. If she expects me to squirm, she'll be disappointed. Dead air doesn't bother me.

I use the opportunity to study her more closely. Her unpolished fingernails have rough, ragged edges. Picked at or gnawed? Her outfit practically swallows her whole. Is it supposed to make her look bigger or smaller? Either way, it's unusually warm out and disgustingly muggy. Dressed like her I'd be sweating like a pig.

She pushes the hood of her sweatshirt back to reveal a short, ragged haircut paired with an alarming dye job. At that instant, a sudden break in the high cloud cover allows sunshine to burst through the window. It hits her head and reflects off the red, orange, and green shards embedded in the black.

"If *we* decide?" The suddenness surprises me. She pays attention and is willing to show it. Is the door open a crack?

"Well, yeah, we both have a say. Just because the hospital sent you, it doesn't mean we're stuck with each other. Finding a good match is what matters."

"Hmph." She crosses her arms; each hand grips a bicep. Resistance? Self-soothing? Both or neither?

"Back to the previous question. The hospital wants you in therapy. What about you?"

"The social worker said you'd help me change my thinking so I won't be depressed and want to kill myself anymore."

"That's one option. Is that what you want?"

"Maybe I like thinking about killing myself." She sounds almost playful as she picks at her sleeve. "What's wrong with that? As long as I don't do it, who the fuck cares?"

"Thinking about killing yourself isn't the same as wanting to kill yourself." Amy shifts her weight; I take that as further encouragement. "Why're you here, Amy? How can I, or someone like me, be of help to you?"

"I have to be in therapy to stay out of the hospital. That's what I want. That place is like jail. It's boring and stupid and the food sucks."

"No question about the food. What's boring and stupid about it?"

She swivels the chair to face the window. The robin's gone; a chickadee has taken its place. "Everyone knows exactly what they have to say to get out, so that's what you hear. No one speaks the truth. They all talk about everything except what's really important."

"Correct me if I'm wrong, but that implies you weren't talking about what was really important to you either. And how can you be so sure about the others? Can you read minds?"

Amy turns the chair back; her hands clutch the armrests. "This is not making me feel better."

I lean in. "I'm not here to make you feel better. If that's what you want, I'm not the right therapist for you."

She sighs heavily and begins twisting back and forth in the chair.

This time I wonder if I've pushed too far. I hope not. In these few minutes, I've gone from feeling fatigue to intrigue. Amy Nguyen puts forth a contemptuous manner, but I see her tap into all her senses to process this new environment. Her head stays remarkably still as she combines the chair's motion with her peripheral vision to take in the entire space. As the air conditioning engages, the cool current travels over the open ceramic bowl filled with dried flowers from my garden, sending a hint of rockrose and lavender in our direction.

Amy draws a deeper breath and stops the chair. I'm curiously relieved when she speaks; I've been holding my breath.

"Were you adopted?"

That takes me aback. "No. Why?"

"Kessler. You don't look like a Kessler."

I laugh. The kid makes connections and has guts. She's also mistress of the conversational pivot. How dare she usurp my position. I slowly unbutton the cuffs of my blouse and fold each sleeve up to the elbow. "Looks, as they say, can be deceiving. But you're right; Kessler is my married name."

"So what are you? Japanese? Chinese? You're not Vietnamese."

"No, I'm Korean American. Born and raised here. My parents immigrated after the Korean War. I'm second generation, like you."

"What about Jackie?"

It takes a second for the meaning to register. "Oh, my grandfather died before I was born. He was a huge fan of President Kennedy. JFK's nickname was Jack, and Jackie was his wife's nickname. My parents honored three birds with one name. What about Amy?"

"My mother liked that schmaltzy book *Little Women*. I'm named after the spoiled brat little sister."

"A spoiled brat with a loving and sensitive heart." The sarcasm doesn't seem to faze her. I can't resist adding, "And she married very well."

She grabs a fistful of her stubby, candy-colored locks. A spark of mutual understanding passes between us. JFK was a catch too.

Time to reclaim my title. "Who did your hair?"

"Is that a joke or an insult?"

"A question. Couldn't help but notice."

"I did."

"Have you always worn it that short?" It looks more shredded than trimmed.

She bristles with satisfaction. "No. My mother always made me have it long, wouldn't let me cut it. It was down to here." She motions with her hand to indicate a position a few inches below her derriere. "Full of split ends. It was gross so I chopped it up to here." Her hand slices the air at collar length. "When she saw, she said I was crazy, so I cut it to here and dyed it. Didn't want to disappoint her."

"The way I see it, everyone's got their own brand of crazy. Do you agree with your mother that this was a sign of yours?"

No response.

I take another angle. "How'd you try to kill yourself?"

"Geez, you go right for it, don't you? Didn't your mother teach you any manners?" I cock my head and raise my eyebrows. She continues, her manner more subdued. "I mean, that's not exactly politically correct."

"Yeah, well, I learned long ago that political correctness only gets you so far. You were in the hospital for a reason. I'm just trying to understand." I hold for a second. "Gonna answer my question?"

"Didn't they send you a report? If you did your job, you'd already know."

"Reports only tell one side of a story. I still want to hear it from you."

I see her do a quick cost-benefit analysis in her head before she responds with what sounds like a sigh of surrender. She grabs the sleeve of her hoodie and twists the fabric back and forth.

"I took pills. Over-the-counter stuff. No one in my family's, like, a junkie. I thought about Tylenol. The irony of ODing on a painkiller appealed to me, but no one would get it. So I took sleeping pills – painless, no stress, no mess. Just fall asleep and it all goes away."

"Only you woke up."

Even I don't think that merits a response. Amy continues investigating the office, this time more openly. Her gaze lingers on my extensive stuffed animal collection lounging across the top of a long, low bookshelf.

"This was the second time you'd been in the hospital, right?"

"No shit, Sherlock." She leans out of the chair toward the plush toys, snatches the chubby brown bunny rabbit, strokes its long, silky ears.

"Good choice," I say. "He's a great hugger." She gives it a tentative nuzzle and I continue. "You were what, thirteen? The report says you hurt yourself, you were cutting."

"Yeah, I cut. What's the big fuckin' deal? I wasn't trying to kill myself, no matter what they say. Other kids were doing it so why the fuck not? Anything to express some meaning." I look at her quizzically; most fifteen-year-olds don't talk like this. "I admit, it was a dumb mistake, OK? It's not like I'll ever do it again."

"Express some meaning?" I ask. The question hangs between us; Amy squirms. I don't want to waste the moment. "I grew up in an immigrant Asian family too. I don't know if your experience is like mine, but Asian families don't talk much. Not about obnoxious stuff like feelings, anyway."

She stares at the floor.

"Is there a scar?" I ask. "Can I see?"

She studies me, perhaps looking for more sarcasm or a hint of pretense. She drops the stuffed bunny into her lap and pulls back the left sleeve of her sweatshirt to expose the inside of her lower arm. There, still clear against her pale skin, is a slightly raised, beautifully formed four-inch-long elongated teardrop, carefully balanced between her wrist and the inside of her elbow. The bulb of the teardrop holds a fairly round circle which in turn holds more crudely carved shapes.

I fetch my reading glasses from the desk and crouch in front of Amy at a respectful distance. "Is that the Earth?"

She nods once, sharply.

I don't know how to respond. I've seen self-harm before; this is different. My first instinct is to reach out and touch it, run my thumb along the delicate curves, tell her I understand. Instead I look up into her face.

"What did you use?"

"Utility knife from art class."

I flinch involuntarily. "How much did it hurt?"

"Like a motherfucker."

"I meant how much did it hurt when you figured out they didn't get it, didn't get you?"

She turns away. "Like I said. It wasn't worth the effort."

I nod slowly. "So if you weren't trying to kill yourself, how'd you end up in the hospital?"

"I started it at home," she says, motioning with her head toward her arm, "but my father kept yelling at me to get out of the bathroom, so I finished it at school. Forgot Band-Aids. Toilet paper didn't work. Some girl saw blood through my sleeve and told the teacher. Long story short, I got to ride in an ambulance, which was cool, but at the hospital my mother and my sister freaked out. Not so cool.

"My mother doesn't speak much English, so my sister always comes to translate. While we were waiting, she yelled at me and said I knew I shouldn't do things like that and I was causing everyone a lot of trouble. Then she went to the cafeteria to get my mother something to drink. That's when the doctor came and asked my mother if she thought I was suicidal and needed to be in a safe place. She just kept nodding and saying yes, which is what she always does because she no understando the lingo. I kept trying to explain but the asshole doctor wouldn't listen to me, the English speaker. That's how I landed in the psych ward."

"He didn't realize your mother didn't understand?"

"No. Not that he cared. Not that it would have mattered."

I picture the scene. It's an old story.

"Your father wasn't there?" I ask.

"He never is. Didn't visit me in the hospital, didn't come to the family meetings. He doesn't give a crap." She picks up the bunny again, tightly wraps one of its long ears around her left forefinger, releases it, rewraps it, and tugs. Her finger turns scarlet.

"This time you took sleeping pills." I imagine myself in the girl's skin, feel the heat of the incision, the spreading lull of the pills. "Pictures and painkillers. You've got quite the gift for metaphor."

The toes of her Doc Martens beat a soft tattoo on the carpet.

I shake my head to clear it and say, "The hospital discharged you on condition you get therapy, which means you're doing better now?" Amy nods. "Okay, so you don't want to kill yourself. Help me out here. How much do you want to live? There is a difference."

Amy replaces the bunny on the bookshelf, turns the chair to face the window again.

"It's a hard question. You can answer it in your own time. The way I look at it, every morning – whether we're aware of it or not – we each make a commitment to make it through another day. It's a contract we make first and foremost with ourselves, to stay committed to life. And it can be incredibly hard to live up to."

I pause to check Amy's reaction before heaping the rest into her lap. "Like I said, you're not stuck here. You have to work with someone, but it doesn't have to be me. Think about it. You decide if you want to come back or not."

The girl shrugs and shakes her head resignedly, sending tufts of hair dancing. "You can't be worse than any of the other idiots."

I startle at another firm knock. I turn to apologize for the interruption, but the kid's gone. I rub my eyes. The clock reads 4:02. Shit. That's right, Taneesha's session ran long.

There's another young face at the door. I do a double take.

"Sorry I'm late," she says. "I didn't know if I was supposed to wait or come back."

"My fault. Sorry to keep you guessing. Ordinarily I'd come get you. You must be Crystal." I offer my hand. Boa Girl gives it a quick shake. As she eases into the swivel chair, she gives me the once-over, spending extra time on my indigo shibori tunic. Hmmm. Curiosity or misgiving? Maybe a bit of both.

I say, "We've seen each other before, haven't we?"

"Yeah," she says, "at the hospital. When I got out they said I need to be in therapy. I got your name from that social worker you were talking to, you know, the one with the stick up her ass." She scans the office; her eyes widen as she catches sight of the stuffed menagerie. "Are you, like, a therapist for little kids?"

"Better watch it. Those are my assistants. They pay attention and they hold grudges."

She looks at me like I'm a lab specimen gone rogue. "Whatever."

"Don't underestimate them. If you ever need a pal, they're here for you."

She takes a closer look at each as if scrutinizing a police lineup. She reaches out slowly and scoops up the scruffy brown bunny.

"Good choice," I say. He's definitely back where he belongs. "He's one of my oldest and dearest friends. He's also a great hugger." She curiously inspects the ear with the permanent wave. "So what're you looking for in a therapist, Crystal? What're you hoping to accomplish?"

She loops the curly ear around her forefinger, tightens it with a tug. "I saw you with that kid and his dad. I want someone who gets it, you know? Someone I can get along with."

For over ten years I worked with the girl who put the curl in that ear. Why do I want to do this, my mother wants to know. I have no idea. But I know I've never considered doing anything else. Is it worth it? After the last three weeks, that's an easy one to answer.

I smile and say, "I have the feeling we'll get along fine."

Acknowledgments

Transitioning from mental health professional to writer has been a multi-year journey. My goal was to write a book I'd want to read; first I had to learn the skills to do that. Major boosts came through Writing by Writers, founded by Pam Houston and Karen Nelson. Pam and Karen, you recruit some of the best writer-teachers imaginable. Sincere thanks to faculty members Sunil Yapa and Alexander Chee. A message for two more, Peter Ho Davies and Joshua Mohr. Peter and Josh, your joy in the written word (and life) is contagious. You have no idea how much I appreciate you. And Josh, in addition to craft lessons, your keen editorial eye and creative zest kept my learning curve challengingly and delightfully steep. Here's to you and Decant Editorial!

Many people contributed mightily to this effort by providing precious feedback and moral support. It really helped that no one laughed when told what I was up to. Thank you a million times over, the Three Js, Harriet Cannon, Karen Fassett-Carman, Mike Fitzpatrick, Erland and Lois Paff Bergen, Carol Pfaffly, Mary Jean and Mike Mitchell, Meg Johnson, Mary Pat Ankerson, Joan Schiff, Diane Schmitz and Bill Stalder, D. Arthur, Roseanne Pereira,

Becky Mandelbaum, Maren Halvorsen, Deborah Föhr, Julie Wood, and Ellen Nelson.

A special shout-out to you, Cybil Flores, for your friendship, enthusiasm, and sparkling artistry.

I've also been blessed with exceptional and courageous female inspirations, my mother and daughters foremost among them. You are my heroes!

Above all else, eternal gratitude to my husband for the forty-plus years of love and support through all that life throws our way.

About the Author

Rhoda Berlin is a second generation Korean American with over thirty years of experience as a marriage and family therapist. She is the co-author of the non-fiction book *Mixed Blessings: A Guide to Multicultural and Multiethnic Relationships*. *See Me* is her first novel.

www.ingramcontent.com/pod-product-compliance
Lightning Source LLC
Chambersburg PA
CBHW061228310726
48971CB00007B/1986